Louisa and the
Missing Heiress

Louisa and the Missing Heiress

—✺—

A LOUISA MAY ALCOTT MYSTERY

Anna Maclean

A SIGNET BOOK

SIGNET
Published by New American Library, a division of
Penguin Group (USA) Inc., 375 Hudson Street,
New York, New York 10014, U.S.A.
Penguin Books Ltd, 80 Strand,
London WC2R 0RL, England
Penguin Books Australia Ltd, 250 Camberwell Road,
Camberwell, Victoria 3124, Australia
Penguin Books Canada Ltd, 10 Alcorn Avenue,
Toronto, Ontario, Canada M4V 3B2
Penguin Books (N.Z.) Ltd, Cnr Rosedale and Airborne Roads,
Albany, Auckland 1310, New Zealand

Penguin Books Ltd, Registered Offices:
80 Strand, London WC2R 0RL, England

First published by Signet, an imprint of New American Library,
a division of Penguin Group (USA) Inc.

 REGISTERED TRADEMARK—MARCA REGISTRADA

ISBN 0-7394-4194-9

Printed in the United States of America

PUBLISHER'S NOTE
This is a work of fiction. Names, characters, places, and incidents either
are the product of the author's imagination or are used fictitiously, and
any resemblance to actual persons, living or dead, business establish-
ments, events, or locales is entirely coincidental.

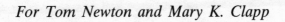

For Tom Newton and Mary K. Clapp

ACKNOWLEDGMENTS

Again, and always, heartfelt thanks to my husband, Steve Poleskie, for his faith in me, his support, his humor and goodwill. Thanks also to my steadfast agent, Esmond Harmsworth, who was my compass and my guide in this process. And thanks to my perceptive and gracious editor, Ellen Edwards.

Dunreath Place
Roxbury, Massachusetts
February 1887

Gentle Readers,

I had a letter from an old friend recently. She
asked if I remembered Dot and if I had ever
thought of writing her story. She is too kind to say
outright but she gently reminded me that youth is
far behind and that what I am going to write, I
should perhaps write now, and quickly. The letter
seemed an omen, for that same day Father had sat
up in bed and asked if I had heard from Dorothy
Brownly recently. His mind wanders and he
thought, that morning, that I was perhaps on my
way to one of those girlhood afternoon activities
that occupied my younger years.

In my youth, I struggled to write and publish stories. Now I am known and I may even admit beloved. In the streets of Concord I cannot even mail
a letter or purchase yarn without being recognized.
That is one of the joys of age and success, though
I admit to occasionally yearning for those younger
days when I could walk the streets anonymously. A
certain anonymity no doubt assisted the events of
which I now wish to write. While I have never shied
away from telling my readers about my family and
my childhood, I have—in part because of the deepest personal reservations—kept silent about many
of what used to be called my "adventures." In part
from modesty, and a wish not to hurt the living, I

have kept secret many of the most interesting years of my life, years in which I found myself in the curious role of lady detective.

I do find myself reticent, however, I who have already revealed so much of my life in my fictional works. What mother would wish to reveal to her sweet children that their beloved author, Louisa May Alcott, had knowledge of crime and criminals, and deeds so dastardly that if known they would require a night-light to burn in the hall? Yet knowledge of them I had. For many years of my life, I found myself surrounded by unexplained death and unexpected danger, as well as holding the unusual and unmerited position of being the only person able to reach a satisfactory conclusion to the mysterious events.

I have decided to go through my diaries and reconstruct the events of some of these years. These, then, are the other stories of my youth, of friends and foes who chanced across my path, sometimes gracing it, sometimes causing such distress I would fall into the Slough of Despond and doubt all, even the words on a white page. I begin with the story of my dear childhood friend, Dot, and her untimely demise.

I trust you may gain some enjoyment through the reading of these tales.

Louisa May Alcott

Prologue

"Listen then," replied the count, "and perhaps you too may share in the excitement of those about you. That box belongs to Josephine. . . ."

I paused, pen in hand, and scratched out the name. It simply did not suit her. I considered following Shakespeare, knowing that my heroine would be as enticing with whatever name God gave her, until I realized that, surely, no reader would become entranced with the lady's plight were she named Maud or Jo.

"Josephine won't do," I said. "People would be calling her Jo, and this woman is most definitely not a Jo. Jo is a homespun name, tomboyish and striving, not given over to frivolity or melodrama. This woman needs a name that is more Italianate, more romantic. Beatrice. Yes, that's it. . . . And her rival shall be Therese."

"Nay, not so strange as one may fancy, Arthur," said his friend, "for it is whispered, and with truth, I fear, that she will bestow the hand so many have sought in vain upon the handsome painter yonder. He is a worthy

*person, but not a fitting husband for a truehearted
woman like Beatrice; he is gay, careless, and fickle, too.
I fear she is tender and confiding, loving with an Italian's passionate devotion, if he be true, and taking an
Italian's quick revenge, if he prove false."*

"And then what, Louisa? Does she give her hand
to the faithless painter, Claude?" breathlessly asked
Miss Sylvia Shattuck.

I stopped reading and began marking on the pages,
crossing out some words and adding others. On some
days the phrases came easily; on others each was a
struggle. This day was a struggle, since I was already
preoccupied with the events to come . . . though I
could not yet know how truly and frighteningly event-
ful the afternoon would become.

Sylvia and I were in the attic writing room in my
family's house on Pinckney Street. She stood beside
my piles of manuscript wrapped in paper and string,
leaning on the huge ancient desk at which I wrote.
Behind her on a ledge stood my favorite, much-
thumbed books: my father's gift, *Pilgrim's Progress,*
and my secret thrill, an edition of Poe's *Murders in
the Rue Morgue.* I have always adored Poe for his
prose and the suspense and thrill of his writing. But,
truth be told, not so much for the mystery of this
story, which I solved long before Poe intended me to,
an achievement I credit to my education in my father's
philosophical methods and the influence of my mother's gift for insight. My parents' careful education in
the ways of the world has made me particularly apt
at arriving at answers to questions of human nature.

The one window in my garret was curtained with
muslin, not lace—I prefer a gentle light when I work,
and of course my family could not waste money on
lace. The floor was bare but scrupulously clean. It was
1854, I was twenty-two, Mother had just lost her job

with the charity agency, and Father . . . well, he had
never had a talent for earning income. Those years of
poverty bleed together in my memory, always overpowered by memories of more important problems.
That was the year following the election of President
Franklin Pierce, and Father, months later, still grumbled to himself about it. We would see him pottering
from library to parlor, from parlor to dinner table,
jabbing the air with his forefinger as he lectured President Pierce in absentia. Pierce was a will-o'-the-wisp,
a moral deficient, willing to do anything for a vote,
including support slavery.

That was also the year my beloved older sister,
Anna, had gone to Syracuse to work as a governess.
I missed her every day, every evening, and perhaps
my friendship with Sylvia grew even deeper because
of that longing for the wise, gentle, absent Anna.

That afternoon, as I finished my work, the slanted
light coming through that window indicated it was
close to three o'clock, the household dinner hour.

"Well," Sylvia said impatiently, reading over my
shoulder. "Does she leave the stage and pledge herself
to the faithless one?"

I considered Sylvia's question, replacing my pen in
its tray. "She must, else there is no story, I fear. But
it will not end happily."

"Claude will love another," Sylvia guessed, leaning
forward eagerly.

"He will be absolutely unreliable," I admitted. "But
Beatrice will have her revenge."

"How exciting, Louisa!"

"Do you think so, Sylvie? Is it, perhaps, too
exciting?"

"Could there be such a thing as too exciting?"

I scratched my nose, leaving a smudge of ink behind, one of my bad habits, I'm afraid. I contemplated
the quality of my writing. It was all blood and thunder.

My natural ambition was, I suppose, for the lurid style.
I could not help but indulge in gorgeous fancies. Perhaps there was no other way for me to write, I thought
as I straightened the manuscript pages into a neat pile.
Yet there was this impulse, deep inside, to tell a true
story, not a fancy.

Even then, before I had published my first work, I
sensed what would ultimately be the real value of my
work. But that day there were three manuscripts on
my desk: *The Flower Fables,* little stories I invented
for the Emerson children and was now working into
a children's book; my true short story, "How I Went
out to Service"; and my tale of Beatrice and Therese,
which I had just named as "The Rival Prima Donnas."
None had yet been published. Next to "How I Went
out to Service" was a rejection letter. I hadn't anticipated how much pain a simple envelope could carry.
The rejection had suggested—no, stated—that I
should pay more attention to domestic duties, as I had
no talent as a writer. The story was one of my first
"real" stories about real people, rather than inven-
tions such as Beatrice and her fickle lover, Claude. In
fact, it was about me, and the rejection had a double
sting to it, for it was my life, my experience that was
rejected, as well as the story.

That name Josephine, though. That was not a
blood-and-thunder name, nor was it a fairy name for
the *Fables.* The name conjured up a fleeting image. A
young woman, a character who sprawled on rugs
rather than sitting primly in chairs, a woman who cher-
ished books over new bonnets and rich husbands. Was
this too ordinary a character for a novel? What would
she say if she spoke? The seed that bloomed into Josephine took root that day . . . but I get ahead of myself.

Whilst some authors complain that they cannot
work without perfect solitude, at this stage in my life
I found being with Sylvia Shattuck more natural and
more helpful than being alone. We had been friends

since childhood, and we had arrived at that wonderful, intimate stage in which words are often unnecessary, so well does one know the other. Of a far less humble background than I, Sylvia was able to enjoy the frivolity that comes with wealth. Unlike so many members of "society," however, she possessed a deep conscience and dedication to help those less fortunate, and, for this and her sweetness, my parents had accepted her into the bosom of our family. "She can't help that she was born wealthy," Father often said, in the same tone in which another person might say, *He can't help that he was born lame,* or mute, or some other inescapable and unearned defect of nature.

And so Sylvia was allowed into my attic workroom. When Sylvia and I were alone, and not working for the poor, for women abandoned by their husbands, or for children desperate to learn, she helped me be less serious and indulge my fancies, my whims, my creativity. Looking back, I am certain that Sylvia was something of an inspiration for me. But I often wondered how we could be frivolous—even silly—when there was so much injustice in the world. Was it that Sylvia and I valued each other not for the fancies and fantasies we indulged, but for what was most subtle in the other's character, for that mysterious promise of what could be?

"What could be," I repeated aloud.

"Another gorgeous fancy?" Sylvia asked. Seeing the look on my face, she said, "Are you thinking again of that letter? You must not let it discourage you. Your writing is marvelous and success will come."

"Sylvia, you are a friend. Meanwhile I write my blood-and-thunders filled with moonlight in Rome, adulteresses with flashing black eyes, madwomen locked in attics, when real life needs to be written. If Father ever read this . . ." I rifled the pages on the desk.

"Now, Louy, you know your father never reads anything more entertaining than *Pilgrim's Progress.* And you may publish those *Flower Fables,* that sweet collection."

"Yes. A children's book. Closer to life, I hope."

"Louisa! Sylvia! It is almost time!" my mother's voice called up the narrow stairway.

I carefully placed the manuscript in a drawer, leaving Beatrice to her fate, and locked the drawer. I extinguished the lamp, for the attic was dark even in the afternoon, and stood.

"We must go, Sylvia. Time to face the terrible siblings and the Medusa."

"Poor Dottie," Sylvia said, also rising.

Dear reader, I must now explain this profusion of friends. Mr. Hawthorne, in one of his calmer moments a few years before, had patiently explained to me the importance of pacing, of allowing the characters time to speak, to be known by the reader, before introducing the next. "Think of it as a play," he had instructed, knowing I was stagestruck in my teens. "Characters appear one at a time, or in couples. Never all at once."

Suffice it to say that before Sylvia became my sole close companion (for as much as I loved my younger sisters, Lizzie and May, they were too young for the adult conversations I had shared with Anna when she was at home), Dottie had also been a close companion. She had, the year before, married Sylvia's cousin, Preston Wortham, and embarked on a honeymoon visit to the capitals of Europe. For months Sylvia and I had speculated on Dottie's daily activities (her visit to Italy had inspired me to place my heroines in peril throughout the Apennines and along the Bay of Naples), and the tea party was our first chance to see her since her return to Boston. Unfortunately, as a price of seeing our friend, Sylvia and I would be forced to endure a visit with Dottie's sisters, and her aunt, a formidable creature we had nicknamed "the Medusa."

Mother waited for us at the bottom of the attic stairs, a basket of just-baked rolls in her hands.

"Bring these for Dottie," she said. "She always liked my raisin cakes. Just imagine, Dottie is a married woman now. Seems like just yesterday she was still in short skirts and afraid of the dark."

"Oh, Abba, with all you have to do," Sylvia said, accepting the basket and giving my mother a kiss on the cheek. Like all of us, Sylvia called Mrs. Bronson Alcott by the familiar name, Abba, short for Abigail. Mother usually had high spirits, but today she looked tired and worn. We worried that she bore too much responsibility on those frail shoulders. Yet she remained my rock, my deepest support in times of difficulty.

"A year seems a long time for a young woman to be away from home and friends." Abba sighed. "These new customs. Why, after your father and I married at King's Chapel we went back to his room at the boardinghouse, and after supper he wrote his lecture for the next day of school. We didn't make such a fuss of things."

"You and Father are the exception to all customs," I said, smiling.

"But to invite you for tea instead of supper," said Abba. "Well, it is time. Send Dottie my love."

I can still see us rushing out of the house in my mind's eye, two pairs of neat, high-buttoned shoes clacking over the wooden floor and down the stairs, and our black cloaks making the whooshing sound of heavy flannel as we dressed for outdoors. I dashed out, chiming the doorbell as I left, both of us laughing with nervousness, dreading the ordeal to come.

Mother, with her housecap askew on her graying hair, waved from an upstairs window and shouted, "Louy, remember to bring back a cake of laundry soap. Now hurry along, or you'll be late! Don't keep Dottie waiting!"

"Oh, true and tender guide, we will not forget the soap!" I waved back a farewell. "And we won't keep Dottie—Mrs. Preston Wortham—waiting!"

Later, I would recall with great sadness the irony of those words.

Chapter One

The Hostess Goes Missing

"I suppose it is some strange new custom," complained Miss Alfreda Thorney. "Inviting guests and then not being there to greet them. I never."

Miss Thorney was the personage we referred to in private as the Medusa, for the thick, curling salt-and-pepper hair that snaked around her forehead and cheeks in a style of hairdressing that had been popular some thirty years before; and because her glance could turn men to stone. Or so I had imagined as a little girl, when the mere sight of her would compel me to run away in terror. Unfortunately, as an adult I found her only slightly less terrifying. There were, after all, those rumors of her instability, of a two-year period when she had been locked into a room with only the family doctor for a visitor.

"Mrs. Wortham is only back from a long voyage," I protested gently, braving the Medusa's stern glance. "I am confident that some pressing matter arose at the last minute, and that she will be home soon. Have another slice of seedcake, won't you?" I picked up the silver cake tray to pass it, but before I could, Mr. Wortham's man, Digby, stepped forward and took it. This sort of formality was not what I was accustomed to.

"I'll do that, miss," he said, and with great state-liness, as if he held the crown jewels, he silently moved around the little circle with it, his highly polished black boots giving off occasional glints of light. Alfreda Thorney visibly cringed as he approached her and stu-diously avoided any eye contact with the servant. Digby, I thought, must be the only man in Boston who intimidates even the Medusa.

Other than Sylvia and myself, our companions in the room were Edith and Sarah, Dottie's sisters, the Medusa, of course, and Edgar, Dottie's brother. Pres-ton Wortham, Dottie's new husband, our host, had briefly greeted us and then disappeared before ex-plaining why our hostess, the new Mrs. Preston Wor-tham, was not present. Good manners forbade a direct question, but I felt distinctly uneasy.

With both Preston and Dottie absent from the room, Sylvia and I were trapped with Dottie's rela-tives, and we shifted around in an awkward silence. I tried to observe, contenting myself with the idea that I might encounter some snippet of conversation, some nuance that might reappear in my stories.

We sat in the best parlor of 10 Commonwealth Ave-nue, one of the new mansions that had begun to ap-pear along that tree-lined boulevard. It was a late-winter afternoon, a season of gray skies and constant damp drizzle. Any disheartened light the sky offered could not make its way through the heavy velvet cur-tains, so all the lamps had been lit and a fire set roar-ing in the fireplace, as well.

I held an alarmingly thin teacup and saucer in one hand and a plate of fish-paste sandwiches—so differ-ent from our less fancy but more delicious fare at home, cunningly (and wastefully, when one considered all the crust and cutaway bread) shaped as shells—in the other. I kept my back straight and my gaze serene, but I must admit I gave in to the temptation to tap my foot, marking time with my impatience, safely out of sight under my hooped skirts, a habit of my girlhood.

"The seedcake is dry," Miss Thorney complained.

"Do try the lady cake," I said, allowing a touch of impatience to creep into my voice. Miss Thorney glared and purposely let her eyes come to rest on my high-buttoned shoe, where the leather had worn noticeably thin at the toes.

At this time in my life, before I had gained success, I struggled with an occasional painful awareness of how others saw my fortunes and my family's. I knew that Edgar and his sisters had heard that my family was at the height—or rather the depth—of its poverty at that time, and I also knew, with the aching self-consciousness of youth, that my white collar was a bit frayed and my hat misshapen from too much hard wear. My wardrobe was often, due to age and stages of being handed down, in a condition that required gentle use, resulting in a toilette often lacking in style or even protection from the elements. Yet I also knew that my worries about my clothes were foolish luxuries when compared to the elemental worries faced by so many less well-off, even people just down the street from the Wortham mansion. I had a loving family, a roof over my head, and wonderful friends. Who was I to sit and worry about frayed fabrics and old shoes?

However, I freely admit that my diminished costume lay in great contrast to the parlor of Mrs. Preston Wortham, for that room, indeed the entire home, was appointed with new carved tables, new upholstered chairs, new carpets, new velvet curtains, all in that condition remarked in envious whispers as *très cher* and usually foreign. Indeed, although I felt such judgments were wrong to make and reflected badly on the superficiality of the observer, I realized how the room might look to Dottie's siblings: as a vulgar display of newness so characteristic of Dottie's new husband, Preston Wortham, and so unlike the charm and good taste of the Brownlys' Boston home. The Brownlys' home was, of course, old, not shabby like my shoes, but old in the tradition of old money and Boston taste.

I found myself wishing that Edgar Brownly, Dot's brother, smoked, for I had decided in a moment of insight into my characters that Claude, Beatrice's faithless lover, would smoke cigarettes. But that created a problem I could fix only through study and observation . . . yet here was I at a tea party when I could have been studying men pacing around the frosty grass on that area of the Commons known as Smokers' Circle.

None of the other guests seemed to notice my restlessness, however. Instead they were busily and happily taking nips out of the reputations of their absent host and hostess.

The lord and master of this house had, ten minutes earlier, excused himself to see to affairs in the kitchen, since his wife was not there to instruct the new cook in the household preferences for garnishing the evening roast. Preston Wortham had accepted such temporary absences as a necessity in his social life, the price of marrying an heiress with a large family and social set. He had learned early in his marriage that ten minutes was enough time for them to vent their spleen, make their nasty comments, and then move on to a new topic of conversation, one that would allow his participation.

Lily, the hostess's spaniel, hid under the sofa and made tiny growls at my ankles. I wished the creature would come out so I might give it a fish sandwich and make friends.

". . .and then . . . oh, Louisa, you wouldn't believe what he said to her! In front of all of us! I still blush to think of it . . ." And the speaker, young Miss Sarah Brownly, did blush, right to the roots of her white-

white lace and pink-faced babes and pleasant evenings before the domestic hearth, I heard again the disapproval in the women's faces.

"Louisa, you will not be marrying, I suppose?" Aunt Alfreda asked.

"I've no immediate plans," I answered quietly, hoping that would end this all too familiar portion of the teatime conversation, for young women were expected to talk of beaus and plans, but I had none and wanted none.

"Nor you, Sylvia," Aunt Alfreda said, turning to my friend. Sylvia turned red.

"Weddings are frowned upon in the convent," I answered for Sylvia, who had recently announced her decision to enter such an establishment. I tactfully changed the subject and carefully balanced my cup and saucer on my knee. "Europe. I wonder if Dottie visited the galleries of the Palazzo degli Uffizi."

"I understand they were not at home during the season." Aunt Alfreda sniffed.

Footsteps sounded just outside the parlor door.

"Hush. Here comes the bridegroom," Sarah said, giggling. Edith frowned.

"He'll probably do her in; wouldn't be surprised," Edgar Brownly muttered. "For the money."

"For the money? Dear brother-in-law, are you talking about the racing season already? How are the stables looking this year?" Preston Wortham threw open the parlor doors just in time to hear Edgar's final words, not the first.

"There's a certain filly I wouldn't bet on," Edgar said darkly.

"Well, you must tell me more when the ladies aren't present. Instead we shall talk about the latest fashions, shall we?"

Preston Wortham was a tall man of powerful build; when he entered a room it felt as if all the furnishings were suddenly tilting in his direction. He sighed, a staged sigh that would read, in the play directions, as *The contented patriarch greets his womenfolk.* "The entire family is here," he said. "Well, almost. My favorite sister-in-law, little Agnes, is missing."

"Agnes is much too young for a tea." Alfreda Thorney sniffed again. "And my niece, your wife, is strangely missing. What is the time?" She fussed with the little gold watch pinned to her bosom. "Four o'clock. And the invitation was for three-thirty. What can Dot be thinking of? Ten minutes is acceptable, but half an hour simply will not do."

"Her hat, I'm sure," said Digby, standing close behind Preston Wortham and still holding the cake tray. "She was thinking of her hat. Her rose toile from Paris blew off this morning in the park and she went out to purchase another."

"Dot and her hats . . ." Mr. Wortham raised his hands palms-up and made a little smile, the kind that husbands make when they are being tolerant. "She has become quite obsessed with style."

"Mr. Wortham, you have said so little of your voyage," I said with forced cheer. "Tell me, did you visit Stonehenge? Did you take a boat down the Seine?" I leaned forward, in eager readiness for tales of foreign lands.

The terrible siblings, Sarah, Edith, and Edgar, sighed with impatience. Boston had everything a civilized person could need. Why this unfortunate need to wander? their curled lips asked. Miss Alfreda's eyes, however, acquired that faraway look as she perhaps imagined herself lounging on a silk-draped barge, floating up the Nile.

"All that is recommended, and more. We were busy to the point of fatigue," Mr. Wortham replied. "Dot would see everything. For me, however, home is the place to be. Can't get this in London or Paris." He picked up a paper, the *National Police Gazette,* and waved it. "Rousing good tales of murder and mayhem!"

"Quite," agreed Edgar, and then cleared his throat, abashed to find himself in agreement with his host on any issue.

In a more serious mode, Preston said, "I do apologize for my wife." He sighed, his voice carrying a note of victory. The family might disapprove all they wish, but Dot was his. "Will you have more tea? I'm sure she will return momentarily. My wife would be so upset to learn she had missed you. My wife"—and this time the emphasis on *my* was heavy as a ship's anchor in stormy port—"my wife has so happily anticipated this little reunion."

Preston Wortham, when he wasn't baiting his foes, had a deep, fine voice and the face and stature of a theater hero, one who could play a Roman caesar or French cavalier and make all the ladies of the audience go home madly in love with him. What he did not have was name or reputation or honest employment . . . so when handsome Mr. Wortham had proposed to and married plain but wealthy Dorothy Brownly, everyone assumed the obvious, even innocent Dorothy, who had commented several times, with an absolute lack of rancor, that "Poor Preston will be much more settled and calm once the family agrees upon the terms of his quarterly allotment." Wives often jest that their husbands are a kind of child, and to Dorothy this was not a jest but a fact, and a fact that suited her, since she had a maternal nature.

Two winters previous, Preston Wortham had been my dance partner, before he had wrangled his introduction to Dot. My feelings for him were purely friendly, but I must confess I enjoyed his beautiful dancing. Yet I fear Preston had feelings for me at that time: In a moment of weakness he professed his admiration but admitted he sought to marry for advantage. "If only you had a bit of money, my dear Miss Alcott," he had sighed.

"If I had it in any quantity, Mr. Wortham, I would buy a trip to Florence, not a husband," I had assured him. And then, because I sensed a certain fragility of character in him, I whispered, "Go slowly and carefully, Mr. Wortham. This business of heiresses can be complicated."

The clock chimed four-thirty. I sighed and stirred, tapping my foot more quickly under the concealing hem of my brown linsey-woolsey skirts. Where was our hostess? Surely she could have tried on every hat in Boston by now. Had she forgotten? Dot had never been the quickest mind—she had wept over fractions and torn her hair over South American rivers—but to completely forget her own welcome-home tea party!

I looked outside the room into the hall. The huge, ornate coat tree was close enough to the parlor that every time I looked in that direction and saw Mr. Wortham's velvet coat hanging there on its hook, I had the eerie sense that someone was standing there, watching. Something strange, hostile, dangerous, floated through that house where newlyweds should have been so happy.

Much as I wished to see Dot, I decided it was time to leave. Abba was waiting for me at home with a basket of clothing to clean and mend for the women's shelter and other tasks with which society could not be bothered. Mr. Wortham was standing at the bay window, looking out into the street. I went to him.

"I do hope Dot is all right. This is not like her."

"I fear a year in Europe may have changed her," he said. "It is liberating to travel, you know." But he was frowning and his dark eyes seemed darker than usual.

"I can only imagine. But do give her my regards. Mother invites you to dinner next Sunday . . . if you can stand one of Father's vegetarian meals. It will be carrots cooked six different ways, but it would be nice if you could come. Mother hasn't seen Dot since we were both still in the schoolroom."

Sylvia joined us at the window, since the terrible siblings had launched a new conversation on the uselessness of charity for immigrants. "How will they learn to support themselves if we give them handouts? Those Irish should not have so many babies," Edith lectured. "Unwed mothers! I never!"

I grimaced, knowing that much of this tirade was for my benefit, since my family spent much of its resources supporting the charities of Boston. "You come for dinner, too, Sylvia. Father would love to see you. He has questions for you, I suspect."

"The conversation will be worth a meal of carrots." Mr. Wortham bent to place a kiss on my hand, in the Continental manner. "We will come. Dot will be—"

But before he could finish the sentence, the front door slammed, and Mrs. Wortham herself, half-visible through the red velvet curtains of the doorway, appeared in the front hall. She was muttering distractedly to herself as she pulled at her gloves.

Craning my neck for a better view, I saw my old friend and was both startled and concerned by the change. She looked more cosmopolitan with her hair draped in the gentler style of French taste rather than the gaudy, silly ringlets of American style. But her walking costume of dusky rose and rabbit fur was the same one she had worn the year before, made by a Boston seamstress. Had she purchased no Parisian fashions? Moreover, Dorothy was hatless, and premature lines etched her pale forehead. How sad she looked!

When Dot finished with the removal of gloves and

coat and turned away from the hall table mirror, she
finally saw her husband and guests, watching.

"Why, Louisa! Alfreda! Edith! Sarah!" Mrs. Wortham exclaimed, her mouth a round O. "What a
surprise!"

Chapter Two

Trouble in Paradise

Mr. Preston Wortham unceremoniously dropped my hand and strode to the doorway for a husbandly embrace. He smiled his tolerant smile.

"Dearest, have you no greeting for me? Where have you been?" he asked gently and slowly, as if speaking to a wayward child. And then, in surprise, "Why, Dorothy, you have changed your clothes! In the middle of the day!"

"What is strange about that?" she asked defensively and with a little anger. Quite unlike Dorothy, I thought with increasing concern. Marriage and travel did affect a young woman, but this Dot, with the distant, almost frightened look in her eyes, with that strained note in her usually gentle voice, this seemed not to be Dot at all.

"I thought it was a new hat you needed, dearest, although we agreed to limit our clothing allowance." Mr. Wortham no longer smiled. Behind him, Alfreda Thorney cleared her throat. A reference to money had been made, in front of others. Quite not the thing to do.

"Hat? Whatever are you talking about?" Dorothy asked.

"Did you forget about tea today?" Mr. Wortham kissed his wife's forehead, and with tenderness brushed back a lock of pale hair that had wandered free. There was something about the gesture that reminded me just then of a play, when the guilty husband has staged a display of just that kind of tenderness that requires an intimate touching of the wife's face before her close friends and family, a superficial pretense of amiability. Whatever had Preston Wortham gotten up to?

"No, my dearest, I did not forget. Tea was for tomorrow. Not today." A scowl appeared on Dot's pale brow.

"No, sweetest, the invitations were for this afternoon. . . ."

"Tomorrow . . ." Dot insisted, and the five guests politely studied the carpet and cleared their throats, for their tones of voice had indicated a quarrel was in the making.

"Today," Mr. Wortham insisted, determined to have the last word.

"Perhaps madam would take a cup of tea?" Digby offered.

"Tea," Dot agreed. "A fresh pot, Digby. I'm chilled to the bone. Though if my guests have been waiting since teatime they are probably ready to float away."

Miss Alfreda frowned at this flippancy and I imagined her thinking, Was this how Europe affected young women of breeding? Made them forgetful and rude? Her nieces, should they wed, would honeymoon in Niagara Falls.

"Just so," Miss Alfreda said. "I really must be on my way. Harriet has asked me to conduct some business for her before the shops close." This, too, was a familiar refrain, for all of Boston society knew that Harriet Brownly treated her sister no better than a paid companion, there to fetch and carry.

"Dear Aunt Alfreda, don't be angry," Dot said, taking her aunt's black-gloved hands and giving her a kiss on the cheek. "I am so sorry. Perhaps you will come again tomorrow . . . I have a present for you, from Venice. But you must come back tomorrow or I won't give it to you."

"Well, dear niece, if you insist. But don't lose your hat tomorrow."

"Hat? Why is everyone going on about hats? Of course I won't. Tea tomorrow, at three. All of you. You, too, Edgar." And that offhand "you, too" indicated a certain lack of affection between brother and sister. Without, I hope, in any way condoning coldness in the family, I could not help but wonder who could blame Dorothy for preferring tea parties without her brother in attendance? Edgar Brownly, the heir and his mother's favorite, in addition to being a glutton, was the kind of spoiled only son who beat street dogs for fun and insisted that his sisters walk behind him on Sunday as they promenaded to church. He had once publicly berated Dorothy for being in possession of a pamphlet on women's suffrage.

But if Dot's tone of voice to Edgar was cool, she was equally cool to her husband. Mr. Wortham put his arm about his wife's shoulders. Dot, with the smallest of movements, shrugged him away.

The honeymoon, whatever it had been, was over, and relations with her family had not mended. I felt my old sense of protection for the girl who was smaller, slower, more vulnerable than myself rise to the surface. And somehow Dot seemed to sense it as she turned to me and began to whisper, "Louy, dear Louy," in the noisy confusion of donning coats and gloves and final comments about the weather. She seemed so curiously weary. She leaned in to kiss my cheek and I smelled a familiar odor: Dr. Borden's Cherry Cough Elixir. Was Dot ill?

The others were out the door, but with a slight pressure on my hand, Dot signaled me to delay for a moment. "So good to see you! And I mean it. . . ." Dot smiled, but even the smile seemed tinged with sadness. "Imagine coming home after months and months away and finding Aunt Alfreda fuming in your parlor!" We laughed, but too briefly, too halfheartedly. Our conversation was making me even more concerned.

"But, Dot, you did forget, and you seem strange. Is there any way I can be of help?"

"Oh, Louy, if only you could. If only I could talk completely openly with a trusted friend. I have made such a mess of it. There is so much sorrow and worry here, because of me."

I felt I had to reach out to Dot, and somehow I had an instinct that the situation was urgent. She seemed so tired, so weary, almost as if she were in terrible danger! I whispered, "Then talk with me, Dot. Remember when you confessed to me that you put the boiled potatoes in your governess's bed because she would not let you sit on the stairs and watch the dancing at New Year's? I never told, Dot. You can trust me."

Dot sighed, and her blue eyes seemed to look into a great distance. "Oh, how innocent we were then. . . . Come tomorrow, Louy," she whispered back. "Early. I must talk to someone. I love him so, yet I am in terror. I must tell him, I must . . . Perhaps you will be the one to understand without judging. Perhaps to you I can explain. . . ."

"Explain what, my dear? Why all this whispering like schoolgirls telling secrets?" Preston appeared suddenly behind her, smiling wolfishly and a little too widely.

Dot's smile faded. "Only how much I hope Louisa will come back tomorrow," she said. "We have so much to talk about. And I have a present for her, from Florence." She turned back to me, her eyes wide. "I do hope you will like it. I carried it around all morning in that awful Italian heat. . . ."

What on earth was wrong between these two? And this talk of presents when something was so amiss? I am sure I frowned or at least looked alarmed. "Of course I will come back tomorrow."

"Well, then. Good-bye, Miss Alcott." Mr. Wortham smiled. The door was closed. Slammed, in fact.

As I turned away, I considered knocking and demanding a second audience with Dot on the spot. But since the door had indeed been shut in my face, the polite thing to do—if there was a polite thing to do—was to leave. I wondered yet again why society seemed so confident in defining politeness in a way that seemed so uncomfortably close to cowardice.

"Well? How did she look?" Abba's right hand was probing the cavity of a freshly butchered chicken. There was a smear of blood on her cheek and feathers in her hair.

I hugged my mother with affection and kissed her clean cheek as my sister Lizzie sat on a stool and helped herself to a cracker from the cracker jar. Lizzie, my "angel in a cellar kitchen," our shy, stay-at-home Lizzie, who was nineteen then, and happier in the family kitchen than anywhere else in the world.

Our simple, lovely kitchen was a relief even to me after the stifling, overfurnished Wortham parlor, with its fragile china figurines balancing on thin-legged tables ready to be toppled by wide-hooped skirts and all those acres of new upholstery waiting for the first stain.

"Abba, I said I would do the kitchen chores today. You were to rest this afternoon," I protested.

"I told her." Lizzie sighed, sounding older and wearier than her years.

"You were late," Abba said. "I thought perhaps

you had disappeared upstairs to your garret to write.
I didn't want to interrupt. Lizzie, leave some crackers
for your father, please."

"I will write today, but later. Let's finish this stew,"
I said, rolling up my sleeves. "It is for the shelter, I
assume, since it has meat in it." I tied an apron over
my dress.

"For the shelter," Abba agreed. "We can make do
with vegetables, but those girls need meat to keep
their strength up. Childbirth is difficult enough, but
when there is no family to support you . . . why, it's
a wonder more of them don't end in the river."

Yesterday one of the residents of the Charles Street
Home for Unwed Girls had been found drowned, tangled in a fishing net. Abba had taken it very badly.
She had known the girl, had tried to cheer her up by
teaching her to knit booties, and to give her courage
by explaining the mysteries of breaking waters and
umbilical cords. The child had been only fourteen and
would not say who the father of her unborn child was,
only that he would have nothing more to do with her,
and her own father, a collier out of work with a broken leg, had kicked her out. She had shown up at the
shelter two months before, carrying her old rag doll
and nothing more.

"Such a tragedy." Abba sighed. "That poor child.
They say suicide. But I wonder if her father, or perhaps the father of her child . . . Men can be violent."
And she probed fiercely into the chicken as if evil
could be found there, and destroyed.

"But tell me how Dot—how our new Mrs. Preston
Wortham—looked," said Lizzie, who enjoyed talk of
crinolines and the new fashions.

"Absent. Abba, she missed her own tea party."

"That is strange," Abba agreed.

"Not that I blame Dot," I said. "Sarah and Edith
and Edgar and Miss Alfreda were all there waiting to

pounce on her. It seemed as though we were having the exact same conversation as we had had last year . . . except, of course, last year Dot wasn't married yet. I have invited her and Mr. Wortham for dinner next Sunday, by the way. Sylvia will come, too."

Abba nodded. "Sunday . . . Louy, your father will be here, so it will be vegetables, but I could make a cake for us," Abba mused. "It isn't like Dottie, though, to miss a tea. She was never as bright as you, but she was always reliable."

"I know. Something is wrong, I fear. She has asked me to come back tomorrow, before the others. For a talk."

"Perhaps she and Mr. Wortham aren't getting along. I hope she doesn't discover this marriage was a mistake. So many were against it from the start. But she seemed so happy. Ah, well, love is a mystery, isn't it? Pass the salt over, Louy."

"Where is Father?" I asked, knowing Abba would appreciate this often-asked question. My father's absences were a frequent occurrence! A typical man, he had absolutely no sense for the domestic sphere, a trait forgiven by his women, as his obliviousness was caused by a deep concern for the welfare of his fellow man. Even when he occasionally infuriated me, I always admired him as someone who had such strong views and did not mind what others thought and said. And my father's convictions and impractical notions allowed Abba and me to indulge our favorite conspiracy: keeping at least one of his feet on the solid, practical earth and preventing his spending all of his minutes on his theories of the virtuous life and harmony with nature.

"In Worcester for the night," Abba said. "Giving a conversation." Father made an occasional dollar by giving talks in private homes, especially after Abba had complained repeatedly of our poverty and his dinner had been reduced from the luxurious abundance of carrots, winter greens, and potatoes to a meager slice of bread and vegetable broth.

"Just as well," I said. "He would not like the sight of you tearing at that chicken. Not even for charity." Eccentric though they were, we respected Father's vegetarian beliefs, borne out of love for his fellow creatures. "And our May? Where is she?" May, in her early teens at that time, was as different from Lizzie as I was from Anna. Anna was calm; I was volatile and moody. Lizzie was shy and found talking to people outside her own family as dismaying as a trip to the dentist for a tooth pulling; May was a butterfly, happiest when in her party dress and out and about.

"With a French tutor, I believe," Abba said. "Or perhaps her music lesson. I can't keep her lessons straight."

When the chicken was in the stewing pot and our own vegetable potage put on to simmer, I folded last night's mending into a basket and put my hat and coat back on. It would be dark soon, and too cold and windy for walking, but there was one last errand of the day.

The Home, as the people of Boston referred to it, was a ramshackle house on Charles Street, once empty and unfit for living and now filled with a dozen girls and women, all in various stages of pregnancy and with nowhere else to go. The building showed the city's ambivalence to this reminder of sin and misfortune among them: One side of the façade had been hastily and clumsily painted in large red letters spelling out the word *whore*; the other side was graced with a new porch and several rocking chairs, courtesy of an anonymous donor. Sylvia and I spent much time there. I realize now that my experience working with these young women was the best education in life I could have experienced.

On that particular late afternoon, last summer's pots of marigolds, now dried and frozen into perpetual ashy brownness, lined the four steps leading to the little porch. Six ragged children played in a makeshift tent made from an old torn quilt. They turned large eyes in my direction as I approached.

"Victoria, are you in there?" I said, as I crouched down before the flap opening.

A little ragamuffin with blond curls and huge brown eyes stuck her head out.

"Hello, Miss Alcott. Do you have a present for me?" Victoria was the fourth child of Miss Amelia Rowbothoms, who, as a resident of the Charles Street home, was waiting for the fifth. Amelia had been born with the dual misfortune of beauty and a simple, trusting nature, a nature that her various employers had amply demonstrated was a liability rather than an asset.

"I do. And for all of you. Apples." I pulled the fruits from my pockets and distributed them, noting sadly that the even the dried, withered winter apples were larger than the little hands grabbing for them, and those hands were caked with seasons of dirt. A certain stability of income, I thought for the dozenth time, was required for good manners and cleanliness. How different this was from Dot's front parlor of 10 Commonwealth Avenue, where no children were yet in evidence but when in good time they did appear, it would be in white-lace christening robes with doting parents and sponsors who would hire clowns and pony rides for yearly birthday parties. Most of the children in the home didn't know their own birthdays, much less celebrate them with pony rides.

Inside, the house smelled overwhelmingly of dirty linen and nappies. There was always a vat of cloths boiling on the stove, always the metallic smell of dried blood. Often there were the sounds from the birthing room upstairs of a woman panting, groaning, screaming, as yet another soul made its way into the world. Yet, surrounded by misery, I felt of use and at home, a sensation foreign to me at the Brownlys' party.

I stood at the bottom of the dark, dusty interior stairs and listened. Except for the low mumble of unseen conversations, the occasional whimpers of babies, the clanging of the metal lid over the steaming vat, the house was quiet. Good. Queenie wasn't in labor yet. It was too soon for the baby, but there had been false labor pains for a week now.

"Queenie?" I called up.

A face, tawny colored, green eyed, not much larger than those of the playing children outside, peered over the stairwell railing. Queenie's rambunctious curls surrounded her face like a messy halo.

"Miss Louisa?"

"Yes. I've a basket. Come pick something for yourself."

The girl, fifteen years old and now as wide as she was tall, made her way carefully down the stairs, leaning backward for balance, keeping one hand on the shelf of her belly and the other firmly on the banister. She sat on the bottom step and stared forlornly into the basket. Her large green eyes moved over the checks and plaids and only slightly stained laces and then looked away again, at the ceiling, at the wall, at her own huge belly.

"See! Pink and green stripes, your favorite colors." I picked out a wool frock and waltzed it before her.

"I can't wear that," Queenie said. "Look at me. Look at it."

"You'll be able to wear it after, I promise. Just keep it for now, and when the time comes we'll give it some alterations. It is much too long, I see. How are you today, Queenie?"

"All right, I suppose." The child leaned her chin into her cupped hands and stared inward, to where the secret was.

"Any pain?"

"Most of the time. I just wish this thing would go away. I don't want it."

"When you hold that little baby for the first time, you'll feel differently." I'm afraid I always told the girls that, even though I knew it wasn't always true. I suspected that some of the girls were here because their own mothers had not been able to hold them and love them.

"Maybe," Queenie said, suspecting the lie.

"Have you heard from your father?"

"I sent that letter you helped me write. He didn't send nothing back."

"He wants to know the father's name. Give him that, and he says he'll take you back in."

"I can't, Miss Louisa." Many of the girls in the ward would not name the father; some for shame because it was their brother, or even their father, others because they did not know which man of several bore the final responsibility. For Queenie, it was different. Her fear was obvious. If she named him, he would take revenge. And no matter what we said, none could convince Queenie that she could be protected from his anger.

"Shall I go talk to your father again?"

"What's the point, Miss Louisa? He doesn't change his mind."

"Don't give up hope, Queenie."

But Queenie only looked back with wounded eyes and went upstairs.

"Don't give up. When this is past, we'll find a situation for you. I promise."

Queenie paused and smiled over her shoulder.

"You're what my ma used to call an optimist," she said.

Tuesday was mild and dry. I stared up at the sky as I emptied the ashes of last night's hearth onto the sooty heap next to the privy. The branches on the oak were brown and bare and carved into the smoky Boston air, reminding me of Beatrice's predicament of loving the faithless Claude. My story was waiting for me, and I had promised to attend for the second consecutive day a tea party! A day such as this in winter was rare, and I would rather have used the little spare time I had to walk along the northern paths out of Boston, to the marshes where the long-legged herons nested and hawks circled, and then, refreshed, go back to my attic and write.

After six years of city life I still missed Concord, missed the ponies and the long walks through forest and field with only squirrels and chipmunks for company, and the occasional hikes with Henry Thoreau or Ralph Emerson. The day after a visit to the Charles Street home usually brought on this homesickness for the clean, quiet countryside.

Yet after my school hours ended and the little Alcott parlor was cleaned of the biscuit crumbs, loose marbles, building blocks, and songbooks that so distressed my father (men can't stand disorder, yet women must!), then were three hours of work at the shelter, helping terrified mothers learn to fold nappies, burp babies, and mend linen, and instructing even more terrified pregnant girls in the nightmare of first labor ahead of them; after that long day, I was now to sit on a silk sofa with my little finger arched over a teacup, as if I had done nothing all day but select an appropriate frock to wear!

Yet even in this period of my life, when my tasks were many and my free hours few, I remember I smiled most of the day. I always knew that Beatrice, or whichever fictional character obsessed me at that moment, would be there on the morrow, waiting, or even later tonight, when I would find a free moment for writing. Both Abba and my father, Bronson, had taught me that an easy life was not necessarily a good one. The life of the mind and the spirit demanded constant testing, improvement, work. And to be the writer I intended to be, I knew that I must live the kind of life that writers live, one of hardship and stamina and reflection. Yet . . . I couldn't help but think, sometimes, that writers of the male sex did have it a little easier. They could work behind a locked study all day, while the women cleaned and laundered and cooked. Even Henry Thoreau, cloistered in his little cabin at Walden Pond, had sent his dirty laundry home to his mother.

"Dottie," I had once confessed as a girl, lamenting female limitations and responsibilities in the world, "I am tempted to don trousers and stride through life à la George Sand."

This statement had agreeably thrilled and shocked Dot, cloistered in her wealth and her family's expectations.

"But then," I remember saying, perhaps a little dreamy eyed, "but then, I read Anne Bradstreet's poems to her husband and think there can be nothing more beautiful than two pure hearts united in love." Dottie had agreed, not knowing then the exhaustion and sadness just a brief period of marriage would bring her.

I did not want to attend this aftenoon's tea. I wanted to walk in the fresh air and listen to Claude and Beatrice argue in my head.

But I had promised Dot I would attend her tea party, and so I would. I admitted to more than a little curiosity. Dot had changed from the quiet, self-contained girl she had been into a quixotic, puzzling young woman. I was lucky to have my companion-at-arms, Sylvia, with me to mull over the odd transformation in our dear friend.

"Even that strange sentence yesterday, something

about carrying it about all morning in the fierce Italian heat . . . Sylvia, that kept going through my mind all last night. Do you remember it?" I said, when Sylvia had arrived and we had begun the walk together back to Dot's house on Commonwealth Avenue. I had changed, as I had to, into my afternoon calling frock, and wore black-lace mittens mended in several places and the requisite hemisphere hat. Although my costume was a lady's, I was in a rush and I realized I could be accused of using my "Concord walk," a fast and long-strided pace meant more for boots and fields than high-heeled button-ups and cobbled streets. I knew I had slipped into such habits, because Sylvia was having trouble keeping pace. And I chastised myself—much as I still do to this day—for worrying about what Boston society thought of me. Why should I care so much what they thought of my walk?

"No, Louisa, I don't," she said panting.

"Well, finally, I did. It is from one of the stories we made up, that summer when we had bonfires every night. But I can't remember the rest of the story, only that a young woman is in great danger, and she carries something about in the Italian heat. . . ."

"Perhaps," Sylvia suggested, pulling at my sleeve in an attempt to slow my pace, "Dot simply doesn't have enough to keep her occupied. You often say that hard work and 'good drill' keep the mind clear."

"Do I? How righteous I must sound, Sylvia. You know, of course, I am counseling myself to keep out of the Slough of Despond. I miss Anna, and I am worried about Dorothy."

"Dorothy did seem changed yesterday," Sylvia agreed. "Certainly she is different from her old self. She used to be shy. Now she seems secretive. She was gay; now she frowns very often. Do you think Wortham has caused this?"

"Your cousin is charming, but unreliable," I said as

we approached once again the Commonwealth Avenue mansion. "He claimed to become a new man when he fell in love with Dot. But Abba says people cannot change their nature, and I think I agree. I know Dottie, being Dottie, even knowing of his earlier exploits, forgave perhaps too quickly, too easily. But I admit to feeling uneasy."

"I know." Sylvia was breathless. "I can tell by the length of your stride."

At two-thirty we knocked once again at the Wortham front door.

Wortham opened it, except he wasn't his usual debonair self. His hair stood on end; his shirt was open at the collar and rumpled. He smelled of whiskey.

"Oh, dear." I sighed. "Dot isn't here, is she?"

"Miss Alcott! She's been gone all day! She left before breakfast, didn't leave a word for me, never came home for lunch. . . . Miss Alcott, I'm worried something has happened!"

Chapter Three

Dottie Is Discovered

"**D**ot is gone! She's been gone all day!" Preston exclaimed again, tearing at his hair in an overwrought manner.

"Stay calm, Mr. Wortham. I'm sure there is an explanation." But even then I wasn't at all sure. "Let us go inside." I placed my gloved hand on his elbow and guided him into his own parlor.

I had never seen Preston Wortham in such a state until that terrible day. He was beside himself, unable to sit, shaking, wild-eyed. I later realized he was overreacting to a wife who had acquired a penchant for absentminded late arrivals. Something was very wrong in this household.

Tea was already set up and Digby stood by, towel on arm. The parlor maid shifted nervously on her tiptoes and wrung her hands in her apron. No one else had arrived yet.

"Mr. Wortham, have you and Dot quarreled?" I was convinced a direct approach was called for.

"Quarreled?" Preston Wortham's eyes grew even larger, and he again ran his hand through his bristling hair. "Quarreled?" he repeated as if the word were new to him. "Of course not!"

Digby cleared his throat and stared straight ahead. The parlor maid giggled.

"I see," I said. "Well, we must sit and wait and hope that Dot will be here soon."

Wortham sat in his armchair, and Sylvia and I perched on a little settee. The first cups of tea were poured. And finished. A second cup poured. Lily the spaniel was nowhere to be seen. Occasionally Mr. Wortham bolted from his chair and paced over the expensive Aubusson rug; then—perhaps I had gazed at him rather sternly—he sat back down.

A half hour passed. The doorbell rang.

"Finally!" Mr. Wortham ran to the door and was about to fling it open when Digby, with a gentle clearing of his throat, discreetly stepped before him into the hall. Gentlemen do not answer their own doors.

"Preston," growled a woman's voice, "I have come again to tea, as Dot pleaded. I hope she is here for a change." Alfreda Thorney marched into the parlor, stopping only to let Digby take her wrap. There was a frozen moment of hostility between Digby and Alfreda (Did no one notice it but I?); then she recollected herself. "Ah. I see she is not. Good thing I did not remove my gloves. Really, this will not do. I will cease calling on her." She folded her arms over her meager bosom and glared.

"Good day, Miss Thorney," Sylvia said, rising and extending her hand.

"It is not a good day. I do not like being mocked in this manner."

"I'm sure Dot doesn't intend—" I began.

"I'm no longer sure of what Dot does or does not intend. Her hasty marriage to this gentleman seems to have altered her. She has lost her breeding. No tea, thank you. I won't be staying."

Preston Wortham turned beet red with anger.

"Perhaps if her own family had been more sympathetic to her nature, Dot wouldn't have wandered so far from home when she made her vows," he growled at Alfreda. "She told me about her sixteenth birthday, when for a gift you brought a physician who specialized in weight reduction!"

"For her own good. She had spent the summer in Newport and ate too many ices!" Alfreda roared back, and then jumped, surprised that she had raised her own voice.

"I think this kind of conversation will do us little good," I suggested, stepping between them, for Mr. Wortham had clenched his fist and seemed on the verge of violence. The doorbell rang again. Digby quit the parlor and returned with the Misses Sarah and Edith Brownly.

"Oh my," Edith said. "Dot has done it again, hasn't she?"

"We had better get to the bottom of this," I said. "Digby, did she by any chance lose her hat again today?"

The irony was not lost on Digby. He smiled ever so slightly. "No, miss, not that I know of."

"Did she say where she was going? Do you know when she went out?"

"No, miss. On both accounts." Digby seemed a man of few words.

The parlor maid giggled louder and raised her hand. "Miss," she said softly.

Mr. Wortham, his black hair standing on end, turned to the little maid and roared, "Speak up! Speak up!"

"Well, sir, if you yell at me like that . . ."

"I'm sorry, Brigid. Tell me, please, what you know of Mrs. Wortham's absence," he said in a low voice between grinding teeth.

"She went out to buy a raisin cake, sir."

"A raisin cake?" four voices shouted at once.

"I'll be damned," said Preston Wortham. "I wonder if she's got herself in the family way. This just is not like Dot!"

"Quite so," agreed Alfreda. "Though I must add that any discussion of . . . of . . . is completely out of place in the front parlor."

"Discussion of what?" asked Edgar Brownly, appearing in the curtained doorway. "I let myself in," he said. "No one seemed to hear the bell ring. What is the commotion?"

He was breathing quickly, panting almost, as if he had been running or in some way exerting his large frame. I noticed a water stain darkening the hem of his trouser legs and I looked to the window, where the cold winter sun still shone, though it was low in the sky.

"Ah," Edgar wheezed, looking at the group. "Dot is not here."

Digby tried to placate us with tea and sandwiches and seedcake, but the cold silence that filled the parlor as Dottie's family sat on silk-covered settees and carved armchairs and again began their wait was palpable. Silver spoons tinkled against thin bone china; somewhere from deeper in the house a canary sang. Edgar slurped his tea. Alfreda sniffed. Sarah and Edith sat stiffly close to each other, one right-handed, the other left-handed, reflecting two images of the same person drinking tea and nibbling at cake.

"Well," Alfreda said after ten minutes, looking more like a Medusa than ever. "I'll not return. Tell that to Dottie. Digby, my wrap." And she sailed out of the room, her indignation puffing out her thin chest and making her sharp chin jut like a ship's prow. Her steps grew dim; a door quietly shut. Alfreda Thorney did not slam doors, even when her patience was tested beyond endurance.

Preston Wortham continued to pace and tear at his

hair, and in a few moments Edith and Sarah also rose to leave. He paid no attention to them but let Digby see to their wraps and the door.

I sat on the silk sofa across from Edgar, and waited. This was no longer a formal call, so for once I felt permitted to remove my hemisphere hat. I leaned into the sofa, prepared to stay until Dottie arrived, and then find the cause of this odd behavior. I felt a strange twinge in my chest, a sadness not yet named but already being born. The whole affair was quite alarming.

There was no pretense of conversation. I had the eerie feeling that we were all characters out of one of my tales. The friend, waiting, terrified. The indifferent brother who stayed simply because he had no other engagements. The husband, guilty, already remorseful about words shouted in the morning over coffee or perhaps the evening before . . . or perhaps guilty of a deed worse than a raised voice.

Perhaps Preston Wortham had struck his wife. Perhaps Dot, at this very moment, was in her mother's parlor, weeping out the tale. A black eye would certainly keep a new bride from her own tea party. But was Mr. Wortham capable of violence? And if that were the scenario, why hadn't Dot sent us all a note telling us not to come this afternoon?

No. It was worse than an uncontrolled squabble. Much worse. I was not leaving the parlor till I knew what had happened to my old friend.

An hour later the doorbell rang once more. Sylvia was reading a scurrilous newspaper she had found; I had borrowed a book from the Wortham library. And so I looked up from my preoccupied perusal of *The Scarlet Letter,* hoping it was Dot, and that Dot had merely forgotten her appointment, forgotten her key . . . and knowing it was not.

Preston Wortham, now slumped in a chair and staring morosely into thin air, let Digby answer the bell.

The manservant returned a moment later, followed by a tall, red-haired stranger wearing a loud plaid suit and a leather badge on his chest. A nightstick dangled from his right hand and in his left hand he held his quickly doffed stovepipe hat.

"Constable Cobban of the Boston Watch and Police," he announced, pausing in the arched doorway.

When I saw Constable Cobban, I knew my world had shifted a little on its axis. I had a premonition that Dottie and I would never have our talk.

"Are you Mr. Wortham?" the man asked, looking with obvious distaste at Edgar Brownly, whose tight scarlet waistcoat had popped a button and gaped over his belly.

"No, I am Mr. Wortham." Preston Wortham stood and did not extend his hand. A paid rather than volunteer safety patrol was new to Boston, and the social status of the new policemen was uncertain.

"I have terrible news, I'm afraid. . . ." The constable looked nervously in our direction. "Perhaps the ladies should leave the room?"

"Out with it! Tell us!" Preston Wortham shouted, unable to control himself.

"Mrs. Wortham . . ." He paused.

"She has been in an accident? A carriage . . . she doesn't realize how quickly they go, sometimes, especially the light two-horse-drawn . . . Has she been injured?" Mr. Wortham was frantic.

"No, sir. I mean, maybe, sir." The man cleared his throat. He had been gently swinging a nightstick in his right hand, but now it fell motionless to his side. "Fact is, sir, she's drowned. Found her at the landing down by the Customs House."

Sylvia and I gasped; Wortham grew strangely calm, and smiled.

"Well, then," he said with hearty good humor, "it can't be her. She had no business down by the wharves. It is not her part of town. You've come to the wrong house. Yes, the wrong house." He rocked back and forth on his heels with relief.

The patrolman cleared his throat once more. "Sir," he said, "we must, of course, have a proper identification of the person. But the fact is, her purse was in her hand and we found some correspondence in it with her name on it, and this address."

"Constable, have you brought the purse with you?" I stood and extended my hand toward him.

"Ah. Yes. A little wet there, miss . . ." He passed me the sodden needlepoint bag, its design of roses and cupids now almost buried under harbor muck. I showed it to Preston.

"It's Dot's. Oh, God!" He groaned, sitting back down.

Slowly, with a little click, I twisted the purse open and gazed inside at a handkerchief with a fancy D embroidered in the corner, a little gold case that, when forced open, revealed several of Dot's own calling cards, and a soggy and disintegrating envelope addressed to Mrs. Preston Wortham. There was nothing else in the purse. Looking back, I realize this was the moment that my mental training, aided by judicious reading of Poe, began to take effect. It began with a simple conjecture: The moneyless purse seemed odd, sinister perhaps, for, even when out for a mere walk, a lady did not leave home without a coin purse for tipping doormen and such.

No one had spoken after the officer made his announcement. Preston seemed to be in a state of incomprehension, frowning and trying to make sense of the aberrant situation, as if English had become a foreign language. Edgar had put down his teacup and sat with his hands in his lap, pressing his thumbs against each other and grimacing.

"This will seem the stupidest of questions, Constable, but by any chance was there a bakery box found with the body? Perhaps floating, and with a raisin cake inside?" I asked.

Constable Cobban frowned at what he perceived to be a strange, even trivial, question. "No, miss. No cake. But we will need someone to come to the morgue and properly identify the body."

"The morgue." Preston Wortham's voice was terrible. "My Dottie . . . No, it isn't possible. This is a mistake. We breakfasted together. She had tea and toast and marmalade. She gave half her toast to Lily. . . ."

"Lily?" Cobban repeated.

"Her little spaniel," I told him.

"Ah," the officer said. He studied his shoes.

"Yes?" I asked.

"Well, there was a dog found with the woman. Drowned, just like her."

"Oh, Dottie." I sighed. It was the dog, finally, that convinced us, that made this truth inescapable. The tears gathered and clouded my vision, and I felt them rolling down my pale cheeks.

But it was Preston Wortham who rolled his eyes up, went limp at the knees, and fell to the floor in a faint. Just like the husband would in a play.

Chapter Four

Reflections at the Morgue

As Preston seemed unable to attend to the tragic task alone, none of the terrible siblings seemed to have a free hour (suddenly Edgar had acquired a whole Wall Street of appointments), and Dottie's mother was an invalid, it was left to me to accompany Mr. Wortham to the morgue that afternoon to certify whether or not the drowning victim was, indeed, his wife, Dot.

The morgue was a rough, cold room beneath City Hall, poorly lit, but even the few gas lamps revealed all too clearly the face and figure of Mrs. Preston Wortham, née Dorothy Brownly, there on the morgue table.

She had been twenty-one years of age. Young to die, I thought, studying her through swimming eyes. Dot's hair and clothes had dried but still clung to her, almost lovingly, as if reluctant to be parted from the spirit that had brightened them for so short a time.

Yet there was no way that Dot's stillness could masquerade as a simple sleep. The river had left moss and weeds in her hair and streaming over her bosom. Her little black shoes were slippery with slime and bursting at the lacings because the water had already begun to bloat the body. Her quilted silk and fur coat was now matted and stiff and of indistinguishable color, and her once white blouse was stained brownish yellow. Her hands—dainty hands that had once been declared her one beauty—those hands were blue and stiff and cold, the skin swollen tightly around her garnet-and-diamond wedding ring. There was no sign of Lily, the puppy. Of course, the city of Boston would not waste money on a simple dog. Its little body had probably been tossed into a dustbin for disposal. Poor Dot. She would have wanted Lily to be buried in the garden next to the puppies and cats of her childhood, with a proper marker and a memorial climbing rose.

Preston Wortham looked so terrible I asked him, "Are you able to bear this? Shall I take you into the outer room?"

He gulped and his eyes blinked, but he stood his ground.

"I am . . . as well as can be imagined. Thank you for coming with me, Miss Alcott." He turned away from Dot's corpse and looked faintly about for a bench or chair, but there was none. There was nothing but death in the room, and regret, and those are not substantial enough for a man of weak character to lean upon.

The morgue attendant was a small, mustachioed man whose eyes seemed not much brighter than those of the corpses resting on the marble slabs in the room. He wore a white apron much smeared and stained with ghastly substances that I chose not to contemplate. When Preston turned away, he moved as if to draw the sheet back over Dot's head. Constable Cobban stayed his hand. He had removed his hat, so that his thick ginger-colored hair stood about his head like a halo, a strange effect for a man of his profession.

"Well?" asked that young officer.

"It is my wife. It is Mrs. Preston Wortham. Dorothy.

Dottie." Wortham's voice was unsteady and low. "She slipped, of course. It was a wet day; she wore little leather shoes instead of sturdier boots. She slipped into the river. There is no question of suicide," he said.

I held my breath and would not look at him. Had Dorothy been so unhappy she had ended her own life?

"I asked only for identification, not explanation," young Cobban said. I realized then that death is never simple, especially when the dead person is young, healthy, and extraordinarily wealthy.

"She will have a consecrated burial," Preston murmured.

"No one has mentioned suicide," Constable Cobban repeated.

Wortham once more bent over the body and placed a kiss on the cold white forehead. His task completed, he turned to leave this room of death.

"Brownly? Was that her maiden name?" Constable Cobban called after him.

Preston turned back in his direction. "It was. Come along, Miss Alcott; you appear overly strained." Though it was he who had turned white and then green.

"In a moment, Mr. Wortham," I remember saying, bending over Dot so I could also give her a final kiss.

How peaceful Dot looked. I hoped that indeed she was at peace, that she had forgiven all there was to forgive and been forgiven her own sins. What sins could young, kind Dot have ever committed? She had been goodness itself. But what she had said yesterday? *There is so much sorrow here, so much worry, because of me.* What had she meant?

"May I?" I said to Constable Cobban, who stood next to her now, ready to pull the sheet back over Dot's face now that the identification had been completed. "I would like to keep her scarf as a memento mori. . . ."

"Of course. I don't suppose Mr. Wortham would object, so why should I?" Cobban said gruffly.

I felt his strange pale eyes watching me, and my fingers grew awkward and could not undo the knot in her scarf.

More gently, Cobban said, "Let me untangle it for you, Miss Alcott. It may be difficult and . . ." He did not finish, but I knew what he meant: Now that the final kiss had been given, it was frightening, gruesome, to have to touch that body from which the spirit of my friend had departed. Dot was fled from here, and all that remained was an emptied vessel, a broken promise.

With surprising gentleness, Sergeant Cobban raised the corpse's head just enough so that the scarf could be unknotted and pulled away. Because rigor mortis was already setting in, the whole torso lifted at an unnatural angle, as if a board had been slipped into her garments to keep her straight, as some mothers did with new babes. One of Dot's mud-stiffened curls fell out of the snood that captured them, and swung down over the table. I could not help feeling dizzy, but I stood my ground.

"Here," Sergeant Cobban said, pulling the scarf free and handing it to me. And because Sergeant Cobban was looking at me, and not the corpse, and Wortham was already hovering near the door, either consumed by nausea and grief or simply distracted, I was the first to see them: little blue bruises on both sides of the neck.

"What's this?"

Constable Cobban saw my eyes narrow with concentration and surprise. He leaned closer to the body, poked gently with his fingertips at the marks, rubbed them slightly as if hoping they might erase. They did not.

"Well, now," he said, standing upright and rocking on his heels, deep in thought. "Indeed, this puts the case in a new light entirely." Cobban hailed the morgue attendant, who had been sitting at a zinc table reading a book. We could see the title: Mary Shelley's *Frankenstein*.

The mustachioed attendant put down his book and sprinted over to the officer's side. Obviously he knew Cobban, and knew Cobban was a man you didn't keep waiting.

"Postmortem on this woman," Cobban ordered.

"We're backed up . . ." the attendant started to protest, then changed his mind. "Two days," he said.

"Tomorrow morning," Cobban said.

"Postmortem?" Preston Wortham, who had been leaning against the wall nearest the door, burying his hands in the armpits of his wool coat and stamping his feet against the cold of the room, paid attention once again to what was going on a few yards away. "Does that mean an autopsy? Since when is an autopsy done on a suici—I mean an accident victim? I won't allow the desecration of poor Dot. . . ."

"Mr. Wortham, there must be a postmortem. Wouldn't you like to know exactly how your young wife died?" There was a note in Constable Cobban's voice that made Wortham uncomfortable. I peered expectantly at him, eager for his answer.

"I know how she died," the husband insisted. "She slipped and fell and drowned. And now I am going to visit her minister and arrange the funeral."

"Three days. That's when the funeral will be," Cobban insisted. "Unless you want the body disinterred. The bruises make it a case needing further examination. Medical jurisprudence will be required." Cobban would not be moved. He had decided.

"Bruises?" Preston moved closer and peered down at his wife's exposed neck. He blanched and swallowed hard, then looked defiantly at Cobban.

The two men glared at each other. Preston was the

first to drop his eyes. "Well, if you believe it is necessary," he said. "But on point of order, I protest this autopsy, as will the rest of the family. Not all in the family are without influence," he added.

"I have heard of the Brownlys," Cobban said icily. "I know Mrs. Brownly will try to have my head on a platter. But she won't get it. Now I suggest you all go home. You've had a shock." And to make his point, Cobban ushered us to the door, as if we were children dismissed from school.

I turned to him. "I would like to view the postmortem. They do require witnesses, don't they?"

"Miss Alcott," protested Preston. "Remember that you are a lady! It is unfit, outrageous!"

And that (I knew such comments gave rise to stubbornness within myself that rivaled my father's!) made me insist that I would view it.

"A full jury will view, as the law requires," Cobban said. "Because of your relationship to the deceased and her husband you may not be part of that jury, but I will arrange a place for you to sit among them. Are you certain, Miss Alcott? A postmortem is not an easy thing to view."

"I am certain," I said. A strong determination was firing through my backbone, a determination to search for the truth about Dot.

Cobban studied me as if he were looking for something. He found it. "Tomorrow at ten promptly," he said. As I left, he touched my shoulder, a gesture between a comforting pat and a discreet push. I could not help but wonder: Was that a great tenderness or just polite attention to a lady?

"Take a carriage home, Miss Alcott. The streets are dark now," he said. "And dangerous."

"I'll see to the lady," Preston said, his voice heavy with noblesse oblige.

As I rode home in Preston Wortham's carriage, I

tried to stop seeing Dot, cold in the morgue, and attempted to distract my racing mind by turning my inner eye to a portrait of home, how it would be when I arrived. Abba would still be in the kitchen, kneading biscuit dough for tomorrow. Lizzie would probably be wih her, helping, and May would be in bed, reading a novel. Father would be in his study, preparing a lecture, probably on the free soil movement and abolition. The front door would be unlocked, even though there was no servant to keep watch over the comings and goings of the house, and even though most of Boston not only bolted their doors but added additional bracing. We had no worldly goods to protect and worry over. Yet that home was a paradise.

Poor Dorothy. What had her home, first with her mother then with her husband, been like?

Dorothy was dead. There had been bruises. And whatever had Dot been doing down by the wharves in that part of town?

"We will have to order a wreath, and I must mend my black bombazine for the funeral," I told Sylvia. "The protocols of grief must be observed. I once thought mourning and its many rules to be old-fashioned and melodramatic; loss now teaches me otherwise."

It was the next day, and we were back in the attic. The sheet of paper in front of me was blank. For once I was silenced and literally unable to write. The paper had blisters where mine and Sylvia's tears had fallen on it.

"What did Abba say?" Sylvia asked.

"To trust in God's mercy. We wept together and she is being brave, but it has affected her. So much death . . ."

I showed Sylvia my journal entry, about the dreams of the night before . . . a dream of Dottie as she had been as a child, still in the schoolroom, shy yet brave, slow to memorize dates and names but quick to sense a storm coming, or a puppy on the verge of illness. The dreams were mostly rehearsals of what had been, as are most dreams of loss, but in some moments Dottie turned away from the familiar gestures of childhood and stared into my eyes. "So much to talk about, dear Louy," Dottie said. As she spoke I woke up, still hearing her gentle voice.

Despondent, I felt myself slipping, my friend's death an unwelcome addition to the oppressive weight already loaded on my shoulders.

"Mother gave me a dose of valerian and told me to put it out of my thoughts," Sylvia said. "She seems to think Dot got what she deserved, whatever that means. I admit she has never cared for Dot, not like we did. I wonder why. Is that your story, Louy?" Sylvia touched a pile of pages.

"Yes. The one Mr. Fields deems unsuitable and lacking in talent."

"And to think you actually did go into service. I could never."

"And I shouldn't have, I fear. Abba was right. I spent my nights blacking boots and being chased around the kitchen table. I would have been of more use here, at home." I smiled ruefully.

The house was still. Outside, a dog barked to be let in. Wind rattled withered leaves. I closed my eyes, beckoned Beatrice and the opera house in Italy, the beautiful women with their sparkling jewels and waving plumes, the men with narrow aristocratic faces, opera glasses held high to examine the feminine company in the various boxes. I smelled the champagne and pâté, the perfumes, heard the slight tinkle of crystal from the overhead chandeliers as the velvet curtains parted to reveal the stage, and onstage a set of a castle, a dark night, a new world waiting to receive

its visitors. And then one word entered my thoughts—
Dottie—and the vision of Italy vanished.

"A stage and a blank page have much in common,
Sylvia," I told my companion. "But I can't concentrate
on this story till I discover what has happened to
Dot."

The professions of detective and author, I now
know, have much in common. Both involve an attempt
to understand the deepest nature of human beings, as
well as the act of telling—or uncovering—their deepest, truest stories. Yet when one is overcome by the
desire to help a friend and solve a mystery, at least
for me, it removes the desire and ability to write. It
is similar to the magical time at the end of each novel
when I feel completely consumed by my characters.
When I am in the middle of a mystery, an event that
occurs only when I must save a friend from peril, the
detective work consumes my every effort and the
muse is, temporarily, struck dumb.

"It is nine-thirty," Sylvia said, checking the little
gold watch pinned to her bodice.

"Sylvie, I worry that even for me this autopsy will
prove too distressing," I said. "Are you certain you
wish to come with me? Remember you fainted at the
sight of blood last summer when you cut your foot."

"I shall not let you endure this alone," she replied
staunchly.

I pulled back the muslin curtain and looked out into
the street.

"There is no sun today, only clouds," Sylvia remarked. It seemed undeniably appropriate.

Chapter Five

A Case for Murder

The postmortem was held in the courthouse basement, in a cold and dreary greenish-white room grotesquely shaped like a small theater, with a construction like a wooden stage, and a table on that stage, and rows of facing tiered seats. The gaslight was unnaturally bright and cast deep shadows as people moved. Paid witnesses, mostly hired off the street, filed in and took their places, piling hats and cloaks on empty chairs in the back.

We took a seat in front, center, just three arm's lengths away. I could see that many of the men in attendance viewed this as a rather bold gesture. I suddenly realized that, if I wished, I could breach convention and reach down and touch my dear friend one last time. I knew I would not, but the urge was there. Sylvia was already visibly trembling.

Waiting, I noted every detail, from the dirty rags in the corner, a stained coffee cup on the edge of the soapstone basin, the triangular sooty stains over the gas lighting fixtures. But always my eyes returned to that table and the solitary figure resting there.

Poor Dot. How alone she looked. Her clothing had been removed and her body wrapped in white sheets soaked in chloride of lime to slow putrefaction. Even so, the sickly odor of death wafted through the room. Many of the witnesses held cologne-soaked handkerchiefs to their noses.

Promptly at ten o'clock (we could hear the bell of Old Trinity ringing) white-bearded Dr. Roder shuffled in from a side door, like an actor uncertain of when to enter stage right. But his stooped posture and vague air were misleading. Boston's oldest doctor of medical jurisprudence, he had an intimidating reputation as a scholar in the field, with training that could trace its ancestry all the way back to the famous Benjamin Rush. He had studied technique with Duncan in Edinburgh and Thomas Cooper at the University of Pennsylvania, and was protégé of old Walter Channing himself at Harvard.

It was said of Roder that he could find cause of death in a corpse that had been buried for centuries and then burned for good measure. If Constable Cobban had requested Dr. Roder for the postmortem, then the officer must already suspect foul play.

Roder, well aware that his fame had preceded him, strode to the center of the room, faced the witnesses, and made a little bow. The uncertain actor had become the impresario. There was slight, nervous applause. I turned and glared at the other observers and they put their hands back in their laps and were silent.

"We will begin," Roder announced.

Cobban, who had been standing in a corner, moved closer to the table. He looked down at Dot with pity and a gentleness that spoke well for a young man who had chosen a career that often required thwacking fugitives on the head and sometimes wearing a revolver inside his coat—unofficially, of course. Revolvers had not yet been issued to the new Boston Police.

A young assistant with long dark hair like an Italian poet's unraveled the top sheet, leaving Dot's arms, legs, and shoulders bare, while a second sheet still modestly covered the torso and trunk. Next to me, Sylvia put her hand over her mouth and rolled her eyes to the ceiling.

In the harsh, bright, unforgiving light I could see other bruises on Dorothy's arms. I knew I had to study this gruesome scene with determined concentration. The bruises were small, pale, as if the blood that would normally pool there where the skin had been insulted hadn't had time to complete its own work. Death had halted the process. While I felt deep grief for my Dorothy, the spirit of Poe's Auguste Dupin seemed to fill me with detective zeal.

Cobban had been standing motionless at the head of the marble slab, staring at Dot's now-loosened hair as if wanting to avoid embarrassing her. The doctor and his attendant, however, handled the corpse with an indifferent boldness that seemed to prolong the humiliation of death.

Active now, Cobban leaned over Dot once again, studying the neck, jotting in his notebook where and how the bruises were located, the shape of them. He looked up, so he could see me. His eyes were wary.

I understood instinctively that the marks on Dot's body could not have been self-inflicted. Young Mrs. Wortham had been very roughly handled, and recently. Were the bruises acquired at death, or sometime before? Were the bruises connected with her death? I tried to convey to Constable Cobban through my eyes and expression that we were thinking alike.

Dr. Roder started the examination at the head. He swept to one side the wealth of loosened pale hair and leaned close, pulling up the eyelids, swabbing out the ears, and prying open the mouth.

"It would appear," he began, speaking loudly, "to be a case of dynamic death, rather than mechanical. The woman is young and with no evidence, yet, of ill health or disease that would cause bodily failure. She was pulled from the harbor, yet there is no sign of river water in her mouth. In cases of drowning, a negative poisoning of the blood ensues, since the blood, suddenly deprived of the influence of the oxygen of the atmosphere, becomes unfit to vivify."

Heads in the gallery nodded to indicate comprehension. One very ancient top-hatted gentleman in the back row was already nodding off. He would be paid his ten cents whether he stayed awake or not.

"There are bruises on the throat seemingly made by a hand," Roder continued. "Moreover, there is a large lump over one ear, invisible to the eye because of the healthy thickness of the subject's hair. But it is a lump, nonetheless, suggesting injury before death. A man, or a woman, may fall alive into water and die there without being drowned, as when she receives a fatal injury by falling with her head hitting a rock. But when a woman in falling into the water receives a fatal cranial injury whereof she dies before she drowns, then she is certainly not drowned, but has fallen dead into the water."

Roder paused and looked at Cobban. "I am, of course, suggesting unnatural death," he said, in case his train of thought hadn't been followed. The paid witnesses leaned forward, interested now.

"Could the injuries have occurred after she fell into the water?" Cobban asked.

"Forensics is a science that sometimes provides more questions than answers, but in this case I would say no," Roder said, poking again at Dot's throat to test for sponginess in the tissue. "There is no swelling of the sinuses that follows a death by cerebral hypostasis caused by drowning."

He moved from Dot's head to her right side, where he lifted her hand and used a sharp little knife to scrape under the nail of her index finger. He then held a magnifying glass over the knife tip.

"There is no sign of sand or wood or any other substance that the deceased, in her death throes, might have attempted to clutch," Roder said. "In my great experience"—he endowed the usually monosyllabic *great* with three syllables, I remember noting—"accidental drownings always have some such refuse under the nails, left during a vain attempt at self-rescue; but many drowning suicides have similar refuse, as if, in the last moment, they have changed their minds and now wish to reverse the decision of self-destruction."

Roder put Dot's hand back at her side. He pressed gently on her chest, then again peered into the open mouth.

"No evidence of tracheal froth, produced when inhaled fluid mixes with the natural mucus of the passages."

"An indication she wasn't breathing when she fell into the river," Cobban said.

"You have been studying my papers. Well done, Constable," Roder said. "But the absence of tracheal froth could also indicate that putrefaction has already begun," he corrected him. "Gas is forming in the abdomen." Roder pressed at the base of Dottie's rib cage. "Most telling, however, are the lungs. They are not expanded, in fact are firm and crepitating. In a victim of drowning, the lungs distend and acquire a spongelike consistency. The torso would be misshapen by now."

Roder paused and reached to a tray an assistant carried. He picked a large, shiny knife. I flinched instinctively and fought the urge to cover my eyes. Next to me, Sylvia gasped. Her hand flew to her mouth, covering it.

"Time to open the cavity and examine the organs," Roder announced.

Another assistant pulled away the last sheet covering Dot's hips and legs and she lay there, naked and completely vulnerable, exposed to friends and strangers alike. I had to keep from crying out in protest. How Dot would have hated this, Dot who would not even pull up her stockings before other women but always retreated to her chamber or the water closet to make any adjustment of clothing, now lying there as naked as a newborn for all to gaze upon. Just as well that none of the family were here . . . this was not the way to remember the young woman, greenly white, blue eyes staring dumbly at eternity, the rest of the body as exposed as any lamb ready for slaughter.

How—why—had she been brought to this? What awful circumstances and passions had led her on this course?

Two factors already argued against suicide. First, the coroner's statement that most suicides preserved, somewhere in the destroyed body, the wish to undo, to live, and Dot's corpse had no such evidence. Could her grief, that secret despair she had worn upon her return from the honeymoon, have been so deep as to thwart even the most instinctive instruction to live?

I concentrated on the past and suddenly remembered how Abba had once described Dottie: *A little simple, sometimes, but full of love, the kind of woman who will live a long life and never regret a moment of it.* No. Dottie could not have overcome her own nature, which was to live. No one could forget her trials on the gorgeous chestnut pony she had received for her tenth birthday—and avidly shared with all of us, her friends. The pony was a beauty with a horrid disposition; it bit, stood its ground, and whenever Dot gained her rightful place in the saddle, without so much as a by-your-leave the pony would buckle and throw her to the ground. Eventually even Mrs. Brownly put her foot down and insisted the pony be returned, but Dot, more stubborn, cried for days. She hated to give up.

At the postmortem, though, I looked down upon Dot's bruised, naked, lifeless body and realized that this was the final insult to whatever injury had quenched that fine spirit. Even her modesty had been annihilated.

Death was a destroyer, and Dot's virtues had been destroyed along with the rest of her.

Roder was beginning to lift organs out of the opened cavity of Dorothy's body.

"Louy," Sylvia pleaded. She had turned pale green.

"We must get you into the air," I said, helping her from her seat. "We have seen enough here. Too much for you, I fear."

It was late morning when I left the bowels of the morgue and returned to the thin light of a cold winter day, much as Orpheus strode back to life, away from the underworld and his beloved Eurydice. The dead live in a place that the living cannot abide. I had visited that place, and now had to pick up again the threads of my own life.

Sylvia recovered after many deep breaths and some mild fanning with a handkerchief, and apologized for her weakness. Bravely, she suggested we finish the morning with a visit to Mr. Wortham, so he might hear of the postmortem from us and not a stranger.

"After what I have seen, I am not ready to converse with him," I remember replying. We both felt, at that moment, a dawning antipathy for the man who had once been a friend, albeit not a close friend. Weren't husbands supposed to keep their wives safe from harm?

"We will walk for a while and get our bearings," I suggested.

Without planning, we found ourselves turning east, toward the Customs House and the harbor, where Dot had been found.

Who had been there with her when she fell? Whose

face had been her last vision of this life? Her husband's? Unlike most heiresses, Dot had married for love above all other considerations. Yet yesterday, the last time we had seen her alive, the marriage seemed to have already soured. Was Preston Wortham a murderer? No. Impossible to think so. Murder required cunning, an urge to action, which lazy, good-natured Preston lacked.

"Waldo Emerson once said to me, when a stable boy much beloved by the locals of Concord had been found guilty of burglary, that if all criminals wore their guilt like a garment the world would have no need of inquiries and investigations," I said, thinking aloud. "Dot was seen in the morning, at breakfast, and then discovered later that afternoon. She had died—been murdered?—in full daylight, in a very busy part of Boston. How?"

The morning fog had not lifted, and the great ships and smaller schooners of Boston Harbor rocked gently on the swells like gargantuan birds, their wings tucked under, barely visible through the drifting mist and spray. Rigging creaked; watch bells clanged; the voices of the shoremen and dockhands echoed and repeated, bouncing off that thick pea-soup fog. A laborer carrying a hogshead of rum on his shoulder as if it were no more than a five-pound sack of flour bumped into me and almost knocked me into the water, so thick was the weather.

"There was no fog on the day Dot died," I continued, accepting his apologies and straightening my hat. "Something else concealed the crime. What could it have been?"

"It is bustling here, Louisa," Sylvia complained. "I can barely hear you."

"Of course. There was a distraction of some sort," I said. "Thank you, Sylvia."

"You are welcome, I'm sure," she said, only a little confused.

The heavy, fetid smell of death mixed with the sea spray on our faces, with the gray clouds jostling in the sky and adding depth to the landlocked fog, with the curses and yells of the sailors and dockworkers. Another body, moving quickly through the blinding air, bumped into me, and I clutched my reticule closer, between arm and side, trying to foil the pickpockets who worked this part of the city. It was noisy here by the Customs House, bustling with feverish activity, with street sellers calling their wares and fishermen mending nets, and workers carrying bundles to the great stone house, the heart and soul of Boston commerce.

Had Constable Cobban said exactly where Dot had been found? No. Only that it had been very close to the Customs House.

"Well," I said to Sylvia, "I will make inquiries."

A little kiosk badly in need of paint and offering sugared water and crab cakes leaned on the right side of the Customs House, not quite touching, but close enough that the larger building protected the tiny one from the strongest winds. The crab-cake seller was an ancient woman, a sailor's widow, whose vision and hearing had been dimmed by time but whose curiosity made up for those weakened faculties.

"A woman hound? A bitch you are seeking?" the crone screeched in response to my first question.

"No, no. A woman drowned. Yesterday. Do you know where she was found?" I yelled back.

"Ah, poor thing." The crone chuckled. "Indeed I do. Right there, before my very eyes, her body floated." She pointed with a gnarled and trembling finger straight ahead. "Lovely gown," she said. "Will it go to a charity house, do you think?"

Downcurrent, I noted. Then she would have entered the water up there, somewhere beyond the Customs House.

"I could use that coat she was wearing," the old

woman insisted. "Once it dries it will be a fine wrap, even if the buttons don't meet the buttonholes. A shame, a fine coat like that, and her in it all dead and weedy. I've said oft enough they shouldn't let the fine folk and their children come down here. Too rough, I say. But the nobs from Beacon Hill will come to see the ships."

I was glad, at the moment, for the fog and the crone's poor eyesight, for I blushed then, myself a Beacon Hill resident, though never a nob. Abba had insisted when we moved from Concord to Boston that we reside in a respectable part of town, for my sisters' sakes.

"The children be the worst part. They are always falling in and needing to be rescued. Yesterday a child fell in and the nurse screamed bloody horror, running back and forth, not brave enough herself to jump in and fetch the child." The old woman smiled with glee.

"When?" I asked. "When did the child fall in?"

"Let's see. I'd had my soup, so it was after dinner, but old man Burns hadn't come by yet for his crab and pickle, so it was before five. Quite a commotion t'were. The shipowners and managers screamed almost as loud as the nurse, for most the men stopped work to watch. They'd been working steady till then, no other distractions."

A commotion in the afternoon. And perhaps, farther up harbor, a woman was hit on the head, strangled, thrown into the water, and no one heard; no one noticed.

"It could have happened like that," I said to Sylvia. "Pull the woman—I know it sounds strange, Sylvia, but if I say 'Dorothy' just now I will weep; I know I will—pull the woman out of view, behind one of those piles of crates waiting to be loaded, at the moment when the commotion is at its greatest, and you could commit murder in broad daylight, in the busiest part of Boston."

"Murder, Louisa?" Sylvia asked, unwilling to believe.

"Would you find suicide more believable?" I asked firmly.

"No. Of course not."

"Second day in a row." The crone was chuckling. "Day before, another little girl fell in. Pretty little thing she was, before she was sodden, that is. That be strange, two days in a row. Them nobs should stay at home. . . ."

"Thank you," I said. "If you need a winter coat, you can get one at the charity house next to Trinity Church. I'll make sure there is one there for you."

"The young woman's? That fur collar looked warm."

"Perhaps," I said. "I'll have to ask her family."

One part of the mystery had offered itself up to possible answers: the how of Dot's death. It was too soon, I felt, to think about the next question: Why? The why would, of course, lead to who, and that part of the mystery must be approached cautiously, slowly, gravely.

But one other question taunted me. Dot, as a girl, had often remarked that home and hearth, not adventure, were her joy and she had spent her entire honeymoon year traveling, as fashion dictated, and, I suspected, Mother Brownly required. Surely Dot had grown sufficiently weary of the sight of ship and sea! So what had she been doing at the harbor in the first place?

Chapter Six

A Mother Mourns

"Abba, it was not an accident," I said, hanging my coat and hat on the waiting hooks by the front door. My mother was on her hands and knees wiping away sticky biscuit crumbs and drops of honey-sweetened milk from the bare wood floor of the hall.

"Dot's death was not an accident," I repeated. The words tasted strange, like burned onions, bitter and heavy on the tongue.

"Is that what the doctor said at the postmortem? Hand me that bucket, Louy. What is it about arrowroot biscuits? I swear they could use them to glue bricks together. Now, tell me about Dot." Abba continued scrubbing the floor, well used to the necessity of blending manual labor with domestic conversation to conserve precious time.

I, heedless of my gown, got down on my hands and knees and started wiping dry with a towel those areas my mother had just scrubbed.

"He didn't say it in so many words," I said. "But that was the gist of his deductions. Dot was already dead when she was thrown into the river. Some crumbs over there, Abba. No, I can reach them." I scraped at the sticky drops with my thumbnail. "There were bruises at the throat, a wound on the head, and no water in the lungs or sinuses. Oh, Abba, you should have seen Dot—Dot's corpse—there on the marble table. . . ."

"Poor child." Abba sat back on her heels and wiped her forehead, and that one phrase, intoned like a prayer, included Dot and me as well, as I had spent the morning studying the result of violent death.

"What poor child? Where have you been, Louy?" My father, tall, silver-haired, and still handsome despite his fifty-some years, came out of his study and hooked his thumbs behind his suspenders. His black trousers bagged at the knees, the elbows of his jacket had worn through, and he had forgotten to shine his boots. Yet still he maintained the aura of an Olympian, albeit a down-at-the-heels deity, especially when viewed from floor level, where Abba and I still searched for crumbs. Father did as well as a philosopher can in a money-loving world, but one could never describe his appearance as prosperous.

I smiled up at him, glad to have him safely home again. We all brooded about Father, about whether he had remembered to eat, to sleep, to wear a clean shirt collar.

I felt warm when he came home, but I felt a reserve with him that I did not with my mother. Perhaps because he often called me his topsy-turvy Louisa in a tone of voice that indicated doubt in my ability to amount to anything; perhaps it was because I could not completely be myself with him but had to hide some of that intellect, that ambition, that was all my own, for the sake of domestic peace. I had learned this difficult lesson at an early age. Yet I loved him, and knew that anything real I would write would contain elements of him.

"Your father has been cheated once again." Abba sighed. "Promised ten dollars, and paid one."

"Promises have been broken," Father agreed.

The wealthy, we had noticed, promised considerable fees and often forgot to pay them later.

"And the conversation went well enough. But I am alarmed at the superficial readings that are popular today," he said, pulling at his suspenders and rocking on his heels. "Too many are reading the sensational trash published in today's papers. Adulteries and murders and men competing for a faithless woman. . . ."

I studied the floor with complete concentration to force down the blush rising to my cheeks, since my own story in progress, "The Rival Prima Donnas," fell into that very category my father now so robustly condemned. If it were to be published, I would have to use a nom de plume. Oh, how that thrilled me! Flora, I quickly decided. In honor of *The Flower Fables,* which, if they were published, could be published under my real name. Yes, Flora Fairfield, authoress of "The Rival Prima Donnas!"

"I must carefully consider what allusions I use," Father said, lost in his own train of thought as he often was and not noticing that I, too, was daydreaming, "as most are lost completely, as a result of people reading trash. Would you believe that Iris Barfoy wasn't familiar with Epicurus's essay on the phenomenon of atmosphere?"

Mother and I exchanged covert glances.

"Shocking," I agreed solemnly.

"But we digress. I distinctly heard the words 'poor child' and inquired if a child of mine was in some distress."

"Not a child of yours, Father. But a child you have known. Dorothy Brownly is dead," I said softly.

"Ah. So soon. Is the child alive and well to console its bereaved father?" Father had assumed that since Dorothy had been a young and healthy woman, she had died while—or soon after—delivering a first child. Many young women did.

"It wasn't childbed fever, Father. Dorothy . . ." I had almost said *drowned,* but that no longer seemed the case. "Dorothy was found in the harbor."

Father frowned, making a perplexed face.

"The harbor? Poor child, indeed. What measure of despair can drive people to self-destruction?" He scratched his chin. "It is the times," he concluded. "The world has become heartless and depraved and the innocent suffer. Isn't . . . wasn't Dorothy the little girl who got herself entangled with that bounder Preston Wortham?"

"Father, she married him."

"I see. And to think he once came calling on you. I have more than once had cause to thank the Creator for the common sense of my own offspring."

I could not suppress a smile of pleasure. "Father! I didn't know you had even noticed! And to think you remembered such a trivial event!"

"Of course I noticed. I remember the man sitting right there, in that chair." He pointed into the parlor, at the brown velvet easy chair. "I didn't like the looks of him. Like a peacock. Overdressed and probably the kind who never bothered to pay his tailor. As if tailors don't have rent to pay, and children to feed . . ."

I quickly perceived that the philospher's mind would soon digress into more familiar territory, the abuses perpetrated by the upper classes on the working classes, unless I could shepherd his thoughts back onto the subject at hand.

"You needn't have worried, Father," I said. "At the time I had no great objection to Mr. Wortham, as I recall, except that I suspected that being his wife would be much too time-consuming. All that brushing of hats and coats and pressing of trousers. But Dorothy had no such reservations, of course, being of an independent income that allows for maids and housekeepers."

"Poverty saved you, Louy," Father said.

"Just don't say from a fate worse than death. Let's perhaps simply conclude that Dorothy's wealth was not always an advantage," I said. "I will call on her mother tomorrow, and offer our condolences."

Father nodded. "I would come with you, as the head of our household, but I must complete this speech I have promised for the Boston Vigilance Committee."

"Don't give it a thought," I said quickly. "Finish your work." The last thing Mrs. Brownly needed was one of Father's lectures on reincarnation.

I spent the next morning at home seeing to my little schoolchildren, since I had left Abba and Lizzie at home with them the day before and May was still too young for such responsibility. Such days, locked indoors with wailing six-year-olds and sulky ten-year-olds, could be difficult. But even with its moments of drudgery, such work was bliss compared to last year, when I had taken work as a housemaid. I sometimes thought that the world offered women tedious choices when one must select between wiping sticky noses and chanting the state capitals over and over, or cleaning boots and emptying bedpans for strangers.

By two o'clock in the afternoon, Johnnie had been sick all over the carpet and Betty had wept because she could not remember Albany in New York, and Ruthie hit James when he hogged the pickup-sticks at playtime, and I was wishing I could flee to my garret and my desk, and go back to that other world I was creating, the world of Italian opera, with its prima donnas and handsome admirers. "It is whispered—and with truth, I fear—that she will bestow the hand so many have sought in vain upon the handsome painter yonder," I whispered to myself, rehearsing dialogue for the next scene in the story as I cleaned up after my little charges.

But my writing would have to wait. I had a condolence call to make at the Brownly mansion. I dressed with careful attention to each detail of my costume and then made a face at myself in the mirror for even trying, for I knew that I would never come up to Mrs. Brownly's standards.

If the Brownlys of Boston did not arrive on the *Mayflower,* it was the ship right after it, beating even the Lowells to that marshy landing spot near Plymouth Rock. The first Brownly of Boston was a planter with the sense to marry a wealthy widow and invest her fortune in a glass manufactory, one of the first in the country. There was Brownly glass in every church in New England, at one time. Along with wealth the family acquired a retroactive family tree: It was said (in whispered, jealous tones) that every deposit made to the family safe seemed to bring the family one degree closer to William the Conquerer, the most coveted of English ancestors.

The most recent Brownly mansion had been built fifty years before the events surrounding Dorothy's death, on Beacon Hill, of course, and while the façade of red brick and white columns was demure enough to meet even Boston standards, the interior of that home was garish with carved wood paneling, gilt mirrors, marble floors, stuffed peacocks, mounted boar's heads, and overstuffed sofas and armchairs covered with floral patterns.

There were three parlors, and a maid for each, and I had rather hoped myself and Mrs. Brownly might converse that day in the little green parlor, for in that velvet-tufted, Moorish-tiled room hung some lovely Fra Angelicos, which some earlier Brownly had had the wiser taste to purchase than whatever Brownly had commissioned the carved inglenook. The inglenook, large enough for a child to hide in—as I knew from my own experience—and therefore to scorch from the fire both frock and matching lace petticoat, was covered with leering gargoyles and virulent wreathing vines. It had been oft commented that when the Brownly clan rebelled against the simplicity of the Regency style, that rebellion was not subtle. So despite gargoyles and inglenooks, I had hoped to gaze once again on *Madonna and Child in an Olive Grove*. But no, the upstairs maid was sent to fetch me upstairs, to the nursery. Mrs. Brownly was one of those unfortunate women who, after decades of childbearing and child raising, had anticipated a happy retirement from such responsibility, only to discover at the age of fifty that yet one more baby had taken up temporary occupancy in her womb.

The change-of-life daughter, Agnes, had been born six years before, to the chagrin of her father, who had promptly died of apoplexy after discovering there was one more daughter to be provided for, and to the joy of Edgar Brownly, who remained the only son and heir to the Brownly fortune, aside from whatever considerations were made for Sarah, Edith, and Dorothy. And like other change-of-life children, Agnes was largely ignored by her exhausted mother until some event in the child's life demanded maternal attention. Today seemed to be one of those days.

I, unsmiling, stepped behind the maid, past the green parlor, the beige parlor, and the red parlor, up the curving polished staircase, and down the hall. I glanced into the green parlor as we passed it, hoping for at least a brief glance of my favorite painting. But the wall where it had hung the year before was empty. Mrs. Brownly must have tired of it.

Halfway down the hall I heard weeping, and saw a woman dressed in a brown wool travel suit dabbing at her eyes as she came out of one of the second-floor service rooms—a linen closet probably, I thought.

The maid, seeing my curiosity, nodded at the

woman, who ignored us and struggled to lift a heavy
carpetbag. "She's been let go," the maid whispered.
"Mrs. Brownly said she was negligent and a danger
to the child. Now there'll be more work for everyone,
with the nanny gone." The dismissed nurse sniffed as
I continued the long walk down the hall, up yet another flight of stairs to the attic.

Mrs. Brownly followed the custom of keeping very
young children in the attic, as out-of-sight as possible,
except for rare and brief occasions when they were
scrubbed, becurled, camouflaged with layers of lace,
and, after promising not to say a word, allowed downstairs for brief glimpses of the grown-up world. Most
of the time, though, the child Agnes was simply incarcerated upstairs.

That afternoon the Brownly nursery, large, well
lighted with plenty of windows (barred), and kept
warm with a tile stove, smelled of eucalyptus steam;
Agnes was sniffling and thumbsucking in her little bed.
She looked up at me with big placid eyes and crooned
a little nursery song to her dolly, a song soon interrupted by a fierce spell of coughing.

"A touch of whooping cough, I'm afraid," Mrs.
Brownly said. "One of childhood's many illnesses. It's
just as well she has no brothers or sisters at home to
catch it from her." And she sighed, already anticipat-
ing the long line of other illnesses to follow before the
child would be grown and wed and someone else's
responsibility. "And I've had to give notice to the
nurse. It is so very, very difficult these days. . . . I
don't suppose you . . . ?" That half-asked question
was addressed to me, who forced a smile. Having a
philosopher as a father often meant that neighbors
and friends felt free to offer me employment. Surely
a philosopher's daughter could always use a little pin
money?

"I am already employed, I am afraid," I reminded

Mrs. Brownly. "My little school at Pinckney Street. I hope Agnes is well soon." I gingerly patted the child's head and looked discreetly about the nursery, which was a marked contrast to the children's room at the Charles Street Home. This child's abode was stocked with a painted and gilded puppet theater, a row of bisque dolls dressed in French-silk fashions, a doll's house with minuscule carved furniture and silver plates, and a bookcase of children's favorite stories. I knew the titles, beginning with *Struwwelpeter*, an awful morality tale about a little girl who burns to death from playing with matches. Surely children deserved better to read than those nightmares that promise dire punishment for every misdeed, I thought. My *Flower Fables* would surely be more enjoyable. I would make them so.

The dolls, hand-me-downs from Dottie, Sarah, and Edith, were lined up against the wall in somewhat forlorn condition, worse for the years of childish hands pulling at their button eyes and yarn braids. No new dolls had been purchased for Agnes, I saw.

Mrs. Brownly was dressed in black crepe. But there had been no other sign of mourning for Dorothy in the house. The black wreath had not yet been put on the door, black cloths had not been draped over the mirrors, and hothouse rose bouquets had not been replaced with white lilies. Perhaps with Agnes ill, there had not yet been time to make the complicated mourning arrangements of the household.

"Mrs. Brownly, I have come to offer my condolences and my family's," I said gently, patting Agnes once more and then accepting a teacup.

"Thank you. It is a great loss, Miss Alcott. Cream or lemon? And how is your mother?" The omnipresent tea service had followed us up the stairs, borne by a maid.

"She is well, thank you. I shall tell her you asked for her."

"Do." A pause as the cream was poured. The sound of heavy silver spoons clanking against teacups was reminiscent of a society afternoon.

"May we speak about Dorothy?" I finally asked, when the silver-tinged silence grew oppressive. Agnes seemed to be sleeping.

"What is there to say?" Mrs. Brownly sniffed. "She married against my wishes. And now she is dead. A biscuit, Miss Alcott?"

I could not help it. My teacup rattled ever so slightly on the saucer. A mother who refuses to mourn the death of a child is a mother who has been turned to stone.

"You did not wish her to marry Mr. Wortham?" I said, as if surprised, as if hearing this for the first time.

"Louisa. I may still call you Louisa, may I not, though you are quite grown?" Mrs. Brownly put down her teacup and folded her hands into her lap. "Good. Louisa, let us not be overly subtle with each other. We both know what that man is. A fortune seeker. A scoundrel. What Dorothy ever saw in him—"

"Perhaps she loved him."

"Loved!" Mrs. Brownly snorted. "What did that child know of the kind of love a wife owes a husband? And do not give me that look. I read your thoughts. You think me cold. I am not. I married for love, Miss Alcott. I know a thing or two about that emotion. I know that what passes as love too often is as thin as moonlight. I did not mind that Dorothy loved Preston Wortham."

"No?" I asked, alert.

"No." The mother sighed heavily. "I minded that she did not love him enough to find happiness with him."

"I am confused," I admitted. "Forgive me if I have seemed judgmental. Explain, please, how you came to believe that Dot did not truly love Mr. Wortham."

Mrs. Brownly unfolded her hands and picked a

piece of lint that had caught on the prong of the emer-
ald setting of her wedding band. Her hands trembled.
I wondered that a mother who had just lost a daughter
could seem more nervous than grieving.

"There was another, before Preston Wortham,"
Mrs. Brownly said slowly, uncertain of the words and
what they would convey about her daughter. "You
did not know of it, because I made Dorothy promise
never to speak of it, not even to her closest friends.
She was too young, too inexperienced, for the affair
to prosper, and it did not. But her heart was spoken
for long before she met Mr. Wortham. You see now,
when she announced her intention to marry Preston
Wortham, why this mother's heart did not leap for
joy?"

Dot, who in life had seemed a simple, loving creature, had become, in death, a creature of mystery. I
found myself longing for the friend I had known, and
now, even more, for the Dorothy I seemed not to
have known.

"Do you know this man's name?" I asked.

Mrs. Brownly hesitated. Her face changed; the senti-
ment that had softened it a moment before disappeared and left the more familiar stern lines. "This is
an unsuitable conversation," she said. "I will not discuss Dorothy's intimate life with those not in the family. You were her friend. Think what you will. Mr.
Wortham managed to convince her of impossible joy.
And we all know why."

I said nothing. Mrs. Brownly started angrily. "He
married Dorothy for her money, of course. Well, he
shall see what all his contriving has achieved. He'll
not get a penny. Not him. We'll see."

Mrs. Brownly smiled. "Not a penny. It was arranged
before the marriage that Dorothy's income would
cease upon her death."

Once the initial shock passed—how this family must

hate Preston Wortham!—I found this news reassuring. I had spent enough time considering the exploits of Poe's Detective Dupin to know that a murderer usually has a motive, and that not even impetuous Preston Wortham would exchange a state of married wealth for impoverished widowerhood. I was not overly fond of Wortham, but I did not wish to live with the notion that my close friend had been murdered by her own husband. If her death was murder, as it seemed, then there had to be a different culprit.

"Mrs. Brownly, forgive me for pursuing this train of thought, but can you think of anyone . . ."

"Who might wish my child dead? Really, Louisa." Mrs. Brownly clucked her tongue. "You have always had an overactive imagination. That awful red-haired constable—he is Irish; don't try to tell me he isn't—has already been here and asked questions. It is much to do about a simple death. She slipped and fell into the water and drowned. At least Dorothy had the manners to rise to the surface. It would have been terrible if we'd had to fire off cannon shot to raise the body. So much talk . . . I couldn't have borne it," Mrs. Brownly said.

And with that final comment, a single tear did slip down Mrs. Brownly's cheek.

"More tea, Louisa?" she asked when she had recovered herself.

"No, thank you. May I ask, though, what will happen now to Dorothy's portion of the estate?"

"Why, it will go to Edgar, of course."

Edgar. Who had arrived late to the second tea party, out of breath and with damp trouser cuffs, though there had been no rain that day.

"Perhaps I will take one more cup of tea, if you don't mind, if I have not overstayed my welcome." I persisted. "Mrs. Brownly, Edgar and Dorothy were quite fond of each other, weren't they?"

"Oh, they simply doted on each other." And the mother's tone of voice and inability to meet my candid gaze indicated that even she could not credit that exaggeration.

Thick, ominous clouds scudded over Boston, and the smell of fish and salt water insinuated all the way up to Beacon Hill, forced sideways and through town rather than up and away because of the lowering sky. I walked brisky, my chin high, my stride so long that my hooped skirts must have swung like a pealing fire bell, announcing disaster. *Edgar inherits. Edgar inherits,* I repeated, and my steps kept time to that refrain.

When I returned to my little home on Pinckney Street I found my homestead reduced to chaos.

One of the schoolchildren, little Walter Campbell, who'd always been a rascal and would always be a rascal, had let loose a pet mouse into the parlor, and then had gone home, leaving the thing behind. The little creature had reappeared on a plate of biscuits set out to tide my father over till supper.

Abba was by nature gentle and unflappable, but one creature she could not abide was a mouse, not even the sweet kind that sit on the plate rim and beseech with soft brown eyes. She was chasing after it rather hotly with a broom, my father was chasing after her, reminding her that it was one of God's creatures and not to be harmed, and Lizzie was chasing after him, for Father had ordered one of the boarders out of the house, after catching him talking alone with Lizzie in the upstairs hall. May was jumping up and down and cheering for the mouse.

The bold boarder, one Mr. Alexander Hall, a Harvard divinity student, leaned in the doorway watching the whole circus and scratching his head, trying to find the correct words of apology for having insulted Mr. Alcott's home and sensing that perhaps this was not the best time to initiate a serious discourse.

I studied the strange choreography taking place in the front parlor for several seconds as I took off my coat, discerned the several problems immediately at hand, and set about correcting them, even before removing my flapping hemisphere hat. A piece of cheese was procured and placed in a corner. Lizzie was given a pot and told to put it over the mouse as soon as it reappeared. Father would then slip the morning newspaper under the pot and remove both cooking vessel and God's creature to the backyard, probably near the refuse bin, where it might feast to its little mousy heart's content on carrot peels.

I sent Mr. Hall to Trevelyan's Pipe Shop for some Cuban blend for Father's pipe. It was the one gift guaranteed to soothe him, and I knew that for all his surreptitious ogling of pretty Lizzie, Mr. Hall was a respectable young man and an irreplaceable boarder. He made no noise, rarely ate in, never, ever wanted his meal on a tray, and always paid on time. As for little Walter Campbell, his pockets would be searched from hence, to prevent the carrying of any other contraband into the Alcott schoolroom/parlor.

Peace restored, we made ourselves comfortable in the worn furniture of the little room and had a good laugh at ourselves. Abba was dusty, Lizzie was blushing, and Father couldn't remember why he had been so harsh with young Mr. Hall, nor how he came to be holding a mouse in his palm. May was sweet-talking the little brown creature and threatening to turn it into a pet. My hat flopped before my eyes and I swept it off my head and into the corner with a flourish.

"I cannot abide that hat. From now on I will wear caps and cloches," I said.

"I never liked it," agreed Father, now looking somewhat less stately since he and the trembling mouse were eye-to-eye in steady contemplation of each other. "Hats should never hide the windows to the soul. It was of the soul I was writing before this domestic crisis called my attention elsewhere. Louisa, you will remember in *Pilgrim's Progress* that fine moment when the pilgrim first senses the divinity of his own—"

"Bronson, take the mouse outdoors," Abba said sternly.

"Ah, yes, the mouse . . ." And he ambled back into his study, still eye to eye with the creature.

"Another sentence left unfinished by Father," May crooned.

"That, too, is an incomplete sentence," I said. "Go back to your lesson, May."

"Do I have to?" complained the child, and Abba and I responded, "Yes!" in unison.

I went to my mother and hugged her.

"It was awful with Mrs. Brownly." I sighed. "She barely wept. A single tear, that was all. She was afraid of the talk." I looked at my mother, at the small parlor with its ragged furnishings, thought of the vegetable meals, the worn linen, the long workdays, and the damp-bottomed schoolchildren . . . all precious to me, since they were part of a destiny that had saved me from having a father who died of apoplexy because another daughter was born to him, or a mother who calmly poured tea and said of that daughter's death, "It is a great loss. . . . Cream or lemon?"

Chapter Seven

The Heir Is Taken Unawares

The next day, Tuesday, after my schoolchildren had been dismissed, I decided to pay a call on the Brownly heir, Edgar, he of the gobbled fish sandwiches.

This was a trickier business than that of the day before, since Edgar Brownly spent most of his time at a little studio he rented near the Customs House, and Boston society frowned upon single maidens paying visits to unwed men in their studios. The way to get about that difficulty was to invite Sylvia to join the occasion, and to have her bring someone as chaperon. To avoid gossip, Sylvia chose not the usual vicar but Father Nolan, a Roman Catholic priest we had met during our social work.

We made a strange sight, two young ladies with a black-frocked priest in tow, making our way through the narrow, dingy streets of that part of Boston, where sailors leaned in doorways and dockhands trudged to and fro carrying barrels and sacks on their well-developed shoulders. I enjoyed it, especially since I had exiled the hated hemisphere hat and wore a little cloche I had found in my grandmother's trunk, and the smaller, simpler hat no longer obscured my vision but allowed me full sight of the world as it unveiled itself before my curious eyes. It also allowed the world to fully see me. We received looks and even a few catcalls, though Father Nolan glared like a guardian dragon at any young men who looked too long.

Mr. Brownly's little studio was the top floor of an old warehouse. Stray cats glowered from the inky corners of the stairwell, and there was a smell of absinthe and beer, but the building overlooked the harbor, so naturally Sylvia and I expected that Mr. Brownly's paintings would be of that picturesque motif. When the shuffling landlady had shown us up the stairs and into the suite with a heavily accented, "You wait here. Mr. Brownly be back soon," our misperception was quickly corrected.

The studio door swung open onto a quite unexpected scene. It was absolutely, uncontestably Bohemian, a room of plain, almost shabby furnishings, uncurtained windows, wine bottles lined up on an unclothed table, and rumpled sheets avalanching off a settee that also seemed to function as a daybed. A pair of black stockings, hastily removed and abandoned and then forgotten, it would seem, snaked out from under said moth-eaten and suspiciously stained settee.

"Oh, dear Mother in heaven," muttered Father Nolan, turning beet red and making a quick sign of the cross as he looked about. The studio was filled with canvases in various stages of completion, each with the same theme: a nude woman. "Extremely nude," I commented aloud. "No wonder Mr. Brownly preferred to set up his studio outside the family home. Imagine what the maids would think."

"Can you imagine if Mrs. Brownly wandered in, expecting to see pastoral scenery or waterscapes of Boston Harbor?" Sylvia asked, grinning.

"Mother in heaven," Father Nolan repeated, mov-

ing closer to a particularly large, almost life-size canvas of a coy peasant girl dressed in a scrap of gauze
strategically draped to call attention to that portion of
the anatomy that it failed to hide.

"The background of poplars and the ruined castle
is, I admit, well drawn and colored," I commented.
"See how the brushstrokes of ocher mimic the shadows cast by a strong Italian sun at high noon." But
elderly Father Nolan studied not the background but
the model who, at a certain angle, could be said to
leer at the viewer.

"Perhaps we should sit over by the window and wait
for Mr. Brownly," Sylvia suggested, gently taking her
priest by the elbow and steering him away from that
particular painting. His color was beginning to look
unhealthy.

"Yes," he said. "We shall sit and wait for this sinner
and see if he might not be brought to redemption."

"Father," I said kindly but firmly, "we are not here
to redeem, but to offer condolences. Please remember that."

"And to ask questions," Sylvia amended.

"Perhaps a few." I grinned. "We need not ask, however, why it is that his landlady so freely gives admittance to all who seek entrance here. 'All' being young
women. It would also explain the very strange look
she gave our guardian."

"Sweet Mother, indeed," agreed Father Nolan. "Do
you think she thinks . . ." And he grew silent, unable
to complete either sentence or thought.

Sylvia and Father Nolan settled uncomfortably to
wait, since Mr. Brownly had equipped his studio with
some plush chairs and footrests, in addition to the
settee on which Sylvia refused to sit, having seen it—
and its activities—in several of the canvases. I, however, prowled about, hands behind my back, stepping
over palettes and paint tubes, my eyes moving this

way and that. I stopped before one canvas and frowned. I lifted a hand as if to touch the painting, and then stepped back in dismay.

"Louisa?" Sylvia asked, noting my increasingly somber demeanor, but just then footsteps were heard coming up the stairs, Edgar Brownly, puffing and panting, and between stentorian gasps singing a music-hall song whose lyrics could not be repeated at a family gathering.

Mr. Brownly yanked the door open and merrily called out a name . . . Katarina, or Katya, I couldn't tell which, for the ending of that greeting was gulped down when he saw us. He stood there on the threshold, wide-eyed and trembling and looking much as a rabbit does when the gardener bears down on it, hoe in hand.

"Are you going to tell Mother?" were the very first words the thirty-year-old Mr. Brownly uttered.

I glided forth and offered my hand as well as a warm, conspiratorial smile. Diplomacy was the key to good detective work.

"Do forgive this intrusion. We come to extend our condolences on the loss of your sister," I said.

Edgar Brownly wiped his profusely sweating brow and sat in the first empty chair at hand.

"Dot," he said. "Oh, yes. Dot." He seemed not overly grieved.

"It must be painful, losing a beloved sister," I tried again.

"Oh, yes. Very painful," Edgar Brownly agreed. He might have been talking about the weather. *Poor Dot,* I thought again, watching how coldly Edgar Brownly discussed her death. How few people seemed to have actually loved her. Had there been a flaw in her nature I had not seen? Or had she simply been one of those unfortunate few, deserving yet rarely receiving affection? I began to regret my decision to come.

"Of course, your fortune will be enhanced by the diminution of the number of sisters to be seen to financially," I added smoothly, getting to the point.

"Not at all," he protested. "That bounder Mr. Wortham will receive Dot's share. I profit not at all by Dot's death." In that moment Edgar reminded me of troublesome little Walter Campbell, who, shuffling his feet and with hands held behind his back, would utter the baldest lies to avoid blame.

"That is not your mother's knowledge of the situation," I gently corrected. "Mr. Wortham is cut off from Dot's inheritance."

"Mother told you that, did she? Oh, yes, now I remember. There was an agreement," Edgar mumbled sheepishly.

I decided to become somewhat more aggressive in my line of questioning.

"Mr. Brownly, you had no great love for your sister, much to profit from her death, and you might also be described as a man of . . . singular morality." I looked about the studio. "One might wonder if the loss of a sister was a goal you actively sought."

Edgar Brownly turned red. He breathed with wheezing difficulty. His eyes popped, much as had Father Nolan's when first looking about at the pictures. Then breeding showed. Money does not purchase contentment, but it does provide a certain composure in difficult situations, such as when one has been accused of murdering one's sister. Mr. Brownly straightened his ascot, leaned back in his chair to allow his compressed lungs more access, and smiled with equanimity.

"Dear Dot's death was an unfortunate accident. Miss Alcott, you have been reading romances, I suspect," he said. It was my turn to blush, for I was not merely reading romances but also writing them, though the Brownlys knew nought of that.

"The postmortem suggested foul play," I persisted.

"Did it? Well, I suggest they reconsider their findings. There will probably follow a request for money from the family, and then, lo and behold, whatever quack performed that unwarranted desecration upon Dorothy will change his mind." Mr. Brownly sighed heavily. "Wealth is a burden, Miss Alcott. The world spends much of its time trying to rob you of it . . . as Dorothy discovered, I'm certain. How is Mr. Wortham? Weepy and guilt-ridden?"

"Well," I said, rising to my feet, "we will be on our way, Mr. Brownly. I am sorry if we have interrupted your work." And I managed to say *work* in a tone of voice that sent the blush back to Edgar's face, and a smile of victory to mine. "But might I ask a favor, Mr. Brownly? An escort home?"

Breeding provides composure but also noblesse oblige. "Certainly, Miss Alcott, though it is a bit inconvenient. I have an appointment this afternoon. Maybe some other time?" He seemed not at all pleased to be inconvenienced and made a point of fetching his gold watch from his waistcoat pocket and peering at it intently.

Feet sounded again in the outer staircase, lighter, faster feet, and I suspected that Mr. Brownly's appointment for the afternoon had arrived. This satisfied me no end, as I had never before met the kind of woman a gentleman would refer to as an "appointment."

The door swung open and a woman, young and exotic and dressed in the most garish of scarlet costumes, stood there, as surprised to see us as Edgar Brownly had been. Her mouth dropped open when she saw Father Nolan, and she murmured, *"Madre Dios"* several times. When she saw me, a dangerous fire glittered in her dark eyes.

"So," she hissed, glaring at Mr. Brownly and flaring her nostrils. "So soon you will replace me? We shall see about that." And she raised her hand to slap him. We did not interfere. The slap was a good one for a smallish woman, loud enough to echo in the studio. Mr. Brownly gave a little yelp and raised his own hand to strike back, though a true gentleman never, ever strikes a lady . . . or a woman, for that matter.

At that moment, I thought it wise to step between the two.

"You are misperceiving the situation. I am a friend of the family," I said to the woman.

"A friend of the family? Ha! What would family do here?" the woman shouted.

She had a point, I thought.

The woman backed out the still-open door, muttering foreign phrases that sounded like curses, and flounced back down the stairs, her high heels clacking like castanets.

"Well," Edgar Brownly said between clenched teeth. "My afternoon schedule has been freed, thank you."

I had a flash of recognition, caused by my clandestine habit—which I hoped no one guessed—of poring over the popular papers and reading about the stars of the stage.

"Was that Katya Mendosa?" I asked, and I could not contain the awe in my voice.

Miss Mendosa was the most popular opera star of the season, not the least for which reason was her famed temper. She had stabbed a rival the year before, undeterred by the logic that stated that her rival, the man's wife, had more right to the man than herself. Some mysterious working of justice had resulted in an acquittal; it was said that the judge was a great fan of opera, or at least of female operatic performers.

"It was. Past tense seems appropriate." Mr. Brownly looked longingly down the stairwell.

"Since you are now free, perhaps you will fetch a

horse and buggy and accompany me on an errand, for
I do not wish to do it alone and Sylvia and her companion have other chores to attend to," I said.

"Yes," Sylvia agreed, understanding my hastiness
was a ruse, "come along, Father Nolan. Louisa, will I
see you tomorrow?"

"Yes. Come to the house, Sylvia. Father still wishes
to speak with you."

And so we parted company, Sylvia to have tea with
the priest and a long talk about the Holy Trinity, and
me to my own purposes, which fell out as follows:

A hired carriage was sent for and I required that it
not be a closed brougham, but a cabriolet with the
folding top down, though it was a winter day and the
air was fresh. Mr. Brownly, the only male in a family
of five women and therefore accustomed to whims,
agreed without a quarrel, but was peevish and uncom-
municative. Although his "appointment" for the afternoon had, apparently, canceled their rendezvous, all
during that crosstown ride he kept checking his pocket
watch, as men do when they wish to indicate their
time is being wasted.

Only when we arrived at our destination, the
Charles Street Home, did the heavy glare leave his
face. Once again he looked somewhat like a rabbit
about to be pounced upon, an image enhanced by his
bulbous nose and heavy, rounded cheeks.

"Will you wait a moment, Mr. Brownly?" I asked
sweetly, once the driver brought the cab to a full stop
in front of the dilapidated porch of the home, with
the flower box and rocker on one side and the red-
painted *whore* marking the other. The omnipresent
children playing on the porch pointed and laughed
and came out of their quilt tent to stroke the horses'
soft mouths; Mr. Brownly had no recourse but to wait
as the ragamuffins swarmed about.

Queenie was upstairs, curled up on her cot but not
sleeping. There was a plate of uneaten flapjacks on

the floor and a glass of water made milky and noxious with a dose of Hostetter's Stomach Bitters.

"Queenie, are you well?"

"Well as can be expected." The girl sighed. She was of gloomy countenance, barely able to eat, to talk, to breathe, so heavy was the weight bearing down on her small, young shoulders, I picked up a much worn book that lay open next to the girl.

"*The Gold Seeker's Manual, a Practical and Instructive Guide to All Persons Emigrating to the Gold Diggings in California,* by David Ansted," I read aloud. "Queenie, when this is over, are you going to search for gold?"

"That's a funny one. No. The camps are for men. But if I had my own stake I might go west and set up a boardinghouse, a new place where no one knows me," Queenie said. "Might as well long for the moon, though when this is over I'll be on the street."

I put my arm about the girl's shoulder and pulled her up into a sitting position. "No, you won't," I said. "I won't let that happen. Come to the window, Queenie, and tell me what you see. Prepare yourself first for a shock, and then have no fear."

I brought her to the window and made her look down into the street. The girl squinted, then drew back in wide-eyed terror.

"It is him," she whispered. "He said he would kill me if I told. . . ."

I put my arms more tightly about her and held her for comfort.

"He can't hurt you, not more than he already has," I said.

"Oh, yes, he can. You don't know him," Queenie said between clenched lips. I drew back, frowning. The expression on Queenie's drawn face spoke of great fear. "You don't know him," she repeated. "He's a devil."

Just at that moment Edgar Brownly looked up at the

window. His face seemed to have changed completely. He was no longer the bland, childish, and chubby darling of the Brownly family, but a man whose repugnance for this house and its inhabitants showed in his darkly knitting brows and the furious line of his mouth.

Queenie and I stood behind the yellowed curtain, where we could see and not be seen, and Brownly did not know that when he raised his clenched fist at that house, I observed the gesture and tucked it into my memory for safekeeping.

Two mysteries had been solved, at least: the mystery of how Queenie came to be pregnant, and why her portrait had been leaning against a wall in Edgar Brownly's studio.

On Wednesday, Mrs. Dorothy Wortham was interred in the Old Boston Cemetery, next to a long line of Brownlys who would keep her company for eternity. The service was subdued, the eulogy brief. It rained all the while, a steady, cold drizzle that soon soaked overcoats and bedraggled the black feathers in the women's hats.

The deceased's brother, Edgar, provided the parting words for Dorothy, since Mrs. Brownly was not strong enough for public speaking, even graveside. He seemed to have great difficulty thinking of pleasant things to say about Dorothy and concluded with the simple statement that she had been the youngest daughter of the Brownly household and loving wife of Preston Wortham. Edgar sneered slightly at that.

Edgar also gave me several sidelong looks of such distaste—indeed, hatred—that Sylvia, standing beside me, didn't understand until I whispered to her the events of the day before, and the murderous look I had spied on Edgar's face through the window.

"Certain men can't stand to be reminded of their sins," Sylvia whispered back from behind her prayer book.

"Certainly when other, even more grievous sins may be awaiting discovery," I whispered back.

During the service the Brownly daughters and spinster aunt stood straight and calm, and they turned away to return to their waiting closed carriages as soon as the prayers were finished. The phrase *indecent haste* sprang to my mind.

Preston Wortham, however, wept copiously. He embarrassed his wife's family, and Edgar loudly muttered that perhaps such a quantity of tears was unmanly . . . or even insincere. Then he, too, with one last darting glance at me, absconded for the carriage and was gone.

Ashes to ashes, dust to dust. Amen.

Sylvia and I stayed on to have private final words with Dorothy. We scattered yellow rose petals over the coffin before the gravediggers began shoveling the dirt back in the long, narrow grave. We were alone then, the three friends, Sylvia, Dorothy, and I, for the last time.

I wept, finally. I had been unable when the Brownlys were present. We shared Sylvia's handkerchief, for I hadn't brought one of my own.

But even then my ability for observation was not deterred.

"The family has left no room for Mr. Wortham," I observed, looking about. "He cannot be buried next to Dorothy. I don't think she would be pleased about that."

"He is young and healthy. I expect it will be a long while before he is buried anywhere," Sylvia said.

I frowned, and did not respond. Bruises on the throat made by a hand, Roder had said at the autopsy. Then she was certainly not drowned, but had fallen dead into the water. Already dead when she was put into the river.

It was bread-baking day in our household, and Abba made the best bread in Boston, so I had reason to become more cheerful. Yet it was not to be our gayest meal, since when the invitation had first been extended, Dorothy had been alive . . . out shopping for a hat, or gloves, or some such thing, and Preston had accepted a dinner invitation on their behalf. She wouldn't be coming—ever again. She had joined the immortals.

"But the body must be fed," Abba insisted. "Sit there, Sylvia, next to Louisa, and tell us your plans."

In addition to carrots cooked six different ways, Abba had supplemented the fare with a dish of boiled potatoes and wilted greens and a wheel of farm cheese, one of the few animal foods that Father allowed. We drank plain water and ate off a worn linen cloth that had never known a scrap of lace, and the meal was, for Sylvia and me both, a feast, for as young as we were, we could feel grief and hunger at the same time and hadn't yet eaten that day.

"Does Queenie really think Mr. Brownly capable of acting upon his threat? Surely he wouldn't actually kill her if she revealed his secret paternity," Sylvia said, slathering a thick layer of white cheese over still-warm bread.

I found it hard to give a reassuring answer. It was not uncommon in Boston, especially in the waterfront tenement area, to find the bodies of obviously pregnant girls who had died violent deaths . . . supposedly murdered by gentlemen friends who did not wish to be encumbered with a family, though such murderers were rarely discovered.

"I don't know," I admitted, pushing carrots around my plate. "The entire family seems strange to me, and, more than ever, I wonder how sweet Dot ever fitted into that household. Just to be certain, though, I have sent a message to Constable Cobban and asked that one of his watchmen check in at the home periodically. I told him threats had been made."

"A fortuitious coincidence that you found Queenie's portrait there in that plethora of canvases," Sylvia said, reaching for more bread.

"Wasn't it," I mused. "Though I had wondered. . . .
Do you remember, Sylvia, the day of the second tea
party, the day Dorothy died? Edgar Brownly arrived
late, and out of breath."

"May, go into the kitchen and fetch us a fresh
pitcher of water," Abba said, not wanting my youngest
sister to hear the details of probable murder, but also
not wishing to cut off a conversation that was obviously important to me. May grumbled, but did as she
was told.

"Tea parties. I disapprove completely," Father
mumbled through a mouthful of potatoes. "Serving
tea and biscuits at an hour when working folk are
sitting down to their hard-earned dinner. Frivolous."

"Edgar is perpetually out of breath, due to an abundance of food and lack of exercise," Sylvia said, following my train of thought. "Did you see him at the
funeral today, sneaking caramels out of his pocket
during the service?"

"Yes, but he was particularly out of breath that day.
And the bottoms of his trouser legs were wet. I remember remarking on that, for the day was dry. If he
had been to the Charles Street Home to spy on Queenie, or threaten her, that would explain the condition
of his hems. You know how they are forever mopping
floors there, and carrying about basins of water. Of
course, if he had been at the waterfront, his trousers
would have been dampened there from the spray. . . .
Oh, if only I knew why Edgar Brownly's pant legs
were wet that day!" I put my fork down and leaned
my chin in my hands, frowning.

"Enough about Mr. Brownly's wardrobe," Father
protested, hemming a bit to get my attention.
"Though I am sorry for little Dorothy's demise, and

unfortunately not surprised to hear of her brother's secret life, there are other matters I wish to discuss."

But before we could continue, the doorbell rang, and I sprang up to answer it. "Who could that be?" Abba asked, frowning. "Louy, were you expecting anyone else?" I returned to the dining room a moment later, and with me, to their great shock, was Preston Wortham, dressed in evening clothes. My eyes met Sylvia's and read in her face what she herself was already thinking: Was this how a husband grieved, by paying calls? What manner of man, indeed, was Preston Wortham?

Chapter Eight

An Arrest Is Made

"You see before you a lonely man, scorned by all," he said, holding his top hat in his hands and looking absolutely distraught. Though he was well—even flashily—dressed, in white shirt and vest and a swallowtail frock coat, his hair stood on end and there was a smudge of ink on the tip of his nose. To whom had he been writing? I wondered. And what?

"I hope I am not unwelcome." Preston Wortham looked, at that moment, pitiable and quite innocent. Those we pity often seem incapable of doing harm, a lesson soon learned by overly lively children with a tendency to knock over tables of knickknacks.

"I will take your coat," I said, springing forward. "Mr. Wortham, you have come out in the cold without your new Saville Row greatcoat."

"Misplaced." He sighed. "Dot takes . . . took such good care . . ."

"Poor Mr. Wortham, you sit right here," Mother said, pulling another chair to the table for him. And so he joined in that small circle, and the dim candlelight on his pale face made him seem even younger, even more in need of protection. We were still gape-mouthed with shock, but Abba had gathered her wits first to do the right and the sensible thing. Which, in that case, was to feed a man who seemed not to have eaten or slept for several days.

"Preston, I hear you have lost your wife," Father said, putting down his knife and fork and peering over his spectacles.

"I have," Preston admitted.

"A bad business," Father concluded. "Very bad. A wife is a good thing, one of the greatest goods in this life. . . ." He paused and beamed at Abba. "You have my sympathy, sir, for your loss."

"Thank you." Preston absentmindedly chewed a piece of bread and butter and stared at the tablecloth. His bravura entrance having been achieved, he now seemed confused.

"Dot's family asked that I not call upon them. Nor will they call upon me. They are not a forgiving family. I don't think I have ever before been this alone," he said in a forlorn voice.

"Quite defeats the whole purpose of proper mourning, which is to unite, not divide," Father observed.

"I called upon Dot's mother yesterday," I said. "She has grown reclusive and bitter, it seemed. Perhaps you should not think overmuch about Dot's family." I had been twirling a bread knife in my fingers. Suddenly it dropped and fell to the floor. I went down on my knees to fetch it from under the table. Once there, I did what I had intended to do all along: I looked carefully at Preston Wortham's trouser cuffs. They were dry as a bone.

I thought back to the year I first met Preston, Dot's husband. It had been during a holiday, two weeks in Newport, in the huge "cottage" on Oceanview Drive that belonged to Sylvia's family, which Preston, Sylvie's cousin, was also visiting. He was already a grown man then, and as good-looking, and always in trouble with his family, hence his frequent trips from New York and pater and the family business, to Newport, where he might sleep till noon and drink till midnight, his favorite occupations. Sylvia was madly in love with him and his dashing top hats and silk dressing robes (not worn concurrently), but later that young and foolish emotion turned to antipathy and often revulsion in her more mature breast.

That summer, when Dorothy, Sylvia, and I were fifteen and dreaming of wild romance in Rome, Preston Wortham seduced the upstairs maid, a young woman called Marie Brennen. His predation was discovered some months later, when the fruit of her seduction began to mound under her white apron. The poor girl was paid off and sent back to her mother in Worcester. Sylvia's father gave Preston a tongue-lashing that echoed through the house, and afterward they shared a cigar and glass of brandy as the older man, in more subdued conversation, fondly remembered the misdemeanors of his own youth. It was lucky neither father nor son spotted my girlish form eavesdropping on the stairs, not out of simple curiosity, but because I knew instantly the conversation would provide essential research for a novel.

It proved to be a particularly interesting summer, as Marie Brennen was not the only fallen woman of the season. Several young society girls had also been discovered in compromising positions, a fact learned only after the girls had been sent home to New York or Boston in disgrace. Dot, the most innocent of our close threesome, had been especially upset by the discovery of Preston's ungentlemanly behavior.

Even Preston, in his moral slumbering and enterprise, could not have been responsible for all the trouble stirred that season, but his name began appearing in whispered conversations much too frequently. His reputation suffered greatly, and with reason. Dottie wept often that summer, and all could see she had formed a higher opinion of him than his nature seemed to justify.

Preston, sitting now at our Pinckney Street table, chewed a bit of bread and swallowed it down with a large gulp of water. Judging from the look he gave the glass, and the way his hair stood on end, it was safe to assume he had been drinking stronger stuff before arriving at our house. He put his hands on the table, rested his chin in them, and stared beseechingly at me.

"Miss Alcott . . . do you think perhaps it . . . it wasn't Dot we saw there, in the morgue . . . in the coffin?" he asked.

"Oh, dear." I sighed. "Yes, Mr. Wortham. I'm quite, quite certain it was Dot." Mother and I exchanged looks.

"Well, it's just that . . . you know . . . you know, it seems like she will walk in the door any minute. She'll smile and say, 'I forgot the time. Have you been waiting long?' She was like that in Rome, during our honeymoon. Forgetful. It doesn't seem like Dot, you are thinking, but she did change, somehow. And I have been hearing things. . . ."

"Things?" I asked, raising one eyebrow.

"A woman. Laughing. Whispering. Then footsteps down the back stairs to the kitchen."

"Where were you, and what time of day was it when you heard this?" I asked, now frowning and leaning forward.

"Early morning. In my bedroom."

"Perhaps you were asleep and simply believed you heard real noises," I suggested.

"No. I was awake, I assure you. In fact, I hadn't yet been to bed."

"Mr. Wortham," I said with great gentleness, "I assure you, to our great sorrow Dorothy is dead. You have not heard her in the house."

"Well, I've heard someone," he insisted. "Did she love me, do you think?"

"Why, Mr. Wortham! Why else would she have married you?" Abba protested.

"Women have their reasons," he said darkly, and then grew silent.

It was an uncomfortable dinner. Father lectured May, Lizzie, and me on the importance of consistency, of making life true to one's beliefs. All the while he spoke, I had been studying Wortham, while Wortham had been glaring into his plate of vegetables, unable to eat.

"Well, it is an important principle," Father said. "Especially for women. The domestic sphere must above all be the place where men and women stay true to the higher principles. It is not my experience that women are the best material for philosophers and mystics, but instead must guide and comfort the home."

Abba and I exchanged another glance, this time one with an unspoken message about Father, not Mr. Wortham. As much as we loved him, his nonprogressive views on women were often grating. I felt it necessary to hide my monthly copy of *The Lily* since Father scorned the feminist press and praised Mrs. Harriet Beecher Stowe more for her femininely modest refusal to give public appearances than for her novel, *Uncle Tom's Cabin*.

And so, that difficult conversation was brought to a conclusion, for the time, and having reached that conclusion we realized that there was nothing else we wished to discuss. Dot was on our minds, but there was her husband, drinking a second glass of after-dinner port that Father could not really afford to serve. We lapsed into silence, and when we took more comfortable seats in the worn, soft chairs of the parlor, Abba and I fetched our sewing baskets. May went upstairs to bed, and Lizzie stayed in the kitchen, washing up and putting things away. After, I heard her soft steps creeping up the kitchen stairway, away from the parlor.

The fire crackled and hissed. The clock struck eight. Wortham stared morosely into the flames. We darned thin stocking after thin stocking, trying to get another season of wear out of them.

At eight-thirty the doorbell rang again. Preston jumped and turned pale. "Dot?" he muttered. I wondered if his confusion might indicate a strong disturbance of the conscience.

"You stay, Abba. I'll get it," I said, glad to be free of the darning needle, and strode into the front hall.

When I returned, I was as white and dazed as Preston. Constable Cobban was with me, dressed in his plaid suit and with the conspicuous badge of his office pinned onto his lapel.

"Mr. Preston Wortham," he said, "I have come to arrest you. You will accompany me to the Watch and Police Station, and then be held at the courthouse until the time of your trial."

Preston, who had risen to his feet, looked even more confused than he had before.

"Jail?" he said in a small, disbelieving voice.

I stepped forward. "Mr. Cobban, what is this about? On what intelligence do you base this arrest?"

"We have received an anonymous letter that places Mr. Wortham at the docks at the time of Mrs. Wortham's death. And we questioned once again the downstairs maid at the Wortham residence, and she has stated that husband and wife quarreled that morning. In fact, most mornings. There is motive, and now a witness."

"An anonymous witness. Really, Mr. Cobban. And if you arrest all husbands and wives who quarrel, well . . ." I glared at him. He glared back for a moment, but then dropped his gaze.

"Sorry, Miss Alcott," he said. "I had hoped he wouldn't be here, so that this scene could have been avoided, but he is here, and now he must leave with me."

Preston smiled as if he were just stepping out onto the porch for a smoke. He did not yet quite comprehend what was happening. When Constable Cobban stepped forward with handcuffs, Preston ceased smiling. Beads of perspiration broke on his forehead, despite the chill of the evening.

"Is that really necessary?" I asked rather sharply.

"Afraid so. This is a murder investigation, Miss Alcott." Cobban addressed his comments to me, as if no one else were present. Our eyes met. His seemed to ask for understanding.

"As you see fit," I said. "But remember and believe that we are innocent till proven guilty, and treat Mr. Wortham accordingly."

"Yes, miss."

"Miss Alcott?" Preston was hunched over now, miserable, his hands cuffed behind his back. Constable Cobban, with a hand on his shoulder, turned him toward the door.

"Just a moment," I exclaimed as Cobban led him away. "Mr. Wortham, were the footsteps and woman's laughter the sounds of the upstairs maid, perhaps?"

"No. She does not come upstairs until ten in the morning. Dot is very strict about that," Preston said. "Jail?" he said again.

The gathering in our parlor waited, shocked, as the front door closed and we heard the constable's steps, and Preston's, marching down the wooden porch. Gone.

"We should have seen them out," Abba said weakly, realizing there had been a breach in manners.

"I think Mr. Wortham preferred we did not," I said, shaken.

"Well," said Father. "Well. Louisa, you do ask strange questions, wanting to know housekeeping arrangements as a man is being led off in cuffs."

And so concluded the evening. Sylvia could see that I wished to be alone with my thoughts, so she prepared for departure.

"This is a puzzling, sad business," I said, holding her coat and absent-mindedly stroking the sheared beaver collar as Sylvia backed into it. "I fear it will grow yet sadder." I sighed.

"Preston would agree with that statement, since he stands a fair chance of being hung," Sylvia agreed. "Perhaps he will simply be sent to a lunatic asylum instead. He seems to have come unglued. All that nonsense about hearing Dot in the house . . ."

At which point Father began one of his familiar sermons on the evils of capital punishment and the inadequacies of our housing of the criminally insane. He was in fine voice that evening, and his words carried all the way out onto the moonlit, rain-dampened street.

I spent several late night hours in the attic, trying to compose my story of star-crossed lovers and Italian nights, but more often than not the sentences turned into thoughts of mourning for Dorothy, and confusion over Wortham.

The next morning, after a night of tossing and turning and finally falling into fitful sleep for an hour or two, I received a letter from Preston Wortham:

My dear Miss Alcott (the hastily penned and smeared message read),

Constable Cobban seems to be of the opinion that poor Dorothy was merdered, and that I am the culprit. I am shoked to the bone, needless to say. I was fond of my wife, more than I am willing to admit to the casual observar and I am not complety insensable to comments whispered about my afections for her, that they might be based on merits other than her own charm and virtues. Such was not the case, and you will believe me or you will not.

I believe they mean to hang me in due proces. Miss Alcott, for the sake of our earlier friendship, plese help me. I swere I am inocent of this deed.

Would you also be so kinde as to stop at my rezidence and fetch a few articles for me. Digby will get them redy for you, from the enclosed list.

Yours in iternal frendship,
Preston Wortham

"He is most certainly innocent of the laws of the English language," Father observed at the table, reading over my shoulder. "I believe he was tutored by Charles Henry of the Harvard Classics department. It seems to have had little positive effect on his writing style."

"What will you do, Louy?" Abba asked. We were in the midst of our breakfast when the missive from Preston arrived, and Abba was busily moving around the table depositing a grayish, gelatinous mess of porridge into everyone's bowl. While Mother's bread was excellent, her morning porridge was one of the reasons I remained slender.

"I will go to Mr. Wortham and see in what way I may assist. I owe Dorothy that much, for the sake of our friendship," I answered. "Immediately." And with my excuse ready-made, I pushed away my bowl and went back upstairs to finish dressing.

Society women might spend an entire morning donning their stockings, chemise, corset, hoops, crinolines, gowns, underskirts, lace sleeves and caps, shoes, false curls, and such, but for me—thank goodness—dressing was an activity that occupied all of ten minutes.

Abba did not, for which I was thankful, require me

to wear corsets or wear them herself, and my father considered such devices unhealthy and also wrong, because the obtaining of whalebones was necessarily cruel to the whales, who preferred to keep them. Hence, my costume usually consisted of a chemise, drawers, hooped crinoline, stockings, and a linen bodice buttoned onto a matching skirt, all of which could be donned in seconds, since I moved with both speed and efficiency, having trained my left hand to be as strong and coordinated as my right. My hair was thick and wavy and required only a brushing and a twisting into place to form the neat, winged chignon I preferred to more elaborate ringletted coiffures.

And, of course, I wore no cosmetics whatsoever; no lady did, though more of them than would admit rubbed stove black on their eyebrows and powdered cornstarch on their noses. Nor did I ever engage in the dubious habit of drinking vinegar to whiten my skin; I preferred a healthy complexion, and the family budget would not allow such vanity.

So, when I had declared "I must get ready immediately," my family knew I referred to matters other than dress: Usually it meant I had fallen asleep in my garret, at my desk, and wished to be certain the pages I had written during the night were safely stored away during the day in my metal tin box. I realize now that my writing life was an open book to my family.

My quick, tapping feet flew up two flights to the attic; and, I imagine, there followed the usual mutterings and exclamations, noises of drawers opening and closing and then a silence, as I quickly reread my work of the night before. I was still embroiled in my love story of fickle Claude, passionate Beatrice, and unwitting Therese, and had come to the realization that one or several of the triangle must die for the story to resolve. Blood and thunder, indeed.

When I returned back downstairs I suspect my family knew from my expression that my writing efforts of the previous evening had not passed muster. I could feel that my eyes were lowered, my mouth tight. My skills at disguising my true feelings have always been blissfully inadequate.

"The story is almost finished, but I am not pleased with it," I said to my mother.

"Louisa, you must not give up," Abba said, understanding.

"I will not. But it is discouraging."

"You must persevere." Abba stroked my hair and I leaned against her for comfort. "You will achieve great things," she whispered in my ear.

"Your faith in me will see me through." I kissed her lined forehead.

Later, after I had helped Abba with the household chores, I put my old cape on and went out. The streets seemed particularly busy that day with even more small newsboys than usual offering the afternoon edition to hurrying pedestrians. A hasty sketch of Wortham had made the front page, with headlines announcing the murder of his wife, and to read of Dorothy in that casual and callow manner, to hear her described as plain but vivacious and privileged, took all the pleasure out of my walk. Instead of enjoying the movement and freedom, I was struck again by the dinginess of any city in late winter, when sooty smoke covers everything and people's faces are pinched and drawn with cold. When my family and I first moved to Boston years before, I had ached for Concord, for the clean countryside, and now that ache returned. The bustle and dirt and change sent all lovely images and restful feelings away.

Servants don't necessarily grieve when ill fortune finds their employers, I reminded myself later, when Digby answered the door at 10 Commonwealth Avenue. He had so successfully hidden his worry about Mr. Wortham that I discovered whiskey on the manservant's breath and a curling black hair on his gray jacket. He appeared not to have shaved for several days, and his side-whiskers needed a trim. Digby, to use a phrase, was letting down the home team.

Even more surprising, a very flustered Alfreda Thorney exited the house just as I prepared to enter. "Oh, Miss Alcott, oh, my," the Medusa stammered. "My, what a surprise. I have been here picking up the glove I left last week at our party." Miss Thorney appeared quite alarmed at seeing me, and she all but jumped with fright when Digby touched her elbow on her way out.

I wondered what on earth could be behind Alfreda Thorney's demeanor. But just as I was about to question her further, Digby said in his gravelly voice, "Yes, miss. Her glove."

I looked at Alfreda Thorney's hands. She wore two oldish gloves with yellowed fingertips and did not carry a third as she rushed away from the house.

Digby quite noticeably did not step aside so that I might enter. In fact, he blocked my way, and I had to use the "let me in" glance, that raised-brow, tilted-head command that young ladies learn when they first make calls and their ambition leads them astray, to parlors where they were not expected. But my glance was successful, so Digby reluctantly stood aside and gave me admittance.

"I have come at Mr. Wortham's request, to fetch some articles. Here is the list." I handed over the paper and Digby frowned in concentration, trying to discover the meaning of words such as *shurts, raiser, stripped trawsours,* and *tartine waste.*

I stood on tiptoe and peered over his shoulder while he read. The house seemed empty and quiet. Too quiet, with that ominous silence one hears immedi-

ately before restrained giggles can no longer be restrained. My instinct told me Digby was not alone.

It was not unknown for valets to entertain lady
friends when left in charge of an otherwise empty
household. But had Digby brought in a friend while
his employer was still in residence? Were those the
sounds, I wondered, the steps and whispers, that Mr.
Wortham had heard? And whatever had the Medusa
been up to? If she had come to fetch a forgotten glove,
why had there been no mismatched third glove in her
hand when she left? More likely, Miss Alfreda Thorney had decided to take advantage of Mr. Wortham's
absence and abscond with the sugar tongs she had
admired the week before.

"That would be his new plaid waistcoat," Digby finally deciphered, squinting at Preston's handwriting.
"If you will wait in the second parlor"—the second
parlor being the second best—". . . in the second parlor," he repeated, in case I hadn't understood the insult, "I will be down in ten minutes with a valise. Will
he be wanting soap and towels, do you think?"

"Yes. And bed linen. At the time of his removal to
the courthouse Mr. Wortham may not have realized
the nature of his accommodations," I said. "I will wait
in the front parlor. I see there is a fire there." The
front parlor being, of course, the best parlor. Digby
frowned, but said nothing. *Why is it,* I wondered, *that
some servants are even greater snobs than their
employers?*

The front parlor had not been unused since Preston's departure. A tumbler stood on a side table, the
half-empty bottle of whiskey next to it, and next to
that a creased opera program. The morning paper was
crumbled on the settee, slippers rested underneath.
A woman's black lace shawl had been tossed onto a
footstool. I picked up the shawl and sniffed it. Attar
of roses. A paper carnation had been pinned to its

collar, giving it an exotic look. I folded it and put it on the back of the settee, near the disheveled morning edition. I peered down at the paper. It was opened to the society page, the wedding announcements. Several names in that column had been circled boldly in ink. Digby, like many men of his station, seemed to have an inordinate interest in the doings of the upper class.

Footsteps overhead announced that the manservant was busy upstairs, probably toing and froing from the wardrobe to an opened valise on Mr. Wortham's bed. I picked up the paper and refolded it to the front page.

There was the sketch of Mr. Wortham, making him look older, diabolical, capable of anything. And underneath, of course, the headline: *Fortune-hunter Arrested for Murder of Wealthy Wife.*

Overhead, I heard the manservant and a new set of footsteps—the woman who wore attar of roses? Murmurs, then laughter floated down the stairs. A minute later Digby returned. I couldn't help but note that the man was smirking and his hair had been ruffled out of place.

"Well, thank you," I said somewhat coldly, accepting the valise he had packed so hastily that a shirtsleeve hung out the side. I made a point of putting the paper back on the table, front page up, with the drawing of Preston Wortham visible.

Digby sighed. "I fear," he said somberly, "that Mr. Wortham's past may be catching up with him. He has not always been known for his prudence."

"What do you mean, Digby?" I asked.

"Ah. I will say no more."

"Well, if it is any reassurance, I shall look deeply into this matter, Digby. Your employer shall not be punished unless he is proven guilty of this terrible deed."

Digby cleared his throat and studied the floor.

"That is reassuring, miss," he said after a long pause.

On my way out, I passed the carved oak hall tree, with its mirror and antlers and umbrella bucket. Preston Wortham's Saville Row coat was hanging there.

"I'll take that, too, Digby," I said. "He will need a warm coat. Strange. He had said it was misplaced."

"Perhaps he forgot to look for it on the coatrack, Miss Alcott," Digby suggested with more than a suggestion of a sneer.

"Well, then, Digby. Thank you for your help." I stepped toward the door. But Digby but not step forward to open it for me. He cleared his throat once again.

"Ah. I almost forgot." He sighed. "Tragedy makes one lose track of things. Mrs. Wortham brought you a present. From France, I believe. She would want me to present it to you, I'm certain. Will you wait a moment?"

He disappeared back up the stairs and was gone a full ten minutes before he returned, looking somewhat strained and carrying a slender tin box.

"I had some difficulty locating it," he said. "It is bonbons. Marzipan, I believe. Good day, miss." And he ushered me out the front door.

Chapter Nine

An Interview with a Murderer

At the courthouse jail, Preston Wortham was over-joyed to see me. He was most in need of a friend.

"A visitor. A lady," the guard called out, even though I already stood in front of the little barred room where Preston had been ensconced, and he could see me quite clearly.

I thought I had prepared myself for the sight of Mr. Wortham in captivity. I knew what the secured room looked like, since my father and other men of the committee had visited it three years before, during the troubled time of the case of Simms, the runaway slave who had been arrested and held in that room. The room was bare, small, and dark, with only one win-dow, and that one almost to the top of the wall, and barred. A heavy wire grille across the doorway pre-vented the occupant from leaving. It was a room from which there was no escape, being on the third floor and heavily guarded. The room smelled fetid, and I averted my eyes from the chamber pot in the corner.

Preston sat on his bed, a bare lumpy mattress on a rusting metal frame, absurdly still dressed in his eve-ning clothes and looking like a gentleman who had partaken a little too freely of entertainment the evening before and been accused of disturbing the peace, not murdering his wife. Men with Preston's looks and childlike intelligence carry an aura of innocence about them; they seem like naughty boys caught stealing from the cookie jar, I thought, studying him.

He had been deprived of his shoes and put in leg irons, since he stood accused of a vicious act of murder. When he politely rose to greet me, the leg irons clanked and the sound startled both of us. He was terrified.

"They will say I murdered poor Dorothy for her money," was his greeting to me. "I am doomed."

I had the awful feeling that life too closely ressembled my blood-and-thunders. The guard brought a chair and I sat opposite Preston, but outside of the barred room.

"I have brought your valise," I said. I set it on the floor, where he could see it. "Soap, razor, sheets, clean clothing. And your coat. It may be chilly, if they let the fire go out at night."

"I wondered where that had gone to," Preston said, reaching for the coat through the bars.

"Here, here!" The guard leaped forward and intercepted the coat. "I'll have to check those pockets first."

"I haven't brought a file, if that is what you are thinking," I protested. But the pockets were checked, and the valise, too, before the guard would pass them on to Preston.

"I'll just have to confiscate this," he said, taking the razor. "Desperate men consider desperate plans."

"How will I shave?" Preston wailed, as if that were his worst problem.

"If you have the money, you can hire a barber to come in," the guard said.

"Well, money is one thing I do have," Preston said darkly.

"Are you certain of that?" I asked, studying the ceiling as Preston unpacked and examined the small clothes that Digby had packed for him.

"Of course I'm certain. Dorothy was even wealthier than I suspected," Preston replied, frowning. "I say, are you sure Digby packed the clean stuff? As far as I can tell, Dorothy's family owns a large portion of the state of Georgia, and the cotton that comes out of there, in addition to the manufactories and the Newport estates."

"They do?" I was genuinely surprised. Dorothy had supported slavery?

"They kept it quiet, for the very reason you have just turned pale, Miss Alcott. Philosophically, they are abolitionists, I suppose. But they own a plantation. Dot didn't know. They kept it from her. Edgar revealed it to me one night in his cups. My brother-in-law does not hold his liquor well."

"You're certain?"

"Look at this shirt! Why didn't Digby press these things? Well, after Edgar spilled the beans I met with their banker for lunch one day, and asked the right questions." Preston smiled, pleased with himself. He had stolen a cookie from the cookie jar. "They are wealthier than you even suspect, Miss Alcott. Wealthier even than I suspected. Certainly wealthier than Dorothy knew. They kept the poor child in the dark, skimping on her clothes allowance, keeping her out of family meetings. When I told her about the plantation, she . . . she wept. She hadn't known, you see."

"And when was that, Mr. Wortham, when you told Dottie about the plantation?" I asked, leaning forward.

"Let's see. We were still unpacking. Two weeks ago. Yes, just two weeks ago. The week before . . ." His voice trailed off. *Before she died,* I finished in my thoughts. *Before she was murdered.*

"There was quite a to-do when we visited her family that Sunday," Wortham continued. "She confronted them, and, well . . . I was asked to leave the room for that discussion. They weren't overly eager to accept me into the family. But you already know that."

"Yes. I already know that. If it is any consolation, I'm sure that by the time you and Dorothy had filled the nursery, they would have grown more accepting. They needed time."

"I'm not at all sure. Edgar, in particular, has taken a rather strong dislike to me. And I to him, I freely admit, though he seemed to dislike Dorothy almost as much as he disliked me. I don't understand that family. You'll think I'm being fanciful but I've often wondered if they didn't have some deep, dark secret. Aside from the slaves. Have you ever wondered about them, Miss Alcott? Do you really think they might have grown to accept me?"

I stared at the stained ceiling for a few moments before answering, uncertain of how openly I wished to discuss this matter. Preston was—rather, had been—Dot's husband. He might also be Dot's murderer. I decided to answer vaguely, and borrowed one of my father's favorite sayings, a quip from the earlier philosopher William Byrd, that that song is best esteemed with which our ears are most acquainted. Of course, it went right over Preston's head, but he nodded and pretended to understand.

I decided it was time to get to the point.

"Mr. Wortham," I said in a low voice, since the guard was not more than ten feet away, "did you and Dot sign a marriage agreement?"

"Of course. It is what our class expects." Now Preston looked deeply confused. "What a strange question."

"And do you know the terms of that agreement? You did read it, didn't you?"

"It was very long, I recall. And filled with clauses. Yes, that was the day that Edgar and I drank champagne with lunch and then the lawyers came with the papers. . . ."

"And you signed after having had too much champagne." I sighed. "I suggest that Dot's brother is not the only man who cannot hold his liquor. Really, Mr. Wortham, one would suspect—"

"Tell me quickly what these questions mean," Preston said, putting his chin in his hands and looking as if he might weep.

I plunged in, since there seemed no way to soften the blow. "Dorothy's mother told me you are cut off from the family wealth, now she is dead."

"Impossible," he said.

"Very possible. You yourself signed the papers. Those very long, clause-filled papers that you seem not to have read."

"Not even an allowance?" Preston moaned so that the guard, half-asleep leaning against the wall, started forward. I held up my hand to indicate all was well, or at least not at emergency level.

"Not even an allowance," I said.

"Does this mean you won't be wanting a shave in the morning?" the guard asked, smirking.

A tear trickled down Mr. Wortham's chin. I looked away courteously, though I felt chilled.

Later that afternoon, Sylvia and I were together again in the kitchen of the Charles Street Home, boiling water for one of the residents. A Miss Miller (she refused to give her first name, and all knew that last name was an invention) had decided to give birth that day, and her labor was in progress—had been, in fact, for several hours already—when we arrived.

Sylvia and I assisted by supplying pails of hot water,

linen, and the occasional teacup of whiskey the mid-wife required to keep up her strength.

"Tear this worn sheet, Sylvie. It will make fine swaddling. I will tell you first about that brown pack-age, as it is a shorter tale," I said, puffing a little with exertion. "It is my new story, Sylvie. Finished. I completed it last night. Though I am dissatisfied." Steam from the boiling vat had curled my thick dark hair and reddened Sylvia's cheeks. Our gowns clung wetly to us.

"This is as close to a Turkish bath as I hope to get." Sylvia wiped perspiration from her eyes, tore the old sheet into foot-wide strips, and handed them to me. I then dipped them in boiling soapy water and hung them on a rope strung through the scullery.

From the upstairs birthing room came the sound of a young woman screaming at the top of her lungs, and the scream was followed by a string of curses that made one wonder where Miss Miller had acquired her conversational habits.

"One can only hope never to experience such agony," Sylvia said.

"If you insist on conversion and the convent, you may well be spared it, Sylvia," I replied. A thought occurred. "As has Dot, who has died so young."

Conversation temporarily ceased again as another scream sounded through the house, a scream of agony that sent chills down my spine. The scream, this time, was followed by silence, and then by a high-pitched wail. Miss Miller's child had successfully entered the world and was calling for his first meal and bath.

"Victory!" Smiling, we gathered up bundles of clean linen to take upstairs. "Only eight hours for her labor. An easy one," I said, though I was certain it hadn't felt at all easy to the new mother. "Let's go relieve the midwife. She'll need a rest."

Another hour passed before both mother and child

were nicely cleaned up and resting upstairs in fresh sheets. Miss Miller had come through quite well, considering it was her first (and last, she insisted), but her lack of curiosity about the infant was troubling. He had been swaddled and laid in a cradle, for Miss Miller would not have him in her bed, nor would she give him her breast. So the poor little tyke sucked goat milk from the pierced finger of a glove and burrowed into a pillow rather than his mother.

"Those who say motherhood is instinctive and natural are talking balderdash," I commented to Sylvia in a low voice. "Maybe for some women it is, but it would seem that love of a baby does not necessarily follow from that brief and often bitter union between a man and woman."

"It's wailing. Take it away," Miss Miller called from her bed. "Take it away!"

And so the new little person was bundled up and taken away by the midwife, to be brought to a wet nurse and then, perhaps, adopted into a good home that would not question too deeply the child's parentage.

"I suspect when I go home, Father will want to hear about Miss Miller and the baby, and then discuss the meaning of life and the transference of souls," I said. "Hard to think all that blood and gore today had any meaning to it at all. Perhaps we should adjourn to a place where one can order a strong cup of tea." And so to the Commonwealth Tea House we went, and found a table in the ladies' side, and ordered a pot of China black and a whole plate of buns, with fresh butter.

"Now," Sylvia ordered, pouring her cup, "tell me about Preston in jail." It was twilight, and the serving girl came and put a little oil lamp on the table. I described my visit to Digby and my audience with Preston in jail.

"He shed tears over lost money, when he had not cried at Dot's autopsy," I said. I shivered again, as I had earlier that day outside Preston's cell.

"But if Preston doesn't inherit, then he doesn't have a motive, does he?" Sylvia said, opening her purse and putting a dime on the table for the tea.

"My turn, Sylvie," I said, opening my own thin coin purse. Sylvia let me pay, knowing I would be embarrassed if she did not.

"Don't you see, Sylvia? He didn't know he wouldn't inherit. When Dot died, Mr. Wortham still believed her death would enrich him."

On our way back to Beacon Hill, I decided to stop and have a chat with Constable Cobban.

"Come with me, Sylvia. Just for appearance' sake."

It was windy, and last year's half-rotted leaves whirled down the street as the world readied itself for spring, for renewal. One leaf, still showing the red and gold of its last year's demise, flew onto my little flat pancake hat and stuck there with determination, as if a milliner had arranged it.

"If you are worried about appearances, then you are not blind to what I have already suspected. Constable Cobban is smitten with you," Sylvia said.

"Don't be silly." I reached up and removed the leaf. Sylvia smiled.

Constable Cobban was just ending his shift, and rolling down his shirt sleeves in preparation for donning his brash plaid jacket. He blushed a bit when I walked into his office, but very courteously pulled out chairs for both of us and sat back down behind his beat-up desk. There were papers everywhere, and a spilled pot of ink no one had thought to wipe up had dried and left a black continent of stain. In the rare spaces of open, uncluttered wood were years and years of penknifed graffiti. There was one deeply etched phrase directly in front of where I sat: *Three down,* it said. (For years I mused over that phrase, wondering.)

"How can I be of assistance?" Cobban looked steadily at both of us, but I was aware his attention had gathered and focused on me.

"You say there was an anonymous letter accusing Dorothy's husband. Might I have the details of that letter?" I asked boldly.

"The Wortham case," he said with a note of impatience, which surprised me. I hadn't considered that he would be working on other matters at the same time. Dot's death had changed me and my world, though I was just beginning to suspect the forces of those changes. How could it not have similarly affected everyone else? How could young Constable Cobban look at me so brightly and say, "The Wortham case," as if it were no more than a matter of a milk jar stolen off a back porch?

"Yes, the Wortham case," I said.

"Not the actual letter, of course," Cobban said, no longer smiling. "That must be retained as evidence. But I will tell you exactly what it says. That a tall man wearing a fancy, expensive greatcoat with a high collar was quarreling with a woman near the docks on the afternoon of Mrs. Wortham's disappearance. The man is described, and meets Mr. Wortham's description. The woman with whom he quarreled met Mrs. Wortham's description."

"Even so, it is a fact of life that husbands and wives do sometimes quarrel, and sometimes in public," I said.

"Sadly true," Cobban agreed. "But when a wife is found murdered, the quarrel takes on significance."

"And you have no idea who sent this anonymous letter?"

"Usually, with an anonymous letter, that is the point, isn't it?" Cobban said gently, patiently. At that moment, for some reason, he reminded me of my father, and I felt exasperated by his masculine manner of trying to impose philosophical logic into the more feminine corners of a disordered world, not accepting that intuition is a companion to, not a substitute for, logic.

I returned a gentle, patient smile. "Exactly. But the method of delivery, the quality of the paper, the slant of the handwriting itself, might provide some information about the sender, their class, the part of Boston in which they reside. You might take a closer look at the letter.

"And there is another point I wish to make," I continued, ignoring the blush that rose to his cheeks. *Redheads blush so easily,* I thought. "Constable Cobban, I have talked to a woman who spends her days at the dock, the crab-cake seller, and she said that on that afternoon there was no quarreling couple, not anywhere near the place were Dot was later found. It was the day the child fell into the water, and there was a large commotion over that, but she says there were no other distractions that afternoon. And my witness is not anonymous."

I rose, and could not resist a smile of victory.

He rose, too, keeping his desk between us, as if he needed restraint.

"Maybe her eyes and ears and concentration failed her for a moment," Cobban offered.

"I think not. She is elderly, but her faculties are sharp enough to witness a public quarrel."

"And she is not so busy selling cakes that she would miss an event of that nature were it to take place near her kiosk and in a manner that caught the attention of others," Sylvia added.

His blush had died down, but now there was harshness in the set of his mouth, and he tapped impatiently on his desk.

"Miss Alcott, do you really believe him innocent? What is he to you, that you seek to defend him?" A brief flash of jealousy in Cobban's placid blue eyes . . . and then composure again, official indifference, professional distance. I thought, at that moment, that he was a man of great passion, and such men can easily be moved to violence.

I took a deep breath before answering his question. "He is innocent till proven guilty," I answered. "That is what he is to us all."

We walked back to Beacon Hill. The first stars were already out, and clouds moved over a slender moon, making of the night a theatrical event of flickering light and shadows that came and went. We could hear cats rustling through the hedges, dogs barking as their toenails tapped on the cobbles. Sounds of a piano, a polka, came dimly through the darkness. Sylvia and I passed a house where voices were raised, a man shouting, a woman weeping. . . .

"What course now, Louisa?" Sylvia asked.

"Now we must determine the condition of that marriage," I answered. "It is not enough to speculate on individual natures, since once merged in matrimony, nature changes or is at least enhanced. We must discover Mr. Wortham's nature, and Dot's, and the nature of their union." I gazed up at the moon, which was playing a disappearing act with the clouds.

"Preston is vain and foolish," Sylvia said. "Dorothy was gentle and, I must say it, a little slow, and in rich abundance of those instincts termed maternal. Their union was based on her love and his greed, with perhaps a little friendship thrown in."

"You simplify, Sylvia. We must both try to look past the superficial and examine the subtleties."

"I am trying, I'm sure. But it is my nature to take things at face value."

"Ah, Sylvie. You don't yet even know yourself. I predict that when matured, when tempered with time and experience, you will look back and see yourself for what you already are . . . a woman of many layers, many purposes."

"You describe yourself, Louy."

Chapter Ten

The Weird Sisters Plot a Voyage

The next day I called on Edith and Sarah Brownly and their aunt, Alfreda Thorney, at the Brownly Beacon Hill mansion. It was not far from my own modest home, but the few blocks made a firm demarcation, a Mason-Dixon line, separating the very wealthy from the not wealthy. Each step from my own little Pinckney Street home toward the Brownly home brought forth disconcerting change: The houses grew larger until finally they were nothing less than palatial mansions; the front gardens grew more elaborate, sprouting daily trimmed yews shaped into peacocks or green versions of the *Mayflower*; the servants dashing to and fro grew more numerous and more finely uniformed.

By the time I arrived, I felt that I might as well have arrived on another planet. Neither Sylvia nor I had often visited Dorothy at home, though the Brownly family had regular calling hours on Wednesday afternoon. Even Dorothy had been uneasy in that large, intimidating redbrick version of a Georgian town house.

In a way, I had arrived in an unknown world: The information that the Brownlys owned shares in a plantation had affected me deeply, and now I could not but help view this manifestation of wealth as the most ill-begotten of gains, since it had been won upon the backs of slaves. Till that news had been proffered, I had believed the very rich Brownlys, though eccentric and often self-absorbed, were capable of reasoning and moral reliability. Now I had my doubts, and those doubts affected the interview that was to follow.

The Brownly sisters and aunt were at home, the lace-capped servant who answered the door announced solemnly. My coat was taken but not my hat. This was to be a formal call, which meant it must be limited to half an hour or less. The rules of etiquette were very strict on that matter.

The three women sat in the front parlor before a blazing fire, though the afternoon was not all that chilly. This was one of the prerogatives of the rich: a fire even when not needed. They wore black crepe for Dorothy, and had replaced their pearl earrings with jet, but that seemed the extent of any grief they felt or exhibited for their sister and niece.

When I arrived at the front parlor, Sarah was pasting last summer's pressed violets and daisies into a scrapbook. She looked rather pretty and girlish, with dried violets strewn over her lap and a rose petal stuck to her cheek, though the dab of white paste on her nose somewhat spoiled the effect. Edith was polishing a pair of walking boots to a high sheen. She rubbed with such gusto that she reminded me of those curious movements of locomotive machinery. Alfreda Thorney was reading a novel, which she hastily buried under a pillow when she saw me, just announced, standing in the doorway. Women in mourning generally did not read the popular press, but devoted their time to sermons and uplifting poetry.

The overall impression was that these three had

quite successfully managed to restrain their burden of grief for the deceased Dot.

"Oh, Louisa, isn't it exciting!" Sarah cooed, looking up from her scrapbook and pushing her little spectacles further down her nose so she might look over them. "We are to go to the Matterhorn! The Matterhorn! I have always wanted to go to France. It was so unfair of Mother to take Dorothy. . . ."

"That is exciting," I commented, still standing, for no one had offered me a chair. "Perhaps, though, you should visit Switzerland as well, since I believe that is where you will find the Matterhorn."

"No. Really? Edith, you never . . . Oh, you are such a tease to have let me go on like that, believing we were to visit France when all along you knew . . . Oh, you are a tease." And she threw down her little paste brush in a temper, so she could wag her finger at her grinning sister. I knew from my own experience in service that the dab of paste on the polished table would take half an hour of polishing to remove, but since Sarah did not even know that tables must be polished but were looked to by servants . . . Oh, spoiled, spoiled!

"We shall visit France, too," was Edith's cool response.

"I am relieved," I said—and if there was a tone of irony and disappointment in my voice, the weird sisters did not hear it—"that you are not overcome with grief."

Edith looked up from her boot polishing and pushed her spectacles higher up on her nose. "We never liked you, Miss Alcott. I feel free to break this connection, now that your friendship with Dorothy has been severed," she said in her deep, booming voice.

"Now, girls," lectured Alfreda Thorney, shifting on the sofa and rearranging the pillows over her buried novel. "Remember your manners."

"Thank you for your honesty." I addressed myself to Edith. "And for the courtesy you showed me while Dorothy was alive. It was a convenient pretense that we enjoyed each other's companionship, and it pleased your sister. May I sit?"

"Do get to the point, Miss Alcott. We are rather pressed for time. There is much packing to be done."

"Oh, Edith." Sarah sighed. "Try to be a little friendly. Miss Alcott, would you like us to call Mama? She is just upstairs in the nursery with Agnes. Will you take tea?"

"No tea, thank you." I chose a straight-backed wooden chair far from the fire, for the day was damp, though warm, and my dress dripped ever so slightly. I had no desire to stain one of the formidable velvet-upholstered chairs or settees. At my own home there would have been towels and hot-water bottles to greet me, and no concern at all for a chair; but this was the Brownly mansion, where lace tablecloths, knotted rugs, carved chairs, bouquets of ferns and hothouse flowers seemed of more consequence than people. I shivered, and not from the dampness. I carefully turned in my chair so that I might see all three women at once.

"There is no need to disturb Mrs. Brownly," I answered mildly. "I have already offered her my condolences. As I now offer them to you. How is Agnes, by the way? Is her congestion improving?"

"Agnes is much too delicate, as is often the case with these change-of-life babies," said Edith coldly. "How Mother ever—"

"Now, Edith, you know women have no say in these things. We must take as God sends. . . ."

"Bullocks," muttered Edith, resuming her boot polishing.

I stifled a smile. I agreed with Edith on that issue. The day before I had shown Queenie a packet of sheaths, and given her instructions on their use . . . instructions that were all too often pointless for girls such as Queenie, whose babies began in nights of forced rather than willing sex.

I could not discuss such matters with the Brownly girls, of course. If legs could not even be referred to in polite society except as vague and sexless limbs, how to refer to other, more secret parts of the body? No, and that was not the purpose of my visit.

"I hope Agnes grows stronger," I said, pretending to look at a vase of roses but surreptitiously studying the women, waiting for their response. "It would be heartbreaking for you to lose two sisters." I leaned closer to the vase and inhaled the fragrance.

Sarah started, as if the thought hadn't occurred to her.

"Dorothy had grown apart from us," Edith explained in her strange, booming voice. "We hardly thought of her as a sister anymore."

Alfreda Thorney stared into the flames, a dreamy expression on her face, and said nothing.

"Because of her marriage to Mr. Wortham?" I asked, again studying the vase of roses.

"Oh, ever so long before that, when . . ." Sarah bubbled, but did not continue. A look from Edith made her clamp her lips in a thin, tight line.

"She was an unsatisfactory sister," Edith said.

"And an unsatisfactory niece," Alfreda Thorney added. "I do not believe in harsh punishment, but . . ." And she, too, finished in midsentence. "Well, some girls mature too soon for their own good. Are you sure you will not take tea, Miss Alcott? Will you be staying long?"

"No tea, thank you. I'll not stay long." When had this cold distance between Dorothy and her siblings begun? Why? Could I discover the roots of this enmity in the ten remaining minutes allowed for this very formal visit? Oh, the deviousness of society's ridiculous rules on paying afternoon calls! A day, a week, a month would not be long enough to reveal the heart of this bizarre family. I tried to imagine my beloved Anna, so far away in Syracuse, saying of me, "She is unsatisfactory." No. God willing such enmity would never exist among the Alcott brood.

Edith put down one boot, now polished to a high sheen, and picked up its mate. I was now used to the heat of the room, and the clutter, and noted with surprise that the sole of that just-polished boot was quite worn. Surely Edith would want new boots?

With that thought came other perceptions about Edith. Her gown was quite out of fashion, and while Edith was not the kind of woman to pay undue attention to the mode of ribbons and frills, surely she knew that her black crepe was moth-eaten in the sleeves? For a woman of great wealth, she was, when closely examined, rather shabby.

"And now Dorothy's quarterly funds will be divided among you, I understand?" I kept my voice low. "I suspect that will add to your funds for a trip abroad." I knew I had broken one of the cardinal rules of society, which was never to mention income, bank accounts, or family finances, but the circumstances of my visit and the need to investigate Dot's death surely trumped the artificial code of the drawing room. Yet, even as I thought this, I realized that about the only people who would agree were my parents— the Brownlys had always acted as if they believed the rules of politesse superceded in moral importance the Ten Commandments and indeed the golden rule as well.

"Considerably," Edith admitted, so unused to hearing this question that she answered without thinking.

Sarah, for the first time, blushed and looked startled. "Why, Edith, I never thought . . . Are we to travel on poor Dorothy's allowance?"

Edith impatiently threw down the rag she had been using on her boots. "Yes. Don't you think we are entitled?" She grew silent again, casting an evil glance at me.

I stared into the flames of the hearth, holding my breath, waiting.

"Well, there will be so much gossip about us now that Dorothy has gotten herself murdered, I'm sure this will be brought up, too," Edith continued. "Several years ago, when Dorothy turned eighteen, she inherited an uncle's share of the Colby Company, as well as a landholding. In the South. That stupid man left a most curious and inconvenient will, indicating that . . ." Edith faltered.

"He did not believe Edgar would provide suitably for Dorothy, after Father passed on," Sarah said. "Isn't that strange?"

"Sarah!" exclaimed Aunt Alfreda, shocked to the core by this most unsuitable path the conversation had taken.

The Colby Company, as I and most of the country knew, was one of the largest cotton mills in New England, and the managers of it were famous for their proslavery position. It was not uncommon for Northerners to own Southern property and the slaves that accompanied such property. But that information, along with insane aunts kept in the attic, uncles with gambling debts, and the first child that arrived five months after the honeymoon, was never, ever spoken of in polite society.

"Dorothy became the major shareholder." Edith picked up an already shining boot and began polishing again with such vigor that I feared the leather might disintegrate.

"Then Dorothy would also have insisted on rearranging the management of your Southern property," I said quietly.

Of course Dorothy would do that. Of course the sisters would resent her, I realized.

The room grew so still I was sure the three women had stopped breathing and were about to swoon.

Simple Sarah was the first to break the silence. "She would have, I'm sure, except . . . well, there was the accident. She died. We had kept the Colby secret so long. Edgar kept saying, 'Don't tell Dorothy, don't tell Dorothy'. So we didn't." Sarah, with an additional rose petal now clinging to the other cheek, smiled disingenuously. "I wonder how she ever found out."

"It was Wortham, of course." Edith glowered. "Sniffing around the lawyers and bankers. He found out and told Dorothy. Just as he has apparently thought fit to speak of family business with Miss Alcott."

"Surely Louisa isn't interested in all this," Alfreda bristled. "No young woman should be. Really. Most inappropriate. Louisa, I see you no longer wear a wide-brimmed hat but a cloche. Do tell me . . ."

The three younger women ignored Alfreda's attempt to steer the conversation into more genteel waters.

"But really, I never thought we were to travel on Dorothy's allowance; it seems . . . ghoulish." Sarah, still pouting, shivered, and the two rose petals fell from her cheeks to her lap, where they joined the strewn violets. She brushed them away, onto the carpet, and I watched them fall onto a bare patch where years of footsteps had obliterated both pattern and texture.

"It is only fair that we use whatever was left of Dorothy's income," Edith insisted coolly. "Unless you would prefer to give the money to a charity. The Charles Street Home for Unwed Girls, perhaps?"

"Edith!" Sarah exclaimed. "Wicked women should be punished, not aided. Yes, perhaps Dorothy would want us to have her allowance, to see all those cities and sights in Europe she saw with . . ."

"With Mr. Wortham," I finished, deciding to do away with any further subtlety and get to the point. "Tell me, Sarah, do you think Mr. Wortham could have murdered Dorothy?"

"Well, the police certainly think so. I'm sure they are ever so much cleverer than I. Close the curtain, Aunt Alfreda, will you? Those gloomy clouds are upsetting," Sarah complained.

Alfreda Thorney rose and did as she was bidden.

"But do you think so?" I persisted, leaning forward now that the Brownly sisters' faces were partially obscured. Indeed, most of the room was now obscured.

"No. He is foolish and greedy, certainly, but I never saw him as a violent man," Sarah said, gently closing her scrapbook and brushing the leftover leaves and flowers onto the carpet for the maid to sweep up. "He could be sweet sometimes."

"Be quiet, you foolish girl," Edith muttered.

"I will not, Edith." Sarah sat up straighter, pleased with herself. "I am free to speak, am I not? No, Louisa, Dorothy sent us letters and cards when she was traveling and she never complained that Mr. Wortham was cruel. Just the opposite, I would say. She complained that he would not leave her alone with her thoughts, that he wanted to know all her emotions, all her reflections, all the stories of her girlhood. He was jealous that she had been to Rome before he could take her there. No, she never complained that he was violent toward her; just the opposite."

"Dorothy wrote all that to you?" Edith looked devastated. "I did not know about this correspondence. She never wrote to me. . . ."

"I suspect she knew you would not write back, Edith," Sarah said in a small voice.

"I understand husbands can be quite possessive in that way." Alfreda Thorney clasped her thin hands together in her lap. "I once considered—"

But she was cut short by Edith, who said darkly, "Mr. Wortham had a different method of showing his cruelty."

"And how was that, Edith?" I asked.

"Ask his mistress, Miss Katya Mendosa."

"Oh, my, my . . ." squealed Alfreda, now fanning herself vigorously. I imagined her thinking: *Marriages and husbands, yes. Mistresses, no. Do these young women know nothing about propriety?*

My allotted time had expired, and just when the conversation was going somewhere. A mistress! I rose to leave but at the arched doorway turned to ask one final question.

"You are certain about Katya Mendosa and Mr. Wortham?"

"Absolutely," Edith said.

"Oh, my." Sylvia sighed when I reported the conversation to her. "I wonder if Edgar Brownly knows about this. Isn't Katya Mendosa the young woman who stormed up and down his stairs, cursing us the day we visited Mr. Brownly's studio?"

"The same," I said, linking arms with my friend.

"How does Miss Mendosa find time for all these activities, and still appear onstage? She must be a woman of uncommon energy," Sylvia mused.

It was the day after my visit to the Brownlys, and Sylvia and I were taking a constitutional on the Commons, near the Smokers' Circle, so that I could surreptitiously study the men lingering there and take some notes on their posture, the smell of the smoke, and the gravelly sound of their voices.

"See that man nearest the lamppost?" I whispered. Sylvia turned and tried to look, without staring, by gazing cross-eyed at the ducks on the pond immediately behind him. The man to whom I referred was middle-aged and of florid complexion, dressed in a somewhat battered beaver hat and faun-colored suit with a black cutaway coat. He looked as if he hadn't seen his bed in several days, and the gentlemen in his group were guffawing in a somewhat uncouth manner, as if the news they exchanged should have been reported only in the privacy of a gentleman's study, over a glass of port.

"He has an opera program in his pocket," I whispered. "If only I could talk to him, and ask him if Katya Mendosa was in good voice last night and what she wore."

"Louisa, you wouldn't talk to a stranger on the street, would you?" Sylvia was often appalled at my boldness. I prided myself on schooling her in the freedoms given to women of spirit.

"Not if you're going to carry on so. Quick, turn away. He caught me studying him."

We hurriedly put our backs to him and walked in the opposite direction. He took a few steps after us and then thought better of it. We returned to our whispered conversation about my visit to the Brownly sisters.

"Wealth is a chimera, Sylvia," I declared. "All my life I have thought the Brownlys to be wealthy. Perhaps because they are reputed to be wealthy, because they once were wealthy. But, Sylvia, I would swear they have fallen on hard times. The parlor curtains have been patched where the moths have gotten to them, and the wallpaper has faded with age, leaving brighter spots where pictures have been taken down, probably to sell. The *Madonna and Child in an Olive Grove* is gone, and other artworks as well. When Sarah saw me looking about, she had the curtains closed, and put the room in darkness."

"No wonder there was such lack of affection between Dorothy and the rest of the family," Sylvia said. "If they were already suffering financially and she was requiring them to sell off property at a loss. Isn't that what they call it, Louisa, when one must sell too quickly and to cheap bidders? They must have bitterly resented her meddling in the family enterprises."

"Yes," I agreed, deep in thought. "Investigators look for motives, don't they? We seem to have too many, Sylvia. Edith can now prove to Sarah that marriage is not a state to be considered, since husbands have a penchant for murdering their wives. That should keep Sarah unwed and by her side, an interesting if uncommon motive for murder. It would seem that the siblings also would want to prevent Dorothy's meddling in the family banking affairs. And now they inherit her allowance, with which they can scrabble up the Matterhorn. I had no idea they wished to go mountaineering, had you?

"I had no idea Preston Wortham had a mistress," I continued without waiting for Sylvia's reply. "Or at least that he had managed the affair so miserably that everyone, including his wife's family, knew about it. I wonder if Dorothy knew? How humiliating for her."

"Perhaps that was why Dorothy grew silent and sad." And at that, we grew silent and sad for a moment.

"It may be part of it," I finally agreed. "But I keep going back to that change in Dorothy, trying to place when it happened so we might know why." We walked on a bit, musing. "It was as if there had been, at some time, some kind of mortal blow to her very nature, to shake her to the core so that she could no longer be . . . why, be Dorothy, I suppose is what I mean. To change from simple to complex, from merry to sad." We had passed the Smokers' Circle and were now approaching the duck pond, where little children sailed paper boats and splashed each other. They seemed so gay. How could they know how short were childhood and innocence?

"Perhaps when she learned about the Southern property," Sylvia suggested.

"That would not have changed her. It would only have made her more of what she already was: a kind, compassionate young woman of conscience. Besides, that occurred just two weeks ago, and the change we noticed and remarked upon occurred earlier. Something else happened, something before that."

"Perhaps she wished to convert and the family wouldn't let her."

I smiled. "Dorothy was sensible rather than mystical. No, it was not a matter of religion."

"Perhaps she had fallen in love."

I paused in midstep. Since Sylvia's arm was hooked through mine and we had walked in uniform pace, and since Sylvia did not know I was going to stop and Sylvia kept going, we almost tripped over each other.

"You are a clever girl. More clever than you realize," I told Sylvia.

"So you think our Dorothy had a broken heart, Louisa? And yet she married Preston. Hmmm. Another motive."

"And what is that, Sylvia?"

"Jealousy. Preston found out that she had had an earlier romance."

I considered Sylvia and patiently said, "Perhaps his mistress can tell us more."

"Oh, Preston is a cad. To throw wonderful Dottie away for . . . for a woman like Katya Mendosa. Do you think he meant to abandon Dottie? But then he would lose her allowance. Murder does seem a solution," Sylvia said with renewed concern.

"No," I said emphatically. I had studied with great care the voluminous literature on the question of marriage. It seemed harder to find a novel that did not contain a mistress than one that did. "Often when a married man takes a mistress he creates a kind of equilibrium in his life. One woman supplies the heirs, the domestic comfort. The other supplies . . . adventure, I suppose. He grows dependent on both, as if he needs two women to create a whole. No, to my mind the mistress does not provide additional motive. But even so, it will turn a jury against him. As common as affairs of that nature are, society plays deaf and dumb to the erring husband only as long as that husband errs in private. Once it is a public matter—and Mr. Wortham's face has been on the front page for several days now—once it is public, society has no choice but to disavow and punish the culprit. Though it seems to me that hanging a man for infidelity may be extreme."

Sylvia sniffed. "It seems modern husbands have adopted a fashion of murdering their wives. I suspect you share my views and that you are also planning to be a spinster!"

"For a while at least," I agreed. "Perhaps a long while. How can one raise children and care for a home and husband, and write books? Of course, there's always Miss Alfreda Thorney to remind one of the miseries of spinsterhood. There must be a third way, Sylvia. A woman must be independent of others and learn to provide for herself."

"There's the rub. Are we all to go into service to earn our keep?"

I groaned. "Never again, anything but that!"

"We will find other ways," Sylvia promised.

I gave her a strong hug, though she was not prone

to such shows of affection. "But now, my dear Sylvia, I must return home. I've left the schoolchildren alone with Abba far too long and they will exhaust her."

We turned back, arm in arm, and passed the Smokers' Circle one last time. The man I had studied glared at us, and I realized his interest had not been of a friendly nature.

"He recognizes me as Bronson Alcott's daughter," I said loudly enough for him and the rest of the Smokers' Circle to hear. "And he himself is a despicable supporter of slavery. Afternoon, Mr. Crawford. The mill running at profit? Cheap cotton is good for the ledger, isn't it? But not much longer, I hope."

"Go home to your scrubbing and keep out of my way," the man growled. "Cheeky abolitionists." He flicked his cigarette to the ground and crushed it under his boot heel with a leer that suggested he wished abolitionists were similarly situated. The other men in the Smokers' Circle moved away from him. Slavery was still the law of the land, but it was an increasingly unpopular law, in Boston, at least.

"I think what shocks me the most in this awful affair is discovering that Dorothy's family owns Southern property and slaves," I said, turning my back to him once again.

Sylvia tried to cheer me. "Can you imagine how Edgar Brownly must have bristled over her meddling in the finances? A woman not only discussing business, but insisting on having her way. Louy, I just had the strangest thought. Poor Preston has already lost two fortunes at his young age. His father's when he was disinherited after that summer of debauchery, and Dorothy's. He would have lost a third fortune, had Dottie lived and forced the sale of the plantation. Poor Preston," Sylvia repeated, for one can feel a bit of sympathy for the wasted dreams even of a murderer. "What now, Louisa? What further questions do we ask, and of whom?"

I smiled and hummed a little.

"Will you come with me to the theater tonight, Sylvia? Katya Mendosa is singing the lead in *A Girl of the West*."

Chapter Eleven

The Diva Sings

According to the popular press, Katya Mendosa had arrived in Boston three years earlier after a highly successful tour of the Western states that had rivaled, in publicity if not reviews, Jenny Lind's first American tour. Miss Mendosa had been born in Seville, Spain, or Havana, Cuba, in 1832 or 1836, depending on her mood, and she had a dark, exotic beauty that sent young men swooning. What she did not have was a voice, and her engagements were typically short, but always played to full houses, since her gowns plunged lower than any other actress's, and when she danced she contrived to keep her skirts above her knees for the entirety of the dance.

Sylvia had ascertained those details—and hurriedly whispered them to me as we entered the theater—from the various young men of her mother's acquaintance who appeared at the family dinner table, often looking pale and sickly from too many "late evenings," as they discreetly called them. One such young man in particular, she informed me, seemed especially well acquainted with the known facts of Miss Mendosa's life—Johnnie Charles, heir of the Charles wagon-wheel-factory fortune.

Johnnie stood to inherit his father's wealth, but those who knew him had long ago come to the realization that Johnnie most certainly would not inherit his father's industriousness or cunning. Earlier that same evening he had sat at Sylvia's table, his pale face floating among the candles like an apparition, his black evening clothes looking slightly rumpled and dusty so that one could in good conscience come to the conclusion that he had not yet changed from the previous evening's party.

"So, Louisa, I gathered up my courage and simply asked Johnnie if he knew Miss Mendosa."

"And?" I asked, wondering what the end of this story would be.

"He had had much too much to drink and appeared maudlin and sad when her name was mentioned. He had a faraway look in his eyes and he said again and again, almost as an entreaty, 'Katya! Katya Mendosa.' "

"Well," I said, hoping Sylvia would finish her story before the play began, but trying not to be too impatient, "what did he tell you about Miss Mendosa?"

"Of all things, he announced, 'I know the vixen.' Apparently Miss Mendosa, as they say, 'stood him up' last week for an engagement with another man."

Next to me, my father shifted uncomfortably in his chair. I knew he disapproved of gossip and disliked being our chaperon, so I patted his arm reassuringly. Then I turned back to Sylvia and the matter at hand. "Who is her new beau?" I whispered.

"You already know. Edgar Brownly! I almost laughed, but then I remembered our visit to his studio and the paintings we found. But, Louisa, I must also tell you what Johnnie said to me about Preston."

"What?" I asked, becoming convinced Sylvia was enjoying leading me on too much. This sort of storytelling, I thought, was more infuriating than amusing!

"Johnnie told me the men at the club had come 'round to Preston. When he first married Dot, they were convinced it was a match for money. But in the past few months, as Johnnie and the others came to know Preston, they realized he was tremendously in love with Dot. He was so taken with her the men realized it had to be a love match and money had nothing to do with it—they thought it was tragic that she died, as Preston would be a grief-stricken disaster without her."

"I heard the same at the Athenaeum," Father said, indicating that as much as he disapproved of gossip he could not resist it himself.

Dressed in an old-fashioned black cutaway coat and cravat, Father looked decidedly out of place in his music-hall chair, but he had been recruited as chaperon for the evening, since young women could not appear out at night without a male escort without losing their good names. I had persuaded him to serve that role, although he, the philosopher, claimed to loathe the theater. I thought it telling, however, that whenever Father arranged one of his schools, he always included singing and dancing in the curriculum.

I was flushed with excitement, and not just because I loved the theater and few other things in this world could bring me out of my grief like an evening on red plush chairs, before a stage, with the greenish limelight casting its strange shadows. The theater was filled with a dozen different perfumes and the tinkle of women's clinking bracelets; there was a tension in the air as if a storm were brewing: a storm of passion onstage.

Tonight would be different from other theater nights, though. Tonight, after the performance, I might very well have an interview with the mistress of a murderer.

"Strange, though, about Mr. Wortham. And very, very sad," I said in response to the reported gossip of that husband. His grief certainly had been hidden when I had seen him in jail. "So he had been talking at his club about how much he loved his wife. And then she died."

"Would that count as a character testimony?" Sylvia asked.

"Depends on the jury, I suppose. One could assume one of two things. Either he loved Dorothy, as he claimed. Or he was speaking of his love for her, hoping a jury would accept club gossip as character testimony after . . ."

"After murdering her." Sylvia sighed. "It is all such a confusing mess."

"Be brave, Sylvia. We will unravel this." And then three knocks sounded, the orchestra begin playing the prelude with great gusto, and the curtain rose.

Seeing the notorious Katya Mendosa in costume and onstage was a revelation to us. Dropping a handkerchief for a certain young man to pick up and return was as flirtatious as a *bonne famille* young woman could be. But Katya Mendosa was not well-bred, unless one counted a biological inheritance that had endowed her with a strong chin, well-fleshed legs, and flashing black eyes. Her olive skin was smooth and sleek, her movements languid. She was the personification of animal magnetism as she tilted her head and winked, as she ran her hands over her arms and shoulders, embracing herself, as she kept her hips moving in circles as she walked, spinning a web with them. She wore a bodice and crinoline tied up with red bows, and nothing else, except I suspected she had padded her hair . . . and perhaps the bodice as well.

Her voice was thin and often false, striking midnote rather than on key. But few in the mostly male audience seemed to notice. She was a woman who stirred strong passions, and I jotted notes and descriptions during most of the performance. Miss Mendosa could well serve as a model and inspiration for some less acceptable female characters that would flesh out my blood-and-thunder stories.

Father appeared to sleep through most of the performance, but at select moments he would sit up in alarm, exclaim, "How large her feet are!" and then sink back into slumber, to the chagrin of various young men seated around us who were gazing anywhere but at Miss Mendosa's red silk dancing slippers.

The operetta itself, thin as the diva's voice, was a frothy confection of love and lust set someplace referred to simply as "the West," though I whispered to Sylvia that they should have specified: Was it Montana, a free-soiler state; or Kansas, where slavery was supported? Not that abolition was confabulated; it was not. Instead, we were treated to various scenes of a somewhat potbellied cavalry officer alternately serenading Miss Mendosa under a balcony dubiously attached to the façade of a log cabin, or rescuing her from a handful of bandits and red-painted Indians wearing drooping feathers.

"Dreadful," was my only comment, whispered a little loudly and often from behind my fan. It had once been my own ambition to appear onstage, till I realized that it would occupy too much time better spent on writing.

"Dreadful," Sylvia agreed, leaning toward the stage with expectancy as one more dagger-armed bandit approached the fattish hero and shrieking heroine. It was not quite up to van Beethoven's *Fidelio* or Wagner's *The Flying Dutchman*. Yet what fun we had. Such is youth, I reflected, that it can mourn a dear friend, worry about a murderer, sit through four hours of staged rubbish, and have a wonderful time, because the evening is fine and there is hard cider and raisin cake at intermission.

The finale of this folksy opera culminated in a

rather crowded scene of Indians (many of whom, killed in a previous scene, had miraculously risen from the dead), cowboys, cloth cows whose hindquarters did not move in unison with their front quarters, and the hero and heroine clasped in each other's arms, singing of undying love. For some reason unknown to the audience, the stage manager had also decided to have a row of scantily clad girls waving Fourth of July sparklers parade through this melee. The audience stamped their feet with approval. Father sat stony faced, arms crossed over his chest.

When the last Indian had been shot, the last duet sung, and the applause had finally died away—and there was considerable applause, let there be no doubt about it; the theater-going audience loved spectacle, and Miss Mendosa and her dancing Indians provided considerable spectacle—when the theater was quiet again, I rose from my seat and headed not for the exit but toward the curtained wing I knew would lead backstage, pulling Sylvia along after me.

I had enjoyed the show, but other matters now required my attention.

"Miss Mendosa is known for her temper," I said. "Let's see if her passion extends to the murder of rivals."

It was difficult to think of Dorothy as anybody's rival in anything but sweetness, and people did not compete over that quality, but Sylvia followed my thinking. If Preston had been mooning and boasting about how much he loved his wife, his former mistress might well grow impatient of such conversation and wish to do away with the topic of conversation.

"Is my company still needed?" Father complained, pulling his timepiece from his waistcoat pocket. His watch had ceased running some months ago, but he still used it to make a point. "I am not eager to make a backstage visit to this female." People swirled around us, and it seemed that Father would end up backstage whether he wished to be or not, for it was difficult to break loose from that stream of humanity.

An opening cleared, though a man's arms appeared and forged a path in the direction of the center aisle and liberty.

"You may leave these young women in my care. I promise to see them safely home." Constable Cobban emerged from the shadows, making his slow, careful way through the jostling crowd like Moses walking through the Red Sea. He must have been seated close to us, if he could arrive at my side so quickly.

I fought the urge to blush but this time found the battle surprisingly easy to win. I gave an amused glance and said, "Constable Cobban. Enjoying some time away from your duties, I see. And how did you enjoy Miss Mendosa? Or perhaps you have seen the play before." I folded my arms over my chest, talking to him as I would my father, avoiding any appearance of the coquette.

Cobban blushed, where I had not.

"Rather . . . uum, nonsensical," he said. "Don't you think? But did I hear you were to pay a backstage visit? I will accompany you, if your father wishes to . . . be about his business." All of Boston knew that Father's business was liable to be illegal, involved as he was in the abolitionist movement and that phenomenon known as the Underground Railroad, whereby fugitive slaves were aided on their way north, to freedom.

"I do have an appointment for quite early this morning. Thank you, young man," he said.

Cobban winked. "Godspeed," he said.

"Come iiinnn!" the diva sang out as soon as Cobban had pounded on the door, and her voice seemed better offstage than on. Cobban opened the door and a strong scent of attar of roses floated out to us. I held my breath, expecting to see a backstage scenario of swooning suitors carrying armloads of flowers and jewels, hoping for a word from the beloved; stage managers begging to extend the run; a bohemian dressing room filled with colorful costumes and strange mementos.

In fact, the only gentleman in Miss Mendosa's dressing room was a somewhat portly fellow who quickly fled when he saw Cobban, and the only flowers were a wilting bunch of daffodils stolen from someone's window box. The disappointment was almost unbearable. For Miss Mendosa, too, it would seem.

Obviously, from her sour expression, she was expecting a different type of visitor, not two other females and an officer of the law, for Constable Cobban was still in his loud brown plaid working attire, with the conspicuous badge pinned to his lapel. I eventually suspected that the young man, notoriously poorly paid as a Boston policeman, had no other suit. Or perhaps he was one of those men who feel inadequate unless they are clothed in garments of authority.

"I had nothing to do with it! Nothing! Nothing!" Miss Mendosa shrieked upon seeing him.

I know that theater professionals often lead lives less than law-abiding or at least lives of freethinking morality, but her instantaneous denial of a crime of which she had not been accused revealed a conscience more than usually burdened with guilt, I thought.

"I'm sure. But nothing to do with what?" Cobban asked, puzzled.

"Ah," she said, growing quieter, realizing that her defensive outburst might have given away more than silence would have. With a small, almost covert gesture she removed the bracelet she had worn during the performance and tucked it under a pillow on her settee.

I realized that the bracelet was probably stolen. Was Miss Mendosa a pickpocket? That seemed unlikely, as this bracelet was clearly a present a man would give a woman and not something a woman would purchase or even steal for herself. The "weaker sex," I knew even then, are far more practical than the dreamers known as men.

But perhaps it did belong to someone else—someone else's wife—and Miss Mendosa knew she had taken a risk by accepting the gift from a male admirer and not asking many questions. What if the bracelet were Dorothy's?

But at that moment, I thought not of the hastily removed bracelet but of Miss Mendosa herself, who had decided to say nothing about whatever matter had made her so quickly proclaim innocence. She turned to me, her dark eyes glowing with venom.

"So!" she hissed, leaning backward as snakes do before the strike. "You haunt me! Go away! Go away!" Obviously she remembered me from our brief chance meeting at Edgar Brownly's studio.

"I wanted to congratulate you on an excellent performance," I said, posing as an adoring fan. My years of dreaming of my own ambition to go on the stage had not been wasted; I successfully feigned admiration.

Cobban eyed me askance, but he was clever and immediately realized the pretense. He bent to take the diva's hand and place a kiss of admiration on it, a gesture that he performed stiffly and with little enthusiasm. Cobban seemed incapable of gallantry. Such a refreshing change from most men, who wear their "gallantry" as a pose that disintegrates the moment something goes wrong.

"Ohh," Miss Mendosa cooed. She'd had time to remove her plumed hat and dancing slippers and stood there in corset and frothing petticoats. They were none too clean. Feeling cold, or perhaps overly exposed, she reached for the shawl hanging on her dressing table mirror, and wrapped it around her shoulders.

"Miss Mendosa, I believe we have a friend in common," I gushed, sounding more girlish than I had at thirteen. Why did that shawl look familiar?

I glanced at the diva's dressing table. Face powder covered everything with a whitish coat, including a tin box of marzipan, and an overturned perfume bottle released that scent of attar of roses. As Miss Mendosa glared at me, I noticed a little porcelain dish containing many calling cards, with Preston Wortham's on top of the pile.

"Yes. We have a 'friend' in common," Miss Mendosa hissed. "And if you continue to see him I will personally cut out your heart." She no longer cooed happily. Cobban, affecting a nonchalance he perhaps did not feel, peered curiously at me.

"She means Edgar Brownly," I explained, which of course was no explanation at all, not to Constable Cobban. His jaw fell just as his eyebrows shot up. "Edgar Brownly?" he asked in a strangled voice. "You and Edgar Brownly?"

"However, I refer to Mr. Preston Wortham," I said.

"Wortham? Wortham? Yes, I know that name." Miss Mendosa frowned in concentration, her slashing eyebrows tilting toward her nose.

"You should. You are his mistress," I said. Next to me, Cobban inhaled sharply. He tapped his fingers on the lapel of his plaid suit, a gesture I already recognized as one he made when nervous or surprised.

"Was I? Yes, yes, I think I might have been," the diva said quietly. "Before he married that mousy Brownly girl. The truth. We were old friends. Men are so stupid." Her Latin accent had disappeared.

"You must have been devastated when he married," I suggested.

"Devastated? Me?" Miss Mendosa drew herself up to her full height of five feet. "Never! I was glad to be rid of the man! Ayee!" The accent was back, stronger than before. "What a pest he was, always saying, 'Give me a kiss; give me a hug; do you love me, Katya'! No, good riddance. Humph!" And she spat on the floor for emphasis. "He had no money," she muttered. "Always the empty pockets."

I took a step backward, out of spitting range.

Miss Mendosa's bookcase was a tangle of ribbons and paste jewelry and kid gloves, all in open cigar boxes. Were any of those scarlet or blue ribbons strong enough to strangle a woman, to leave marks on her throat? What were those rusty stains on the half-buried glove in the smallest box?

"After he wed, he had plenty of money," Cobban insisted. "Did you see him then?"

"After he married that little nobody?" Obviously Miss Mendosa, whatever her origins, was not a Boston native. Bostonians would never refer to a Brownly as a nobody, not even for spite.

From the pursing movements of her mouth it seemed that the diva might spit again, so I took another step backward. Instead, Miss Mendosa swallowed hard. I gazed over her shoulder and glanced at Preston's calling card, there on her dressing table. Now that I was close I could see a note scribbled on it: *Thurs. at 4. Please.* An assignation?

"No," she said. "Never. He come to me, he beg me to take him back. But I would not. He was bad before, and worse after. Before, just poor. After, married and poor. Not for me." She sighed and lifted a limp hand to her brow in resignation and leaned slightly backward, as if to swoon. It was the same gesture we had just viewed onstage several times that evening. More playacting.

"But Preston Wortham was wealthy," I persisted.

"Before the marriage he was of limited but independent means, and after . . . well, his wife was one of the wealthiest women in the state."

"Yes, his wife give him allowance." The fluttering hand on her brow flew back down to her hip, and now the actress leaned forward again, aggressive, angry. "But too little. Gone in a day. I ask for a new pair of gloves; he say, 'Not this week, my love. Maybe next week.' Now, leave, please. I have people to see. You . . ." She pointed her finger at me. "You stay away from Mr. Brownly. And you . . ." She turned and glared at Sylvia. "You leave my things alone."

Guiltily, Sylvia replaced the wig she had picked up to examine.

"I was trying to imagine her as a blonde," Sylvia admitted once we were back in the hall and the diva had slammed the door on us. "How can a woman of such obvious Latin origins play a blonde?"

"Sylvia," I said, "sometimes you see so much. And sometimes you see so little. You were right in your earlier description. Miss Mendosa is a woman of uncommon energy." I had remembered where I had seen that shawl before. In Preston Wortham's parlor, when his man, Digby, had been entertaining an unseen lady upstairs.

Back in the now-darkened theater and heading for the side door, Constable Cobban gave me the kind of look that little men make when they play king of the mountain.

"Your friend Preston Wortham is a real no-account kind of fellow, it would seem," he said with some satisfaction.

"Make your criticism more specific, Constable Cobban, if you please," I requested gently.

"Cheating on his wife, for one. Odious. But then, to cheat on his mistress, too!"

"Miss Mendosa never accused him of infidelity.

Quite the opposite. In her telling of the tale, he seems to be pining away for her. You must listen more carefully, Mr. Cobban."

"But she said he never had money on him, although he was wealthy. Obviously he was keeping a third woman somewhere." His red hair, cut as short as convention would allow to control its springy curls, glinted when we passed under a gas lamp, and the gleam in his eye was unmistakable. It seemed he was jealous of Preston, because he was my friend.

"Have you noticed," he asked with feigned innocence, "that the maid in the Wortham household is particularly attractive?"

"Why are we now speaking of maids?" I asked.

"Not just attractive," Cobban persisted. "In point of fact, she looks a bit like yourself. If you don't mind my saying."

"I do mind." He was suggesting that some illicit emotion or even act had passed between Wortham and myself, and that the maid was my substitute. It was common enough; even a ribald joke was made of it, that if you wanted to see what a man's mistress looked like, you had only to view the new parlor maid. I paused and turned to stare him full in the face. I was rightly angry. Gentlemen do not engage in and voice such speculations. Moreover, I, as an abolitionist, had to tightly guard my reputation against all gossip, for anything said against me could also belittle my ideals.

"And as for Mr. Wortham having a second mistress," I continued, "I'm not certain that Miss Mendosa's word can be taken as gospel truth. Her values appear rather arbitrary. Good night, Mr. Cobban. Thank you for accompanying us. Oh . . . I almost forgot to ask. What brought you to the theater, tonight, Constable?"

"To speak with Miss Mendosa, of course." He blushed again. "In a strictly professional manner, that is."

"Of course." I smiled. "Good night, Constable."

"I'd be pleased to see you home."

"Not necessary. It is a pleasant evening and it will be refreshing to walk. Won't it, Sylvie?"

He seemed displeased. "As you wish," he said curtly, and turned briskly.

"Actually, Louisa, these shoes pinch. I would have preferred a carriage," Sylvia protested after the young constable was gone.

"I admit that young man makes me nervous," I explained. "Let's walk a bit, and if your feet swell, we'll find our own carriage."

We were both disinclined to converse. As we walked from gas lamp to gas lamp, we studied the still night and our own thoughts.

"Such a muddle." Sylvia sighed once. "It makes no sense. This connection between Mr. Wortham and Katya Mendosa and Edgar Brownly, the lies . . . it is impossible to discern the truth of this situation."

Our shoes clicked on the sidewalk, and that was the only sound once we left the neighborhood of the theater and the little private clubs and ice-cream parlors. The relentless clouds of that season covered the moon, and when the lamps grew farther apart, the night was very dark. We moved from circle to circle of sickly light from the street lamps, feeling ourselves swallowed by the night between those circles.

Sylvia hummed occassionally, for as silly as the evening's music had been, some of the tunes were engaging.

"Be quiet, Sylvia," I said abruptly, once we had turned the corner and headed up Beacon Hill.

"My melody does not warrant such an order," she protested.

"Do you hear something?" I asked, ignoring the complaint.

Sylvia listened. Nothing. And then the distant, gravelly sound of iron-rimmed wheels on cobblestones.

"A carriage," she said.

"Oh, why don't the clouds leave for even a moment?" I fretted. "Where is the carriage? Can you see it, Sylvia?" My eyes were often strained and weakened.

"Not yet. It is too dark." By instinct we pressed closer to the building at our back, skirts flattening like collapsed flowers, for the street had narrowed considerably.

"There!" I exclaimed. A carriage, black and completely enclosed, emerged from the darkness, and the ringing of the wheels grew deafening.

"It is coming quickly," I said.

And before Sylvia could respond, it was upon us, forcing us to cower against the building and cover our faces against the wind of it, for the driver had whipped the horses to a reckless gallop and the carriage passed within inches.

"You madman!" Sylvia yelled at the driver, but he raised the whip and urged the horses even faster, and was gone around the corner.

"That was a close call. We could have been trampled," she muttered. "That driver should lose his cabby license."

"That was not a public cab, Sylvia," I said. "There was a monogram on the door."

"Did you see it?"

"Maybe. I don't say for certain, but I think it was a W."

"Well, whoever the driver was, he should be more careful," Sylvia complained, smoothing her crumpled skirt.

"Indeed," said I, wondering.

Chapter Twelve

New Life and Old Problems

The very next morning, at dawn, Queenie's baby decided to arrive.

I was already up and at my first chores of the day, rolling out biscuits for a first rising, cleaning irons for the next day's laundry, and correcting May's composition written the day before.

When little Brendan from the Home came to announce the event, he used the kitchen door, knowing it was closest to the cookie jar, and that I was always liable to be there, instead of in the parlor. He was right.

"Now? I must go there," I said, tearing off my apron and running to the bottom of the staircase. "She must be terrified. Abba! Abba! I'm going to the Home! It's Queenie's time!"

"Go, Louy," Abba yelled back, leaning over the upstairs railing. "Take a cake of soap with you and some bread. There's never enough there." And then, more softly, "I'm sure you'll be some time, Louy. This being her first and her so little. Keep your courage."

Already buttoning my cloak, I smiled up at my mother. Wasn't that just like Abba? Bread and soap and courage.

When I arrived at the Home half an hour later, a midwife was already there in the birthing room, kneeling beside Queenie and holding her hand. Rather, Queenie held her hand in a grip so strong that the midwife winced but did not pull away. The lamps cast long, well-defined shadows in the small room used exclusively for this purpose. A huge fire roared in the fireplace, and a double layer of curtains had been drawn to keep out all drafts, for it was deemed beneficial for women in labor to perspire and all but melt from heat. The room was so close I could barely breathe.

Queenie was in the bed, with its single well-used sheet over a thick layer of straw to absorb the various liquids associated with this particular process. The linen was twisted and tossed about like whitecaps on a stormy sea.

"The contractions are ten minutes apart," the midwife said, looking up at me. "They have been ten minutes apart for hours now."

I could not help thinking dark thoughts about Edgar Brownly. Oh, if only he could be here now to see his handiwork . . . I asked the midwife when Queenie's labor had begun.

"Last night," the midwife said. She wore a light muslin gown with no crinolines or laces, and I realized for the first time the true purpose of the simplicity of nursing garb—it makes the warmth of the illness room bearable. "Around midnight. I had her walking around the room till just about an hour ago, to get it moving."

I did some quick mental math. Queenie had been in labor six hours. If her labor proceeded normally, it would last about another eleven hours, according to Abba's prediction.

"I don't want to do this," Queenie said, curling up on her side and weeping. "Make it go away." Her voice cracked with exhaustion.

"Ergot?" I suggested, myself on the verge of tears. This was the herb cordial commonly administered to increase contractions.

"She's already had as much as I dare give her," the midwife said. "We could take her to Harvard Medical. . . ."

"No!" Queenie shrieked, trying to sit up but unable. "Not the hospital. I've heard what they do there. They make you go to sleep and cut it out."

"Sometimes it is necessary," the midwife said, stroking Queenie's damp hair. "Didn't Queen Victoria herself let them give her chloroform for her seventh delivery?"

"I won't go there. Miss Alcott, don't let them take me." She twisted toward me, her hands in supplication before her thin chest.

"Hush, Queenie. Rest and gather your strength between the contractions. No, we'll just have to wait a bit more. And, Queenie, you'll have to be strong." I took a deep breath. I'd have to be strong, too.

A new contraction swept over her, and Queenie's face crumpled, her body writhing; she screamed and cursed.

"There'll be none of that language, missy," the midwife said. "There's young'uns out there, a-listening."

The pain seemed to lessen for a moment then, because Queenie stretched a bit and took a deep breath. She closed her eyes, and long, childish lashes rested against her damp cheeks. I had never seen her look younger and more helpless than at that moment, when she was beginning the first and perhaps most dire responsibility of motherhood—bringing her baby alive into this world, and somehow surviving it herself.

The midwife took me off to the side. She looked unhappy. "Too small," she muttered. "The girl's too small."

"Oh, Queenie." I sighed. I knew what that meant. In my days at the Home several expecting mothers had died in childbirth, and for most it was because they were undernourished and painfully thin, too thin to come through the ordeal alive.

Queenie had a long day ahead of her. Perhaps several. Perhaps worse.

"Ether?" I asked, desperately wanting to find a way to reduce Queenie's pain.

"Later, if it gets too bad," the midwife said. "Though I don't like to use it, not like those medical gentlemen from the Boston Medical Society do, and the girl is right to be afeared of it. Ether can kill as well as old-fashioned childbirthing. But get the forceps out of my bag, in case."

At the word forceps, Queenie let out a howl such as I had never heard before. Between waves of pain, she managed to roar, "I'll kill him for this!" her first verbal response to her seduction. "I don't care that his namby sister was found in the water. She deserved it as well as he does!"

I sat at Queenie's side all through the morning and afternoon, and by evening, when Queenie was slipping in and out of a strange sleep between bouts of screaming and pushing, I, too, was exhausted. The midwife was napping, sitting up in the rocking chair. Sweat streamed off both of us from the cloistered heat of that room.

Other women brought us cups of tea and bowls of soup. The lamps had been lighted inside the Home, and the smoke from the roaring hearth in the room mixed with the soot of the oil lamps, creating an interior fog that gave the scene a nightmarish quality. The room had become all angles and shadows, smoke and obscurity, except for the white sheets roiled over the delirious Queenie. She looked so young, so small.

"I wonder if it was as bad for my mother," I mused, trying to slip some of my own soup between Queenie's white, cracked lips. "And to think she went through it time and again, knowing what was to come."

"One forgets the pain, my dear, and remembers only the joy of holding the baby," the midwife offered. "It is true but indeed hard to believe."

I let my thoughts slip back to Dottie. Dot yearned for children and always talked about how she would fill her nursery someday with babies. Perhaps it was because she grew up surrounded by so many sisters and brothers. Strange how the kind, lovely Dot was like a rare, unusual bird compared to the selfish brood that made up the rest of her siblings, always grumbling and thinking of themselves. Suddenly I was struck by an idea. Dot was different from her sisters and brother, truly different. It seemed important to clarify, finally, what had caused that difference, for it seemed a key to her sad death.

But at that moment, Queenie's baby decided to cease her delay.

"It's coming. Thank God," the midwife said, peering between Queenie's knees.

I gathered 'round the bloody theater of new life and watched, holding my breath. What would present first? The top of the head? Well and good. If it was a foot, that was a real problem. If it was an arm, and we saw that the baby was lying transverse . . . well, I refused to think about that one. Most likely both mother and child would die. I saw those gleaming forceps on the table and tried hard to ignore them, to pretend they would not be needed.

Queenie screamed and pushed so hard her teeth ground and threatened to break.

She panted, then screamed again.

The soft, domed top of a head appeared. We fought back the dangerous impulse to pull the infant free and then, one last push, one final scream . . . and Queenie had a daughter.

The noise of it was astounding, and reminded me more than anything of the noise a ship at sea makes, when the waves roll so high that the undertow sucks at the boat and tries to pull it under and the sailors yell for their lives. But this little ship had decided not to let the storm defeat her.

"Queenie!" I shouted, my eyes huge and moist. "Queenie, it's a girl! A perfect little girl. See, ten toes, ten fingers . . . she's perfect!"

She might have had ten of the required digits, but she was also red and mewing and flailing with clenched fists as if she were already having a temper tantrum.

"She's beautiful," Queenie whispered when the washed and swaddled infant was put to her breast. "See! Hair already. Poor thing. I was hoping she'd be ugly—safer that way. Oh, blue eyes."

"All babies have blue eyes," the midwife said, wiping her glistening red hands on a gruesomely stained apron and stepping closer to admire her handiwork.

"Oh . . . didn't know." Exhausted, Queenie fell asleep, words forming on her lips.

"Poor bugger." The midwife tickled the infant under the chin. "They'll both starve or worse, end up in a mill, working and starving."

A moment before, my spirit had soared. Now it sank back to earth. The Charles Street Home enforced a rule that women must leave three weeks after birth to make room for others, for there was a never-ending river of woman abandoned or driven away by their menfolk. Where would Queenie go? Who would be willing to take her in?

"Maybe she can find someone to adopt the infant," the midwife said. "It would be a kindness to her, to let her go. That's what some mothers do when they can't care for the child."

I stood over the sleeping Queenie and brushed her hair with my fingertips. "A kindness . . ." I repeated. I looked at the midwife, startled, then looked back down at Queenie, wondering.

*　　*　　*

The next day I knew I had a fearsome task ahead. I had to brave, of all places, the Boston Athenaeum.

The Athenaeum was a private library founded ages ago by the Puritans of the early colony, and recently relocated to a new Italianate brownstone on Beacon Street, behind the Old Granary Burying Ground. It smelled gloriously of new mortar and wallpaper paste and leather . . . and that sacred odor of books. Boston gentlemen housed their special collections of books there, and went there to read, smoke their pipes, and pursue other gentlemanly activities, safe from the distraction of females and children and domesticity. Women, who frequently traveled *en caravane* with regiments of children in tow, were distinctly unwelcome, had, in fact, been forcibly turned away at the front door. But as the daughter of such a noted philosopher and abolitionist, I had acquired unofficial visiting rights to both the bookcases downstairs and the stacks upstairs.

Later that morning, dressed in a subdued gray wool jacket and skirt, I signed in at the Athenaeum's front desk, adding Mr. Amos Bronson Alcott's name after my own by way of reference.

Charles Agwerd was on duty that day: an elderly gentleman with scanty white whiskers bristling from nose, cheek, and ears and a suit cut in the style of fifty years before, with huge cuffs and a low, ruffled collar. He was old enough to remember having his milk cup broken on the day when Daniel Shays and his fellow rebels marched to the State Supreme Court in Springfield to protest the high land taxation that followed the Revolution. He reminded the patrons of the Athenaeum often of this fact, and usually concluded the rather lengthy retelling of that anecdote and others of his personal history with the opinion that men weren't men anymore, and women certainly weren't women. Despite my subdued costume and lack of prattling toddlers and babes-in-arms, he gave his usual disapproving glance when I signed the register.

"You look sensible," he admitted with reluctance. "Can you make squirrel stew?" he asked testily.

I admitted I could not.

He sighed as though his heart would break and then muttered his old refrain that women had lost their femininity and good sense. Strange, I reflected, how many gentlemen associated femininity with the goriest of tasks. Yet when their own children were born, these men were nowhere to be seen, usually cowering behind the locked and bolted doors of their studies, fingers in their ears. I wondered if a time would ever come when fathers would also help see their own offspring into the world. If so, that should help population control.

Despite my poor knowledge of colonial cuisine, Charles Agwerd allowed me entrance and gave me a tag in exchange for my coat and hat.

Heads, all male, turned as I—that foreign, exotic animal, woman—walked down the long carpeted hall to the head librarian's desk. The long room smelled most pleasantly of leather and cigar smoke, reminding me of Father's study.

"I would like assistance researching the life history of Katya Mendosa," I told the head librarian, who had risen in obvious alarm.

"Katya . . . ?" he repeated.

"Mendosa. An actress. A performer. One who treads the boards. Surely you have heard of actresses? If not, I will explain the profession." One had to get down to business quickly at the Athenaeum.

"No need to explain," he said, turning bright red. "Have you any information other than a name?" His tone of voice was peevish, yet he picked up a pen and prepared to take a few notes.

"Let's see. She is still alive. Is that helpful? I would say she is about thirty years of age, though her costumes and makeup give her a more youthful appearance. She has an accent. Spanish, I believe, though it tends to fluctuate a bit between that language and several others. She is currently appearing on the Boston stage, and before that she toured in the West."

"Newspapers and journals," he said. "I suspect there will be little written of her of a more permanent nature. If you will wait here . . ."

He returned fifteen minutes later carrying piles and piles of yellowing periodicals.

"These are publications from cities of the South and the West," he said, using a tone of voice that preachers often adopt with children. "If you find dates of her performances in various cities, you may also find reviews and biographies and other material." He gloated as he released the pile in front of him with such alacrity that a small cloud of dust puffed out as it landed on the polished mahogany desk. For the first time during our exchange he seemed pleased. He'd had his revenge, he supposed, for my female act of trespass.

What he did not know was that the prospect of that tall pile of popular press gave me a thrill. I had a morning before me filled with news and stories from all over the country. What more could I wish?

And so I passed a very pleasant half day reading several years' worth of news of Natchez, Saint Louis, Nashville, Louisville, Cincinnati, and Wheeling, and several smaller towns along the Western theater-touring route. There were stories from New Mexico, which had been acquired for the Union, and reports from M. C. Perry in the Japans, tales of gunfights and land claims and blizzards and more drama than any writer could seek. There were pages of poems by Tennyson that set me dreaming, and countless reviews of my dear friend Henry Thoreau's book, *Walden*.

There was considerable space and verbiage used to describe the progress of Jenny Lind, who had toured the year before, but notices advertising the appearances of Katya Mendosa were scarce and, even when located, small. It was sobering to think that much of what Miss Mendosa's promoters claimed for her was hyberbole and even invention. I half believed her to be famous and wealthy, or at least as wealthy as a woman of the working classes could become. She was not, as her lack of publicity and reviews indicated little interest on the part of audiences.

I did, however, find a few dates and listings of performances, and scribbled those down on a blotter.

When I left the Athenaeum, there was a closed carriage standing at the curb. The window had been rolled up and curtained, but not completely. Inside, strangely, sat Katya Mendosa herself. She glared as I passed. There was a man inside as well, but I could not see his face.

It felt a strange coincidence, but it was possible that another Athenaeum member might be spending time with the actress and escorting her about in a carriage.

Still, it did feel strange.

"Hmm," I said later, biting my lip and looking at the list, once again alone with Sylvia. "I would have expected more." We were in the small garden that came with our Pinckney Street house, and I was pulling away the pile of last year's leaves that buried Abba's daffodil bed.

"Why, Louisa, is something missing? To think you spent an entire morning in that dusty vault. Is this a weed or a flower, Louy?" She pointed to a small yellow tip just breaking the ground.

"Flower. Don't pull at it, Sylvia. The Athenaeum is well maintained and not at all dusty," I replied. "Certainly it's not a vault. I could happily spend a month in there with all those books, those leather chairs and gas lamps at every desk, no wailing children . . ." I grew dreamy for a moment, and then resumed a brisk manner. "But I prefer not to spend my time there researching such actresses as Madame Mendosa. She was a fairly boring research subject." I took off my thick gloves and pulled from my pocket the blotter on which I had written my notes of the diva's appearances.

"Did you notice anything about this list, Sylvia?" I asked when she had finished reading.

"A certain paucity of engagements," Sylvia said, "with much time between them."

"A worthy observation. We can assume Miss Mendosa has, and needs, other sources of income. Anything else, Sylvia?" I was smiling encouragingly, giving her the kind of look I gave my schoolchildren when I was trying to make them feel clever.

"She had a run in Newport, in that little theater we used to attend as children, because they had ballet dancers and puppet shows in the afternoon."

"Yes. And . . ." I cradled my chin in my hands and watched as the maid from the house next door carried a bucket of ash out to the pile. Sylvia frowned with impatience.

The maid, not knowing she was watched, scratched her red hands and sighed with exhaustion, though the day was not yet over. If her duties were typical, she still had a table to lay, a long wash-up to clean the kitchen after dinner, children to bathe, hearths to prepare for the morning fires. If there was mending, and there always was, she would have to do it by gaslight. She would be working long after the family was sleeping in their beds. If the poor woman had children they would have spent the day alone, probably in the attic, in soggy nappies and with their thumbs in their mouths to quell the hunger, and with that distant look in their eyes that lonely children soon develop.

I sighed, and Sylvia knew I was thinking of Queenie.

"Unfair!" Sylvia cried. "You hint at hidden meanings and then fall silent!"

"Katya's career seems to have begun sometime in 1850, four years ago, for I found no mention of her before that."

"And so? All careers must begin at some time."

"Exactly," I said.

Chapter Thirteen

The Checkered Past Revealed

Boston had a simple system of restraining its criminal population. Offenders of modest ambition—Saturday-night drunks, meat-shop butchers with heavy thumbs and light scales, pickpockets, and others of that ilk—were housed in a small, uncomfortable jail till their fine was paid or their time served. Dangerous villains, however, were quartered in the courthouse itself, a building that I had already visited many times even before Preston fell headlong into his troubles, since my father's Vigilance Committee had rallied there in the past, especially three years before, when the fugitive slave Sims had been held and tried.

Said building, located in Court Square, was a foursquare granite structure of formidable size and austere presence that contained the marshal's office, much of the city administrative offices, and the courtroom itself. It was guarded by an assortment of soldiery and police, and much of legalistic Boston gathered in that place. The dashing young lawyer Richard Henry Dana kept his offices across the way, and Judge Edward Greely Loring spent more time there than teaching in his Harvard law class. Wendell Phillips could be seen pacing the halls with papers in hand to file or present;

Ralph Waldo Emerson, Thomas Wentworth Higginson, and my father, of course . . . the names of the people who could be seen scuffling down those halls at the time of this story read like a history lesson, the law students boasted.

And so three days following the birth of Queenie's daughter, after my own schoolchildren had left and the parlor had been swept clean of marbles and crumbs, I returned to that courthouse to pay a second visit to Preston Wortham. I had some very specific questions for him.

It was about three o'clock in the afternoon when I arrived, and Constable Cobban was just finishing an early workday at the courthouse; we passed each other in the hall.

"Afternoon," he said, grinning and making a little bow vaguely in my direction. He blushed. He seemed to always blush when he saw me, I reflected, and reminded myself I must give him no encouragement.

"Good afternoon to you, Constable," I replied somewhat coolly. He seemed to wish to converse, but I continued on my way.

"I approve," he called after me.

"Approve?"

"Your manners, Miss Alcott. You are right. You should not stop to talk to a man in public. I wonder, though, that you came here by yourself. Perhaps something of Mrs. Wortham rubbed off on you."

I wondered what he meant by that, but decided the conversation would have to wait. There were other matters to look into before I quizzed him on his somewhat harsh attitude toward my friend. It seemed far too soon to trust him with all my reflections on the business of Dorothy, and if I stopped to exchange small talk, he might interpret that as encouragement.

No, there would be time enough for chatting later, and I was in a bit of a rush, fitting, as I was, this chore

between my school day and the domestic tasks waiting
for me at home. So I did not stop and give that young
man a chance to converse. What would he have said
if I had? I felt his eyes on my back, and kept walking.

And, of course, because I was both preoccupied and
rushed and in no mood for small talk or other unnecessary conversation, just as I rounded the corner,
Mayor Van Crowninshield Smith appeared before me,
his top hat reaching to the low ceiling of the third
floor, the carved ivory handle of his walking cane shining through the shadowed interior darkness.

"Ah!" Boston's mayor exclaimed brightly. "Miss
Alcott. Yes, it is Miss Alcott? Miss Alcott, how are
you and your excellent father?"

It is not politic to snub a mayor, much as one is
tempted, so I sighed and squared my shoulders and
prepared to listen to his chatter for a few moments. I
did not particularly like Mayor Van Crowninshield
Smith. He was the kind of person who seeks to be
admired by all and so ends up admired by none. He
had the morals of a kite, Father said, turning in every
breeze that came along and sometimes spiraling in
nonsensical circles. When he met with the pro-slavery
Irish of Boston, he advocated the slavery system.
When he met with the free-soilers, he preached
against slavery.

Mayor Van Crowninshield Smith also had literary
aspirations, and had been an editor of the *Boston
Medical and Surgical Journal.* He fancied himself to
be a man of letters and was always desirous of conversation with other men of letters, so much so that those
more stately men of the town, Mr. Thoreau, Mr. Richard Dana, and even Mr. Emerson when he was in
from Concord, took to ducking down hallways and
behind shrubs when they saw the mayor approaching.
One of the great delights of my girlhood had been to
spy the top hat and bushy eyebrows of the very serious

Ralph Emerson sticking up from behind a rhododen-
dron as the mayor strolled by.

I had no such recourse at that moment. Shrubs are
difficult to find in interior hallways of courthouses.

"Father is well, Mayor. I will tell him you asked
about him." I made the tiniest of curtsies, as women
are expected to do before high personages, and made
to continue on my way.

He took my elbow and turned to walk with me.
Such men usually do. It is one of their irritating habits
to believe that no woman could possibly wish to be
alone with her thoughts when he was available to
them.

"I had a letter to the editor published on Wednesday last. Did you see it, Miss Alcott? Did your father
comment upon it?" the mayor asked eagerly.

"Wednesday last. Let me remember." I pretended
to search my memory, frowning a little with the
feigned effort. "Yes, Wednesday. That was the day
the neighbor's spaniel reached the paper before Father could. How sad! We missed your letter! What
was it about, Mayor?"

This was a fabrication. We had read the letter and
laughed heartily before using the paper to light the
evening fire in the hearth, for the mayor had proposed
that the history and geography of Turkey be made a
compulsory subject at Harvard. Not that we had anything against that esteemed Oriental country; rather it
was transparent that Mayor Van Crowninshield Smith
merely wished to sell more copies of his travel book,
Turkey and the Turks, by requiring the Harvard students to buy it. The book's unimaginative title was
indicative of its unimaginative contents. I had read the
tome and torn my hair over it. "Has he no eyes? Has
he no ears?" I had moaned. "To visit such a place,
and record only street names!"

"Ah. A spaniel. I see. Well. I shall send your father

a copy." The mayor stroked his beard thoughtfully. "I believe I have saved a few," he added, as if his entire front parlor were not crammed with copies of the paper. "Then perhaps we might discuss it."

"Certainly," I agreed cheerfully. "Though Father is just a little busy these days. He still gives conversations, as you know."

Now the friendly mayor grew quite serious. "And it is just that I wish to speak with him about," he said. "Perhaps he could put my name forward. Not that I would wish to be remunerated . . . no such thing. But I believe I could provide some philosophical and literary content to a room of intellectuals and philosophers such as those who gather to hear your father speak. Don't you think?"

He paused and smiled at his own disingenuousness. I was thankful he did not allow time for me to answer, certain as he was that my only possible response could be an affirmation. Then his expression changed, as if it had suddenly occurred to him that he was having this delightful conversation not on the avenue or in the park, but in a dark hallway lined with rooms in which criminals were detained, probably plotting even more dreadful deeds as we spoke.

"Miss Alcott, may I ask your business at the courthouse? You are not in any difficulty? Your father's activities have not caught up with him?" He referred, of course, to Father's work with the Boston Vigilance Committee and the abolitionists. Should we ever be discovered harboring a fugitive slave in our home, we would be fined five hundred dollars (a fortune!) and Father would go to jail. Mostly, the mayor simply looked the other way. Even abolitionst votes were important to him.

"No," I said. "There is no difficulty at home. I have only come to visit an old friend, Mr. Wortham."

"Wortham? The wife murderer? An old friend?

You must reconsider your friendships, Miss Alcott. I am against this murdering of wives, most against it."

I smiled. I must remember to tell my father that the mayor had finally expressed a definite opinion.

"It is not conclusively proven that he is a wife murderer," I answered calmly.

"No. But it will be. And I believe you were also in conversation with that young Cobban."

"We exchanged greetings," I admitted.

"Beware of him," the mayor warned darkly. "Between you and me, he is not a great admirer of the fair sex, not since the day his certain young woman decided to marry another. Bitter. That's what I say. And with a penchant to use force when not required. We've had to warn him."

I studied the ceiling, no longer listening and only eager to end this unwanted conversation. "Yes, well, I'm sure that is none of my business. Good afternoon, Mayor. I will give Father your regards." We were then standing before the barred and grilled door where Mr. Wortham was incarcerated. I knocked on the door myself.

The startled guard looked up from his slumber and fetched the stool for me to sit on. I accepted the stool with a polite if stiff thank-you, feeling Mayor Van Crowninshield Smith's eyes boring into my back.

Preston had been lying on his cot, the newspaper over his face. He sat up when I knocked. He had altered considerably. Jail does that to a man, I suspected. Proof of that alteration was that he did not rise to greet me, as a gentleman would have, even in that place. Perhaps Preston had not altered, but merely become more of what he already was, and a gentleman is not a noun one uses for such a person. I had not fully considered the question of Wortham's nature; it seemed a dark topic, but one I could no longer afford to ignore.

"What did you quarrel about with Dorothy?" I asked.

Preston looked at the crumpled afternoon-edition newspaper he had been reading. "Dibgy used to iron these for me," he said.

A sinister aspect had overtaken his former good looks. His mustache had been allowed to grow wild and now weedily covered his top lip; his thick black hair was in a state of similar unrestrained naturality and stood wildly about his head. He wore a rumpled shirt lacking collar or cuffs, and his suspenders dangled over his legs rather than his shoulders. He no longer looked like a gentleman who had been brought in for a night of rowdy carousing. He looked what he was: a man with a bad conscience who had given up hope; a man who had been discovered for what he really was, which was the kind of husband all young women are warned against acquiring.

"She thought I had broken a promise. That I had renewed an . . . old connection," he muttered.

I looked up at the barred window behind him, high on the wall. Thin, cold sunlight seeped through, but not enough to cast shadows of the bars on the floor.

"Had you?" I asked quietly, lowering my eyes to his and gazing steadily, as if I would read him. "Is it true, Mr. Wortham, that upon your return from Europe you took Katya Mendosa as your mistress?"

Preston rose from his chair with a sudden, angry movement. "She is not my mistress!" he shouted. "Who is repeating this evil rumor?" But at that moment his exertions and quick gestures caused his leg irons to clank. Chastised by the metal reminders of guilt, he sat back down, ran his hands through his already bristling hair, and picked up the paper he had been reading, as if he would ignore further questions.

"It seems to be rather common knowledge," I said. "Dorothy's sisters knew. One could reasonably suspect Dorothy also knew."

From behind his paper, Preston groaned.

"Did Dorothy know, and did you quarrel about that, Mr. Wortham?"

Preston sighed heavily and put down the paper. He looked wild-eyed. "Once. Just once I had dinner with her. Katya seemed so . . . so warm. Like an old friend. But it was just once, I swear. But I was seen. And Dorothy found out," he admitted. "Someone told her. Oh, what a scene there was. Poor Dorothy. I've never seen her weep so. She said she would leave me, that I had never really loved her. She said . . . she said what her family had accused me of all along, of marrying her for her money."

I rose and began to pace in the hall, as I always did when moved by strong emotion that could not be expressed. "Poor Dorothy," I repeated. "Poor Dorothy. Oh, Mr. Wortham, the pain you caused."

"I know," he muttered, wiping at his eyes, though those eyes were dry. "I have not lived a single day since without doing penance of some kind. Can a man never be forgiven? I am no worse than most."

"Certainly no better than most." I sighed. "But answer me this question: When did you have your one-evening affair with Katya Mendosa?"

"A month ago. The day after the paper carried the notice in the society column that Dorothy and I had returned from Europe. How Dorothy hated that, having our names in the paper. I tried to tell her that times had changed, that society columns were quite acceptable, but . . ."

His train of thought had begun to wander, so I steered him back to our course.

"How did you first meet Katya Mendosa?"

"At the theater, of course. She was dancing in the production of *Hiawatha*. Her costume was nothing but feathers, as I recall."

I cleared my throat.

"Yes. Well," he continued, somewhat abashed, for

his memories had wandered down shameful paths. "She saw me in the front row with some friends, and sent a note asking if I would like to have a glass of punch with her, after. I was most flattered."

"Was the note addressed to the gentleman in the front row, or did it have your name on it?" If Preston heard the irony in my voice, he did not respond to it.

"My name was on it."

"And you had not met before that?"

"Not that I can remember. And I'm certain I would remember."

"You spoke of a promise to Dorothy. Did she require you to promise that you would never see Katya Mendosa again?"

"Yes."

A man in Preston's precarious predicament might well be grateful for all assistance shown. Preston, however, seemed unwilling to be quizzed further about this affair, and now resumed his perusal of the front page, which contained a rather lurid account of his seduction of the young maid in Newport some years before. Accused of wificide, he now was fair game for the reading public.

"Mr. Wortham, I must tell you that I saw your calling card in Miss Mendosa's dressing room. You asked for an appointment with her."

Preston sighed and again put down his unironed paper. "To . . . to be certain that Katya understood our friendship was at an end."

"Let's see. You wanted to see her to tell her you wouldn't be coming to see her anymore."

Wortham blushed. "That's right," he said. "I told her I couldn't afford the expense. She expected me to buy her things."

I sighed. Wortham was one of the new men who associated money with morality, perhaps even saw money in its place.

Accept people as they are, Louy, my mother often

instructed. *We each have our own nature, and while we can be improved, we can't be what it is not our nature to be.* All right. I would accept Wortham on his own terms. "Mr. Wortham, your marriage made you wealthy. Surely you had the means to keep . . ." I could not complete the sentence; even the words were another betrayal of Dorothy. *To keep a mistress.*

"A good wardrobe is so very expensive these days." he muttered. "I'm a lost cause, Miss Alcott. Perhaps you should give up on me. Besides, I'm not sure I want to live. I miss her so damn much. I hadn't realized . . ."

"How much you loved Dottie?" I finished. *Or how impoverished you would be upon her death?* I wondered, but did not say.

"Ah, so many regrets." He sighed.

I began to pace again, then turned to confront him.

"And that was the sum of the quarrel with Dorothy?" I asked. "She suspected—discovered, I would say—that you had visited a woman?"

"There were other words and accusations. To be frank, I suspected Dorothy herself was keeping a secret of some nature from me."

This brought me up short opposite Wortham's cot, our eyes meeting through the bars on the door. "Keeping a secret? Dorothy? What did you suspect was the nature of her secret?"

Preston grew pale. "I think there was . . . someone else."

"You suspected Dorothy of being disloyal?" I asked finally, having remembered what Mrs. Brownly said, that Dorothy had loved—and lost—another before her marriage to Wortham.

"I did. Yes, Miss Alcott, I did. There. I've said it. Even during our honeymoon I would come across her writing a letter, and she would hide the letter and pretend it was nothing, just a scrap of paper. And as soon as we were home in Boston, she disappeared for the entire afternoon, and came back red-eyed."

"So that afternoon of the first tea party, when she arrived late . . ."

"I thought she had been with him."

"Mr. Wortham, I don't know what to say. Except, perhaps, this. I knew Dorothy longer than you did, and perhaps even more closely, at least for a few years, as we were growing. Fidelity was her essence."

"People change. Women change. What, then, was her secret? A wife owes her husband complete honesty."

"And what does a husband owe a wife?" I couldn't resist. He did not answer. There was a long, ominous silence, filled only with the intrusive noises of guards coming on duty downstairs, their heavy, echoing footsteps, the mumbled exchange of greetings, a rattling of keys. Outside in the street a water seller called out his wares of cool sips of good well water, children sang and laughed, horses and carriages rumbled past. Life.

"I am beginning to understand," I said softly. "If . . . when . . . you are released, perhaps Dot's family will allow you a proper period of mourning in the Newport house." This was a ruse. At that moment his guilt seemed almost palpable, and I wasn't at all convinced he would be released, but I needed to direct this distressing conversation to other topics.

Preston looked up from his distracted study of his prison floor with a small glimmer of, if not actual hope, than a recognition that such a word as *future* did exist, after all. "If I'm not hanged, that would be a fine idea," he admitted with some longing in his voice. "It will be summer by then. Dot always loved Newport in the summer. So did I."

A single tear trickled down his cheek, and he wiped it away with the back of his hand, as children do. There was something stagey about the gesture, something that reminded me of that first visit at the beginning of this tragic affair, when Dottie had come home and he had gently, but with a larger gesture than necessary, brushed a wayward lock out of her eyes.

"My God," he groaned. "I even miss that foolish little dog of hers. How she loved Lily. The dog looked like a silly little thing, but you know it had a reputation in Rome, when we spent the spring there. Give it a glove to sniff, and it could track the owner all over the city. We used to play at it for fun, with our guests."

So that was why the dog died, too, I mused. It could identify its mistress's killer.

I felt weary. I wanted justice. I wanted to finish this business so that I could get on with living, remembering Dorothy as a gentle, loving girl and not as a murder victim.

"I will find the truth, Mr. Wortham," I promised. "Whether it suits you or not. One more question, Mr. Wortham, before I leave you to your paper, perhaps the most painful of all. It is true, is it not, that some years ago you seduced a certain young girl by the name of Marie Brennen, who then had your child?"

"You have seen the afternoon paper, Miss Alcott. It is now a matter of public record. Of course, what the reporter did not manage to fit into his piece is that I have sent money for the child every quarter since. I did all that a gentleman could be required to do in the circumstances."

I, being a realist, did not point out that he could have been expected not to seduce an innocent girl in the first place. I hadn't come to lecture, but to acquire information. "There were rumors of other seductions that summer, Mr. Wortham."

"Am I to hang for the sins of my youth?" He moaned. "I was young and callow. I have since repented and done what I could to set matters right. I have, in ways I will not speak of, tried to make amends for those I injured. You must believe me, Miss Alcott."

"I am trying. But you must tell me, Mr. Wortham. Did you also seduce Dorothy that summer?"

Chapter Fourteen

Darkening Prospects

"Of course he denied it," I said. "I had, just a few minutes before, accused him of being ungentlemanly in his complaints about Katya Mendosa. Why would he then admit to having seduced Dorothy? When will I learn to better guard my tongue?"

Sylvia and I sat peeling potatoes in the kitchen of the little Pinckney Street house as Abba chopped the shriveled remainders of last year's apples for our supper pie. May sat at the table reading a book, her dark curls held back with a pretty red velvet ribbon, and I could hear Lizzie upstairs, sweeping and dusting.

The room was rich with the fragrances of nutmeg and yeast, reminding me of so many hours spent in warm domesticity with my mother in other kitchens—in Concord; at the Fruitlands, with its yawning fireplaces and immense drafty rooms where wandered Henry David Thoreau, Nathaniel Hawthorne, and Ralph Waldo Emerson, so imposing to others but to me a friendly group to invite to a game of tag; and the smaller, more manageable kitchen of Hillside, where Abba had hung old lace curtains and weekly polished the deal table to a high sheen, never rubbing away the scratchings her growing girls had left in that wood.

It was midafternoon and the sun lingered high as if reluctant to be on its way. Geese flew in the eastern part of the sky, their exuberant honks sounding through the window Abba had opened to let out some of the steam of her cooking. Spring was coming, but I felt none of the sweet expectation of springtime. I had dreamed again of Dorothy, and Dorothy, in that dream, had wept. "I am terrified of him," she had said.

Abba poured hot milk and honey into old chipped mugs for us and gave a warning glance in May's direction. She pretended to ignore us, but I knew the word *seduce* had caught her attention.

Sylvia stretched her arms over her head in animal bliss. Another bread-baking day had come around, so she was supping with us on the foods of paradise.

"Discretion may be a virtue of middle age, not youth," Abba said, turning from where she had been looking out the window, perhaps daydreaming of spring gardens and fresh greens for salad.

Her wisdom was a delayed response to my question, for I had just finished my telling of yesterday's visit with Preston and waited for my mother's reply. "Perhaps, Louy, you should not have asked about his earlier relations with Dorothy, if there were any," that wise woman said, pulling out a chair for herself at the wobbly deal table. She fetched from her voluminous pocket a skein of brown wool stabbed with two needles from which dangled a sock, half-knitted and looking like a bit of seaweed scrapped from a rock.

"The . . . poor . . . child . . . is . . . dead," Abba said, counting stitches between words. "What good is it to dredge up the past?"

Abba looked tired. She had been up all night, indeed for many nights, packing baskets of donated food to help a fugitive slave family from North Carolina, though such secretive night work was never part of afternoon discussion, not even when we were surrounded by family and old friends. Secrecy was paramount.

"Her murderer must be brought to justice, Abba. I owe Dorothy that."

"But what do any mistakes she might have made years before have to do with her death? Isn't the past over?" Abba's needles clacked in time with her words, making an almost-song of it. *Isn't the past over? Isn't the past over?*

The past. I remembered Dorothy as a child who had had difficulty comprehending the passage of time, and simple words such as *present* and *future*. "Now is now," she had insisted, pouting in that very pretty way that seems unique to undersized children with blond curls. She comprehended eternity, in one of her few religious classes, as an ongoing now, with no confusing terms to muddle the moment. I, remembering, shivered and wondered if a child's ease in understanding eternity had any connection to her death at an early age.

"Is the past over? That is what I am trying to discover, Abba." I sipped my hot milk and honey. "We believe that the death was not an accident. That was the conclusion of the medical examiner. So there was a reason for it. Someone wished her dead. Why? Who could wish Dorothy dead? What wrong had she ever committed?"

"Constable Cobban seems certain he has the murderer in jail already, and you have discovered several motives," Sylvia pointed out, reaching for more bread and jam.

"The evidence is far from conclusive. In fact, it is dubious," I said. "And we must operate on a just level, Sylvia. We must maintain his innocence till his guilt is incontestable. No, we must continue to search for both person and reason till the truth of this matter is resolved."

"If she had allowed herself to be seduced, perhaps Edgar Brownly wished her dead to preserve family honor," Sylvia suggested, quite willing, I noticed, to sacrifice Edgar for Preston, one cousin for another.

"Sylvie, are you just now thinking of that?" I asked. "I admit it is farfetched, that family unity could go so astray as to permit a brother to murder a sister. But, as you said, there was little love between Dorothy and Edgar for some reason, and . . . Well. Better not to say quite yet how I assess his character, except to say he seems to have little or no reason to lord it over Mr. Wortham. One is no better than the other. I wonder if they know they have shared a mistress."

"Oh, my. May, run to the store for a cup of sugar, dear," Abba said.

"It's too interesting here," May protested.

"Exactly," Abba said. "Be on your way." May, complaining, took a nickel from the jar and left. Mother got up from the wobbly table and went into the laundry alcove to pour a measure of lye into the vat of water she had put on to boil. The strong wash-day smell wafted through to us, adding a harsher undernote to the room's gentler perfume of apples and cinnamon.

The potatoes peeled and in the pot, I, between bites of bread and sips of milk, picked up a basket from the floor and balanced it in my lap. With the sharp end of a seam ripper I began efficiently popping off the buttons from all of my father's shirts. They would have to be removed so they wouldn't break in the washing; buttons were expensive. After the ironing, they would all have to be sewn back in place.

I pondered a carved wooden button that appeared to have been chewed by little teeth. Probably May's, years before. "Why would Edgar wait so long, then?" I said. "That summer in Newport when Dorothy was in disgrace was many years ago."

"Wait for what?" Sylvia asked.

"To punish Dorothy for her indiscretions with Wortham. For tarnishing the family name, is probably how he would have put it if he had discovered that his sister had been seduced."

"You think he would have killed her for honor?" Sylvia's eyes were wide.

"No. But he might have found her by the water's edge and struck her, never intending the blow to be so hard, so lethal. But why so many years later?"

"I can barely remember that summer," Sylvia agreed. "We were fifteen, weren't we? Is there more bread, please? And some of that berry jelly? I am so tired and hungry!"

"And why is that, child?" said Abba, back from the laundry room and now reaching for her knitting.

"I could not sleep. I am half-convinced my mother has hired one of those Pinkerton fellows to follow me! I have heard steps behind me, and last night when I looked out the window I could have sworn I saw a man in a long coat staring up at my window."

I nodded in recognition; two nights before I, too, had looked out the window and seen a man standing, watching. I cleared my throat and tried to warn Sylvia not to continue this conversation. Abba gave me a sharp glance and was about to ask me something, when the front bell chimed.

"We will talk more about this later," Abba said darkly. I knew that, to my mother, contemplating the mystery of a friend's demise was one thing; ending up in danger myself was not Abba's intent for her daughter. It was comforting to have a mother worry about one, especially at a moment when I myself was becoming more and more worried.

Abba put down her knitting and went to answer the door.

"Sylvia, I had the same sensation earlier this morning, when I walked down Beacon Hill to do the day's marketing. Footsteps, close, in rhythm with my own . . . but no one there when I turned around," I whispered, so that Abba in the front hall couldn't hear.

"At least we know it can't be Preston," Sylvia whispered back. "He's under lock and key."

"In leg irons," I agreed. "Are they really necessary, I wonder?"

Abba returned a moment later, and while she was still thin-lipped with concern, she had her arm through that of an amiable-looking older gentleman with long white hair and a well-traveled dark suit. Abba's eyes flashed with pleasure, and the visitor grinned excessively, abashed to find himself an object of attention.

"Uncle Henry?" I asked, disbelieving. My wide eyes grew wider. "Uncle Henry!" I cried with greater conviction, putting down the shirt I'd been debuttoning.

"Who else? Give me a hug, my girl; it's been a long while." He opened his arms wide and I flung myself into them.

Henry Mapp wasn't really an uncle, merely an old friend of the family who had known us since before we were the Alcotts, having once been a traveling lecturer on the same circuit as Father in his bygone bachelor days. Henry Mapp had taken a different course, though, and instead of being true to his calling as an educator and philosopher, as Father had, he had invested in stocks, earned enough to buy a small manufactory of woolen gloves and stockings, and from there had progressed into wealth and a very comfortable old age.

"I have been in Europe for some time," he explained, accepting a wobbly chair at the table and hungrily eyeing the bread and jam. "Baking day," he said with youthful vigor. "I am lucky."

Abba fetched another plate and mug. "Mr. Alcott will be so sorry he missed you," she said. "Will you be in Boston a day or two?" She did not say where

Father was that day, which of course meant he was involved in one of his many committees, probably at that very moment seeking safe refuge for the runaway slaves Abba had cooked for all last night.

"Much longer," Mr. Mapp said, biting into the bread and leaving rosy dots of jam nesting in the bristling mustachios at the corner of his mouth. "I'm here for good, Mrs. Alcott. I've had enough of abroad . . . all those sauced foods and ancient ruins . . . and now that my two girls are married, I can do as I please. Boating on the Charles. That's what I've in mind. And a little garden with some roses. Louisa, I see you've not wed."

"No, I have not, Uncle Henry." I placed my ink-stained, long-fingered hands on the table, as if to emphasize the point that I wore no rings, no bands of gold.

"No rush," Abba said, patting my shoulder.

"Exactly," Mr. Mapp agreed. "Better to take a while and look around, not rush into anything. Marry in haste, repent at leisure, I always say. Take that poor Brownly girl. What was her name? Dorothy?"

"So you've heard," I said, resuming my work on the shirt. A button popped off and made a little *keplunk* into the button jar.

"Hasn't everyone? I always knew that young man was a rotter. He made eyes once at my Harriet, down at our Newport house, and I gave her what-for. I'll not have that blood mixed in with mine, I told her. She listened, thank God. Sent him packing. Do you have any coffee, Mrs. Alcott?"

Abba rose and fetched a pot from the stove.

"When was that, Uncle Henry?" I asked lightly. I bent over the shirt I was working on.

"Let's see. Just before I took the girls to Rome. Must be seven years ago, already. Harriet was just sixteen, if that old. Come to think of it, that was the winter the Brownlys were in Rome, too. And the McCormacks, and the Miltons. Kept bumping into Bostonians. The old city was packed with Americans abroad. Never had to bother with a word of Italian."

"Were you in the same set, in Rome, with the Brownlys?" I tried to remain calm, and not spice my voice with an edge that gave the question unclear significance.

"Should have been," Mr. Mapp said, taking another large bite of bread and jam, which thickened his speech somewhat. "But Mrs. Brownly and Dorothy pretty much kept to themselves. I understood the girl was in disgrace, had misbehaved the summer before and her mother had carted her off to Europe. Fifteen is a hard age with daughters." He sighed and trailed off, obviously caught in painful remembrance of his own Harriet's girlhood.

I frowned and leaned more closely over my work. Dorothy had been in disgrace in Rome. Because of Newport, because of Preston? Mrs. Brownly had done what any wealthy society matron does when her daughter falls in with a bad lot: taken her to Europe for distraction, for punishment (punishment! I reflected. Oh, to go to Europe!), I forced my thoughts back to Dorothy. Yes, the mother takes her away and hopes she forgets him. But Dorothy had come home and six years later married the man! No wonder her family had been exasperated and alienated.

"Yes, those years between childhood and marriage are hard for a parent with daughters." Mr. Mapp swallowed his bread and jam and sighed heavily. "Not that sons make it much easier. Take my own Herbert. Gambling. The times I have paid off his debts with a final warning . . . Didn't walk the straight and narrow till he met Mary, and she laid down the law. Thank God it took. I think it took." He scratched his beard and stared out the window, wondering.

"Yes. And poor Mrs. Brownly with Edgar, who seems disinclined to wed at all," I added.

Mr. Mapp chuckled. "I think Edgar is well inclined, but his mother is not. Those two are uncommonly close. Or at least were. There is a distance between them these days. Come to think of it, there was talk about Edgar that year in Rome, as well as Dorothy. Seemed he'd threatened to leave Boston and never again speak to his mother, because she took Dorothy on the grand tour, but none of her other children . . . not Edgar, and you can imagine how a young man like Edgar would look forward to visiting Rome and Paris . . . all those opera dancers. Strange, isn't it? I never pegged Dorothy as Mrs. Brownly's favorite. Quite the opposite."

"Stranger and stranger," I agreed.

Mr. Mapp pursued his own train of thought. "There will be no cavorting with Roman opera dancers for Edgar, not with Mrs. Brownly requiring him to keep the books, lunch with the bankers and mill manager, and look to the family interests. Though gossip pairs him off with a few American young persons of the stage. Youth." Mr. Mapp sighed again and fell silent. I had already learned that when older gentlemen mention youth and fall silent they are enjoying fond remembrances best not shared with the gentle sex.

Abba poured another cup of coffee for our visitor.

"But I didn't come for gossip," Henry Mapp said happily, refreshed by his memories and the excellent Alcott bread. He accepted his steaming cup and grew earnest. "I need your help, Mrs. Alcott. I'm setting up a household for myself and I need a staff. Upstairs maids, cooks, valet, the whole kit. Can you help?"

"Of course." This was Abba's speciality, matching the unemployed with households in need of service. "There's Betty Donner, the cook. The woman she was with just passed on without leaving so much as a nickel to her, much less a retirement bequest, so Betty will be needing a new place. And I'm sure I can convince Brigid Connor to come to you. The situtation she has is not a good one. There is a young man in the house who follows her about and makes eyes and they are stinting her wages, as I'm sure you'll never do. Can't think of a capable valet free at the moment, but I'm sure a name will come to mind."

"Maybe that fellow Digby will be free after they hang Wortham," Mr. Mapp proposed a little too eagerly for good taste. "Oh. Sorry, Miss Sylvia. He is your cousin."

"Yes," said my friend somewhat weakly. "More and more distantly."

"Well, speak to that Digby fellow," he said, turning again to Abba. "I've never known anyone as capable as he. Smart, too. Speaks French and Italian almost as well as English. He was in Rome when I visited. Don't know what family he was with, but I saw him at the Pantheon, gazing up in a kind of dull ecstasy. An old ruin, that's what I call it. Especially the west wall, ready to topple down. I hear they've restored it."

I bent down over the shirt and popped off another button.

"Yes, staffing is a problem," I agreed thoughtfully. "Never know who you will end up with. By the by . . ." My expression changed to the same one of wide-eyed innocence I'd used with Katya Mendosa. "I know a young woman who will be an excellent kitchen helper for the cook, Mr. Mapp. Queenie Carter. She's smart and quick and honest."

Henry Mapp squinted at me and twirled his mustache. "Louisa, you're pulling something. I can tell from your voice."

"Well, Queenie has a daughter. A very young daughter. Newborn, in fact." I peered intently at the shirt in my lap; Sylvia looked at the ceiling.

"And her husband? Can he work, too?" Mr. Mapp's squint deepened.

I took a deep breath. "There is no husband."

Henry Mapp wiped the crumbs off his hands and rose to leave. "Mrs. Alcott, if you would please ask Betty Donner and Brigid Connor to stop by, I'll speak with them. They are honest and virtuous by reputation."

My heart sank. If even an old friend of the family would not hire Queenie, how ever would I place her? There were houses on the docks where the sailors spent their money that took in young women like Queenie. *Never,* I thought, and saw the same resolve in Sylvia's eyes. Such women lived lives of such misery and danger that inevitable early death was deemed a mercy. And what would become of her daughter?

"I thank you for your time, Mrs. Alcott. And for that excellent bread and jam. My regards to Mr. Alcott." Mr. Mapp rose and reached for the coat and hat he'd put on the fourth table chair. He stopped and scratched his head. It was obvious he knew he had disappointed me, but, as I knew, the rules of society dictated that one did not bring such women into a decent household.

"Wouldn't you know, I almost forgot my second reason for coming. I've had lunch with old Mr. Wallace—you know, of the Wallace and Wallace Mill Company—and he'd like to have Bronson come by next week some evening and give a parlor talk, a conversation. He'll pay, of course. Do you think Mr. Alcott will be available?" His eyes went to the threadbare curtains and seemed to recognize that if household amenities were an indication, the Alcott household could use some extra income. Pleased with himself, Mr. Mapp rocked back and forth on his feet, smiling.

Abba threw her arms around him. The month's groceries had just been paid for. "Of course, of course," she exclaimed with delight. "Thank you, Mr. Mapp." And because she was a woman who was both grateful and generous by nature, she looked for some way to repay the kindness. My box of French marzipan, still unopened, was on a shelf behind her. Abba reached for the box and gave it to Mr. Mapp.

"Why, thank you, ma'am. I admit to a fondness for sweets. Good day, then." Mr. Mapp accepted the box and left.

"Louy, I hope you don't mind . . ." Abba began when we were alone again.

"Of course not. It was the right thing to do, Abba. And so like you. I would rather Dorothy had brought me a book of Roman etchings than French sweets, if she insisted on bringing me a present at all. She did become forgetful, bringing me sweets when she knew I have no particular fondness for them."

"Well, I must see to the linens." And Abba disappeared into the back pantry, where the vat was boiling.

"Rome," I said, when my mother was gone. "Back to Rome. All roads, especially Dorothy's, seem to lead there." I began clearing away the cups and saucers and pots of jam.

"And she was so very different when she came back," Sylvia offered. " I think it was more than that affair with Preston the summer before. I think she must have fallen in love with an Italian count. But maybe he was already married. Or unsuitable."

"He just now found out," I said, putting the dishes in a bucket under the pump and thrusting my hands deep into my pockets.

"What?"

"Why, Edgar, if he killed his sister even accidentally—oh, how wicked the world can be—if he was capable of murdering Dorothy as a kind of honor killing, why would he wait so long? Because he just found out why Mrs. Brownly took Dorothy to Rome, and not he. He hadn't known about that earlier summer, about Dorothy and Mr. Wortham. Somehow, something occurred immediately upon Dorothy's arrival home. I think I shall have to speak with Edgar Brownly again."

And with that conclusion, I stared unhappily at the ceiling.

"Are the buttons off, Louy?" Abba called from the pantry. "I'm ready for the next batch."

"Coming, Abba," I called back. I smiled at Sylvia. "I don't suppose there will be any more surprise visitors, so now I must get back to the washing and mending of linens. It was good to see an old friend, though. Mr. Mapp hasn't stopped by in a very long time. I hope he doesn't disappear from our lives once again. He has done Father many kindnesses."

"Carrying away the box of marzipans may not count as one," Sylvia teased. "I happen to know that your father, unlike you, does have a sweet tooth."

"Well, you know Father. He'll have forgotten by now that Dorothy ever made a present of them to me, and what's forgotten is not missed."

Chapter Fifteen

A Deadly Habit

"Were you warm enough last night, Abba?" It was morning, and because there had been a late-winter snowfall, my little schoolchildren had stayed home for the day. I was in the pantry with Mother, folding laundry and feeling a combination of bliss and regret, for there would be no children that day (They were sweet; they were messy. They were angels; they could also be demons.), but there would also be no sunshine. Winter grayness had returned with a vengeance, and those geese that had honked so merrily yesterday were probably heading back south, I reflected. A snowfall meant we would have to burn even more wood and coal simply to keep our little home livable, and at that time of the year, when piles were low, the prices were very high.

"Warm enough," my mother answered stoically, clanking down one iron that had gone cold and picking up the second.

I folded the shirt into the basket and reached for the next one. Father had been away the night before, traveling and giving a conversation in Amherst, and Abba had trouble sleeping when her husband was gone. I suspected she had not even retired to her bed until after he had returned, on the first morning mail train, himself yawning and pale with fatigue.

"I do dislike it when your father is gone," she admitted. "Do you think he remembered to eat any dinner, Louy?" Her eyes lifted from her laundry and sought the closed door of his study across the hall. He was already hard at work on his next lecture.

He was gone much of the time, I reflected, folding another shirt and inspecting the frayed cuff. His work—his calling, as he said—required frequent absences, sometimes for weeks, and the house, whatever house we were living in at the time, felt empty without him. The women, his women, would find themselves listening for his steps, for the crackle of the evening paper, the clearing of the throat that preceded his most thoughtful statements.

That name—Josephine, Jo—came into my thoughts again, that character waiting in the wings. Jo would miss her father, would experience that emptiness within the home.

Though the emptiness was not always unbearable. Father could be difficult, too, and even Abba's step seemed a little lighter, freer, when the philosopher was gone.

Tenderly, Abba ran the iron over the collar of Bronson's heavy muslin jacket. "I do miss woolen blankets," she admitted.

Father, some years before as part of his vegetarian regime, had removed from the house almost all animal products, leaving us with cotton blankets and wooden shoes. Leather shoes had been allowed into use some weeks later, since wooden ones caused blisters, but we still were limited to linen and cotton blankets.

"Do you ever miss roast beef?" I asked, grinning.

"I choose not to answer that," Abba said. "Instead, tell me about the story you are writing."

"Well," I said, hesitating, not wanting to reveal the

blood-and-thunder I was writing, "I am thinking about a story set at Fruitlands. Something about wild oats."

"Wild oats. A good title," Abba agreed. I had vivid memories of Fruitlands, the utopian community Father had founded ten years before, where men might reach perfection through rustic labor and the study of philosophy. But while the men had studied, I remembered that Abba, Anna, and I had had to feed the group and work fifteen-hour days at the practicalities of life. It had been a hard time, and ultimately the community collapsed. Father's ideals would not even allow the use of manure on the fields, protesting that we should retain the soil exactly as the Creator made it, and the crops were so sparse we almost starved that year.

"Do you remember the day you climbed the tree and wouldn't come down?" Abba mused.

"Oh, yes. I hadn't been able to keep my temper, as I had promised. And Mr. Lane had made me very cross. I know we are required to love all, but he strained my potential for goodness."

Abba did not respond, for her own feelings for the extreme Mr. William Lane were even stronger. He had tried to convince Bronson to end his marriage to Abba, since individual contract destroyed community integrity. That had been a hard time, indeed, with the small, crowded rustic house filled with bad tempers, wounded feelings, and indecision. But Father had held true. "Till death do us part," he finally told Abba, and they had kissed, and Mr. Lane had left. Even the philosopher of Concord was not quite ready for free love.

"Wild oats," Abba repeated. "Yes. There will be some stories there worth telling."

Abba and I finished the week's worth of mending, bleaching, and ironing, then sat at the little table for our morning tea, wondering if Father would join us.

That morning he was preparing his "conversation" for Mr. Wallace's gathering. He had already decided to speak on the shallowness and uselessness of contemporary amusements, not being able to cleanse from his imagination the sight and sound of Miss Katya Mendosa warbling bad lyrics as fake Indians leapt about onstage and died over and over.

Sipping milky tea and waiting, we heard a sharp cry from his study. In unison, barely breathing, we jumped to our feet and rushed into the little book-lined room fearing the worst, for while Father was in excellent health, he was not young.

He stood behind his battered, paper-covered desk. The morning edition was spread out before him, and he pointed to a headline. There was a look of terrible remorse on his pale face.

"It's Henry Mapp," he said. "Dead. A complete surprise. Dear old Henry. Gone."

"Oh, no, Bronson! Why, he looked healthy as could be yesterday!" Abba's eyes were already wet.

"Our life's a moment and less than a moment," said Father, hooking his thumbs in his suspenders and rocking back and forth on his heels.

"Mr. Mapp?" I said, still wiping my hands on a dish towel. "Are you sure? Do they say how?"

"Yes, it is old Henry. And they think his heart gave out."

I sat quickly in a chair, suddenly light-headed. "Something is very wrong. Not just his death, though that is a tragedy, of course. But how strange that he died the day after visiting us for the first time in years. I . . . I will go to visit his daughter."

"Yes," Abba agreed, also sitting. "We must extend our condolences." She sounded absolutely shocked, barely able to put the words together.

"Sympathy calls are becoming a much too frequent pasttime," Father observed, frowning.

*   *   *

Mrs. Harriet Simpson, née Mapp, was in residence in her father's home on Boylston Street, and she opened the door herself when I called that afternoon. Mrs. Simpson was dressed in black, and her brown hair had been brushed vigorously into the confines of black netting. She looked much younger than her twenty-four years.

"Oh, Louisa." She wept, touching a handkerchief to her wet and reddened eyes. "It's so terrible!"

I embraced her tightly and then we moved as one into the house.

"The house is a mess. Father hadn't even unpacked yet," said Harriet. "Poor Father." The handkerchief swept the eyes again and there were difficult moments of unrestrained sobbing. I searched her reticule for salts but, finding none, decided instead to pour a glass of water from a tray on a table. Harriet sipped noisily. She took a deep breath and pointed the way through the chaos of unpacked boxes.

"Step over those packing crates, Louisa, and come into the front parlor. We can sit and chat. We can catch up on old times. Wasn't it awful about poor Dorothy?" And the sobbing recommenced.

Mr. Mapp hadn't been exaggerating when he had said the day before that he had just moved back to Boston and was still getting his house in order. The hall was barefloored and empty except for the boxes and packing crates. There was not even a coat tree on which to hang my cape, so I carried it over my arm and followed Harriet into the parlor. White sheets covered most of the furniture and the windows were blocked with black cloth to keep the sun from fading the wallpaper. Now the black gauze would have to remain in place for mourning.

Harriet was formally dressed, however, with her mother's braided hair brooch pinned securely to the front of her bodice and her grandmother's jet beads dangling from throat and ears. She had spent the morning with the minister, making funeral arrangements.

"I can't believe he's passed over," she whispered, sitting on a white-clothed sofa and looking strangely like an artist's model, with that grief on her face and all that draped cloth behind her; then I thought that she looked as all women look in a room filled with covered furniture, as if she were about to embark on a long journey. But it was her father who had just begun the longest journey. I shivered, both because of the eeriness of the room and because my feet were soaked. Harriet patted the sofa and indicated I was to sit next to her.

"I feel a similar disbelief. His passing was so unexpected," I admitted. "You know he called on us just yesterday. We were so pleased to see him. It had been a long time, all those years he spent in Europe . . . and now, to come home and . . . and . . ." Because Harriet was sobbing again, I did not finish the sentence. Now, however, the sobbing had reached gale strength. Smelling salts were definitely needed. There must be a vial somewhere in the house. I found the little silver downstairs maid's bell and rang it as loudly as possible.

A moment later a severe-looking woman came in.

"Yes?" she asked haughtily, obviously irritated to have been called away from her duties. She wore a lace-trimmed apron over her blue wool dress, and that was the only thing about her that indicated her servant status. She was tall, handsome, and reminded me of a governess Sylvia had once had, who had frequently locked her in her closet.

"Smelling salts and tea, please," I requested, trying to sound slightly more authoritative than I looked. "Some brandy in the tea, if there is any in the house."

The tall, wraithlike woman sniffed, complained, "As if I haven't enough to do," and walked out.

Between sobs, Harriet giggled. "Isn't she awful? I'm simply terrified of her," she admitted. "Father hired her through an agency. I believe he was planning to replace Mrs. Bradley as soon as he found a different housekeeper.

"Yes, that is why he visited us yesterday, for help with staffing. When did Mrs. Bradley begin her employment?" I asked, pleased that this change in conversation had somewhat restored Harriet, who was most at ease when discussing domestic arrangements.

"I'm not sure. Father mailed ahead instructions—you know how he likes everything orderly so he doesn't have to be bothered with the household—and she was here when he arrived. Even he was a little frightened of her." Harriet giggled again. "Oh, Louisa, I feel so much better already. Thank you."

Mrs. Bradley returned with a tea tray. She glared again and thumped the tray so loudly on the table that the milk spilled.

"Thank you, Mrs. Bradley," I said. "No, please don't leave. Not yet. I was wondering. Were you here last night, and this morning?"

"I was employed as a live-in, miss. Of course I was here." She folded her arms over her chest and glared harder.

"Then did you notice anything amiss about your employer? His death takes us all by surprise; he seemed in such good health." I tried to frame my questions as polite conversation suitable for a condolence call, not wanting to further upset Harriet.

"We'd just met. I knew nothing about him, so I really can't say. Except I did warn him that sweets were bad for the heart. But he didn't listen. Ate the box at one sitting, he did."

"The box?" I frowned.

"Yes, miss. Some candy he brought home. Took it to his room last night and I found it this morning when . . . when . . ." For the first time her iron visage crumpled. Mrs. Bradley had discovered the dead Mr. Mapp in his bed.

"Would you bring me the box, Mrs. Bradley," I said very calmly.

A moment later the housekeeper returned, bearing the tin box that Abba had presented to Mr. Mapp the day before.

"Ummm," said Harriet. "Daddy loved marzipan. And there's one left." She reached for the last bonbon in the tin. It had been completely buried in the powdered sugar so that Mr. Mapp must have overlooked it.

"No, dear," I said, staying her hand. "I will send you some fresh ones." I took the tin from Mrs. Bradley and shut it firmly with the remaining candy inside.

I spent another half hour with Harriet, talking about her father and administering salts as required, but when other visitors arrived to extend condolences I gave Harriet one last embrace and took my leave.

On the front step I hugged the tin to my chest and gazed at Mr. Mapp's house, with its black gauze mourning curtains. My mind was racing at a furious pace. If Mr. Mapp had indeed died from eating the marzipan meant for me, what did that mean? Surely Dorothy would not have wanted to poison me? Not the old Dottie, anyway, but perhaps this new, strange Dorothy who forgot when her guests were coming to tea. Dorothy had changed—if not her nature, then her responses and attitudes. And with reason Dorothy had grown jealous of Preston. Had she learned that Preston had once kissed me? If so, could she have truly been jealous of me, one of her oldest friends, because of a trifle? No. Not Dorothy.

I sent Sylvia a note that afternoon, asking her to

pay a condolence call on Harriet, knowing full well that Harriet and Sylvia hadn't spoken for years because of some silly girlish quarrel. But judging by Mrs. Bradley's severity, Harriet would need old friends about her for a while. Sylvia returned my note with one of her own. She would call on Harriet. But it was to be a trade.

This was the favor Sylvia wished, as explained later: for me to come as a guest to a ball her mother was planning.

"You must, Louisa. You simply must, else I can't bear it."

It was the next morning, after we'd had a brisk walk through the puddling snow on the Commons, and I was setting up the parlor for my little day school, fetching chalks for the slates and a globe for the geography lesson.

"No. I haven't the time," I said. I was in such a rush I thumped pieces of chalk and a slateboard at each of six places set around a game table that had been recruited into the service of education.

"You promised," Sylvia accused.

"You sound like a schoolgirl," I said.

"Well, I felt like one last night, when I got home and discovered that without asking me Mother had sent out invitations for a dance, in my honor, for the Saturday following the next. A dance! You'd think I was sixteen all over again."

"Yes. Not the ripe old age of twenty," I said. "Don't ask me to do this, Sylvia. I'm not in a mood to put ribbons in my hair and trip around a dance floor."

"Think of the music." Sylvia smiled slyly. "There will be polkas and reels. The musicians are already hired."

"I can't, Sylvia," I protested gently but with slightly less conviction. It was to be a meat market, and we were to be the lambs for sale. But I loved music.

"What with this business of Dorothy, and now worrying about Queenie and her baby, how could I spend an evening dancing? How could your mother ask it?" I insisted.

"Her reasoning is simple and heartless. Dorothy was not a blood relative, so we are not officially in mourning." Sylvia bent down and fetched a marble that had fallen off the table. "I can't bear it if you don't come. Just for an hour. Bring your notebook and carry that around instead of a dance card. You can take notes for a story."

I sighed. Sylvia had won the battle. Every experience could be used in one of my stories. Here was grist for the mill. "Well, for an hour or two. For the music. And the dialogue. The Brownly family will not attend because of the mourning, of course," I added.

"Courtesy requires that they be invited, but Mother does not expect them to come. It is much too soon after Dorothy's passing."

"Then since you have determined to involve me in this affair, I will hand-deliver Edgar Brownly's invitation," I said. "And on the way, I will leave the marzipan tin with Constable Cobban. I've decided the police chemist should examine it."

"Louisa, you can't think—"

"I think nothing, Sylvia. But there is a connection, and it must be explored."

"And to think, just a short while ago we believed Dorothy had suffered a fatal accident. Now it's murder, and perhaps double murder. Is the world still round, Louisa, or has it gone flat? I wouldn't be surprised, so much seems to be changing."

"Or perhaps things never were as they seemed," I said sadly.

The front door slammed and Walter Campbell stormed into the room, squealing that he wanted milk and crackers.

"School is starting," I said with a wry smile. Sylvia fled, but only after promising to return in two hours and finish the last hour of school for me, so that I might attend to my errand of delivering Edgar Brownly's invitation myself. and have one more conversation with the Brownly heir.

I moved effortlessly through the lessons of the morning, able to recite all the tributaries of the Mississippi and conduct a second private train of thought in my head at the same time. But my reality had shifted in the weeks since Dot's death. Daughters were no longer loved by their mothers and elder brothers; sisters no longer protected younger sisters; good friends bearing gifts seemed less trustworthy; and husbands . . . well, husbands seemed in general a thing to be avoided, if Preston were an example of the breed.

Much of what I had been taught of that great ambiguity that society likes to refer to as "life" seemed no longer pertinent. Dorothy's death was revealing the underbelly of the serpent known as society, and any cruelty suddenly seemed possible.

When I decided to pay one more visit to Edgar Brownly, Mr. Wortham had been in jail for a week, trying to work with his lawyer to prepare a defense, for the court had decided he would be charged and tried. I feared that if the truth were not discovered soon, it might never be.

"You know how you must quickly spill salt over red wine when it splashes on a white cloth?" I told Sylvia when she returned after lunch. "If the wine dries, the stain can never be removed. I feel this stain is drying, Sylvia. There is no time to lose. Judge Loring will hear the case against Preston Wortham, and an outraged jury will find him guilty simply because someone must be punished. Mr. Wortham will hang, and I will never know for certain what really happened to Dorothy, and why."

"Then you think my cousin innocent?"

"I did not say that, Sylvia." I smiled sadly and put down the black crayon I had used to make my schoolroom maps of the Amazon and Nile and Mississippi. "I said I would never be certain. There. Can you work with this?

"Here is the Amazon. The one with the monkey in the tree next to it. The Nile has a pyramid next to it." I put a second map over the first. "And the Mississippi has a levee. Can you remember those, and place the towns along them?"

"I suppose. Maybe I should just try singing lessons instead," Sylvia suggested, daunted by what she had agreed to do.

"Now, Sylvia, you will never know if teaching children will suit you if you do not attempt it now," I said. "Be brave. They cannot hurt you very much. Only remember little Dicky does bite when he's angry."

I tugged at my waistjacket and gave my hair one last pat into place. I wore my dark blue afternoon "calling" outfit, the same costume I had worn to Dorothy's two tea parties, and I hoped, with those memories, to stir Edgar Brownly's conscience. "The play's the thing," I had muttered as I dressed.

"I will return as soon as I have met with Edgar Brownly and made a short visit to Queenie. I have some new garments for her baby." I rose from the table and, distracted, gave my friend a reassuring kiss on the forehead, as I did with my young students.

I missed Anna more than ever that afternoon, as I walked back to Mr. Brownly's studio. It was unwise, I knew, going out without a chaperon, and if Anna had been at home she would have accompanied me. But she was in Syracuse, May was too young for this visit, Lizzie was too shy, and Sylvia was in the schoolroom. I was on my own. I hoped desperately that Miss Mendosa would not arrive in the middle of this less-than-social visit.

The fickle Boston weather had changed from snow to a drizzle, and I carried my beat-up old parasol—not a prime choice of weapon, but one that would serve its purpose in the sequence of events that day. To save money, I walked to the bay rather than take the public coach, and because the cobbles were slippery, a full three-quarters of an hour passed before I arrived at Brownly's studio. I encountered few people on the street, only those who must be out in wet weather, for over the centuries Bostonians have developed a nose for the weather, and it was the kind of day when mothers stuck their heads out of upstairs windows, sniffed, shouted back to spouse and children that a fog was settling, then clapped the window and shutters shut again, and kept them shut for the day.

The greengrocer was out with his cart of early lettuces and spinach, the milk seller and his donkey made their slow progress up and down the streets of Beacon Hill, but I spied no others braving the dreary afternoon till I arrived at the Common. There, a goose girl raced up and down a muddy path, herding her honking white charges, and at the Smokers' Circle a huddled group of men created a denser fog than that rolling in from the bay.

I went first to the Charles Street Home, to leave a bundle of baby's things for Queenie.

"Oh, ain't that the sweetest!" The new mother sighed, examining the pink sleeping gown with matching cap, the white booties, the miniature woolen coat, all only slightly used and well mended by Abba herself where the moths had made holes.

"How do you feel, Queenie?" I sat in the one rickety ladder-back chair the room contained, and patted Queenie's hand.

"Tired, Miss Louisa. And kind of soft in the head,

if you know what I mean. I can only see today, like there's nothing past it." Queenie hugged her baby closer and the little bundle mewed and stretched, whereupon I spent several minutes admiring the baby's beauty and intelligence, as new mothers seem to expect even before the infant can display any qualities whatsoever other than the primary skill of taking in and then giving out various liquids.

"Are you still reading your books about California? I don't see them here," I said when I felt due praise had been rendered.

"What's the point?" Queenie stared out the dirty, curtainless window at the swirling gray fog. "I can't even afford the coach to Worcester, and I can't walk to San Francisco, can I?"

"Don't give up, Queenie. I haven't. We'll find a solution," I said.

But Queenie only stared out the window and stroked her baby's head.

By the time I arrived at Edgar Brownly's studio, I was very determined. Too many things needed to be set to rights.

The fog had reached the consistency and color of burned pea soup, for the chill had turned to outright cold, and the thousands of chimneys in the city were sending up a fresh allowance of soot and smoke that, encountering the heavier wet mist, simply fell back down to earth.

By the Customs House the fog was especially thick, for there it combined with the salty mist of the bay, and for that I was thankful, I admitted later, for it rendered me just another vague moving object in the false twilight. The sailors leaning in the tavern doorways did not bother with their usual catcalls and whistles. The foghorn boomed and the harbor cats skittered over the cobbles and yowled. Bells clanged from the masts of rocking boats.

The same old landlady who had opened the door to me a week earlier now opened it again and smirked unpleasantly at me.

"Come to see 'im again, have you?" She cackled. "You young women are all alike. Them high-buttoned blouses don't fool me." She opened the door and allowed me into the hallway.

"Is Mr. Brownly at home?"

"Went out for grub. Back in a minute, I suppose. There." She pointed into a deeper shadow. "You remember where the stairs are. I'm not walking up there with you. My knees are something bad, you know."

No gas lamps had been lighted here; the landlady would not waste money on illumination during day hours, no matter how dark the day. The hall was all shadow and fog, for broken windows had allowed the outdoor climate to migrate indoors. The windows had not been broken during my first visit, I thought. There had been some violence here.

"I remember the way," I told the muttering landlady. "There's no need to accompany me. Thank you." I gave the woman a nickel and began a slow, cautious climb upstairs to the top floor. The railing was slick with grease, the stairs littered with paper and bottles and now leaves, which had come in through the broken windows.

As the landlady had said, he was not in, but he had left his door open. That indicated he was expecting someone, and it was not I. Nevertheless, I decided to take the risk and enter and wait.

The room was as I had remembered. Canvases leaned against the walls in wild disarray, rectangles of all sizes and shapes jutting their corners at each other with no little hostility. One unfinished canvas, still on its easel and covered with a cloth, occupied the center of the room.

I lifted that cloth, and Katya Mendosa, dressed—or

somewhat dressed, since the garments were few and brief—as a gypsy dancer gazed back at me. The actress's eyes were narrowed, her mouth pouting. She looked on the verge of a complaint. It was most lifelike. While the canvases were of dubious taste, their execution displayed talent; how Mr. Brownly must have resented it when his little sister was taken to Europe to tour the galleries, and not he.

I replaced the cover and continued my inspection.

The studio, I noted now, was more prosperous than the building. Brownly had brought in a second velvet sofa and positioned it under the window since my last visit. Perhaps he, too, was already making use of Dorothy's allowance. He had also installed a polished table with a good embroidered cloth on it, a liquor cabinet, and a big copper coal scuttle. A folding screen modestly kept from view the chamber pot and washbasin in the corner. There was a "maid's box" next to the fireplace, with the brushes and blacklead used to tidy up hearths, so I knew that Brownly also had a woman come in for the cleaning. His taste for artistic deprivation went only so far, it would seem.

The charwoman probably came in the morning to mop and dust and lay the fire for the day, since the Brownly heir slept at home and would not need a fire in the evening. *For the most part,* I added to myself.

Carefully, moving the paintings as little as possible, I began my cautious search through them, tilting canvas-stretched frames this way and that until I again discovered the painting of Queenie. This I pulled out of its pile and leaned against an empty spot of wall. I sat gingerly on the sofa opposite it, and considered.

Queenie stared back at me out of huge, lustrous green eyes. Her bristling black hair fell partially over her shoulders, and aside from that avalanche of hair, she was as naked as the day she was born. The child— she was barely fourteen when this was painted, I estimated—reclined languorously on a sofa, the same sofa on which I now sat. Brownly had outfitted her with a ruby ring and many strands of pearls around her slender neck. Probably his mother's. How had Queenie, a child of the streets, felt wearing those jewels, reclining on that sofa . . . and wearing nothing else? How, for that matter, had Mr. Brownly convinced her to pose so? Money alone wouldn't be enough, not for Queenie, who, while she struggled to give birth to her first child, had still clutched a blanket modestly over her belly and legs.

I felt my eyes narrow, my jaw grow tense. I looked very closely at the painting, nose-to-nose. The pupils of Queenie's eyes were dilated. Her fingers were loosely curled as if she half slept, despite those wide-open eyes, and the tilt of her head also suggested sleepiness. Laudanum. Brownly had given her opium.

I heard footsteps then, and, leaving the painting where it was, I sat back down, this time in the chair by the table, not on the sofa. As upset as I was, I remembered that ladies, if caught alone in a room with a gentleman, never sit on the sofa, since that could be construed as an invitation to intimacy. Of course, I wasn't really alone with a gentleman; I was alone with Edgar Brownly, the child seducer, the drugger of women . . . the murderer?

He fumbled with the unlocked door and finally kicked it open. His red moon face was obscured by an armload of groceries, bottles and loaves of bread sticking out of net bags, so he did not see me at first. He was humming a tune from *Girl of the Golden West*.

Stooping with apparent effort and exhaling the sound that sails make when the wind suddenly abandons them, he placed his parcels on a side table. He stood, removed his hat, and turned around. He saw me sitting there, waiting, watching.

He sputtered with dismay for a few moments before

finally being able to pronounce, "Miss Alcott! What in blazes are you doing here?"

"The door was open, and the landlady said I might come in," I answered mildly. "I was hoping we might talk for a few moments."

"Most inconvenient!" He turned in a circle the way street dogs do when they have been cornered and have no escape. He could not very well flee his own loft, however, so he decided to take off his greatcoat, hang it on the oak coat tree from whence also dangled an umbrella and his painting smock, and brave the lionness in his own den.

"You are . . . you are not a lady," he sputtered, taking some time to come up with even that mild insult. "You . . . you . . . are masculine in your thinking!" And he meant that as a great insult, indeed, though I could not take it as such.

He sputtered and ineffectually insulted me for several more minutes, scratched his head, started to say things and then paused before words formed themselves, and finally sat on the sofa, looking as if he would weep with frustration.

"I will be gone in just a few minutes," I said firmly. "But I do wish to speak with you about Dorothy."

"Dorothy." He pouted. "It is always about Dorothy. It has always been about Dorothy. Will she never stop plaguing me?"

"Mr. Brownly, your sister is dead. Surely she can bother you no longer."

His pout disappeared. "Humph. Yes, of course. I mean, we grieve for her; we all do."

"Was there ill will between you and Dorothy? Sisters can be a nuisance," I commented in my gentlest voice.

Slow as he was, Edgar Brownly was beginning to follow my line of thinking. "Ill will? No. Of course not. At least, no more than naturally occurs between an older brother who is saddled with the responsibility of overseeing a family of females, and the much younger sister who refuses to take on any responsibility at all. I love my sisters, Miss Alcott. All of them. I have dedicated my life to their well-being."

"Of course you have," I agreed. "Your mother must be quite proud of you, and grateful, I suspect, for your . . . sacrifices. I see a little spirit stove over there, Mr. Brownly. Could I make you a cup of tea? It is such a damp day."

To myself, I invoked a little prayer to Abba, asking for guidance from the woman whose insights into human nature had already taught me so much. What would encourage Edgar Brownly to talk openly? Temper could make him forget his manners and his aloofness. Most liable to stir his temper: that perpetual, deep rivalry between brother and sister, that dire competition for a mother's love.

"Tea would be welcome, Miss Alcott. Thank you . . . Mother. Grateful. I suppose." And he made a little snort, the way children do when they wish for a box of toy soldiers for Christmas and receive instead a book of improving sermons.

I fussed with the spirit stove, lighting it and fetching a kettle of water from the large tapped barrel in the corner where Mr. Brownly washed his brushes. I poured Darjeeling into a Limoges pot and waited for the water to simmer, hoping that as the water came to a boil so would the Brownly heir. If he had mudered Dorothy, even accidentally, perhaps I could hasten the process by which he would arrive at a need to confess, or at least talk to someone about his relationship with her. My eyes swept over the dresser top, where Edgar kept the tea things. There was a tin of marzipan there. Slowly, as if it might bite, I picked up the tin and examined it. It was a duplicate of the box of bonbons that Dorothy had purchased for me.

When the tea was ready I poured in quantites of sugar and brought the cup to Mr. Brownly.

"There," I said gently. "There. Drink your tea, and tell me about it."

"She's never been truly grateful, you know," he said, pouting again. "Mother, I mean. She takes me for granted. Everything I do for her, for Edith and Sarah."

"For Dorothy, when she was alive," I prompted.

"Dorothy didn't know the meaning of the word *gratitude*. She was the baby of the family for such a long time, so spoiled . . . until Agnes came. Dorothy cared nothing for family name, for position. She was the worst of the lot. Oops." He smiled mischievously. "There I go again. Speaking ill of the dead."

"I understand," I whispered. I reached over to pat his hand, just as mothers do with children who have been told they will not be taken out to play that day.

And just at that moment, Katya Mendosa arrived.

As had Mr. Brownly, the Mendosa carried armloads of provisions: little net bags of muffins and biscuits, a cake in a white box, a wheel of cheese. Unlike Mr. Brownly, instead of carefully depositing her burden on the nearby table, she opened her arms and simply let them fall to the floor when she saw me.

The noise they made was somewhere between that of a small avalanche and the impact of a milk cart into a brick fence. Custard cream from a zuppa inglese seeped out of the crumpled box and onto the bare floor; the cheese bounced into the corner.

"You!" Katya Mendosa shrieked, her eyes blazing to where my hand rested consolingly on Mr. Brownly's. "You haunt me!"

"Good afternoon, Miss Mendosa," said I, hastily removing my hand.

"Now now," said Mr. Brownly, rising and moving away from this raging object of his affections. "Now, now, Katya . . ."

"Don't you 'Katya' me, you two-timing good-for-nothing."

Miss Mendosa spent several moments delivering herself of a loud speech, which did little for Mr. Brownly's peace of mind. Nor, for that matter, did it much enhance my esteem to hear myself called man-stealer, slut, and other titles from the pulp press, some of which I had used in my own blood-and-thunder stories.

My ears burning, I stayed in my chair, trying to assess the situation. It was no small task, as the noise level had risen considerably with Mendosa's arrival. As a woman of no little logic and common sense, I was tempted to obey my instincts and flee, for there was a scent of violence in the air as strong as Katya Mendosa's abundantly used attar of roses scent. However, as Dorothy's friend, I knew I must stay and endure. Words were all I had to solve this mystery of what had happened to Dorothy, so words I would hear. And there was that tin of French marzipan sitting on Edgar Brownly's dresser. I would brave the storm and stay.

Katya's jealous-woman tirade that had begun with a melodic though thick Spanish accent took a detour somewhere in the middle, lost its soft consonants and lyrical dipthongs, and became a shrill accent that I soon recognized. It sounded like the strident voice of Mrs. Dougal's washerwoman, who had been born in County Mayo. The exotic Katya Mendosa was an Irishwoman.

It took a full ten minutes for the diva to exhaust herself. When the shouting stopped Miss Mendosa plopped onto the sofa, wiped her perspiring brow, and began to weep.

"You see how he treats me," she complained to me. "Not a word from him. Silent as a stone, and just as affectionate."

I did not think it wise to point out that he had not

had a chance to speak, had in fact been shouted down several times when he did try to speak. Mr. Brownly was, at that moment, on his hands and knees, fetching pieces of cheese and rolls from the floor.

"My dear, of course I am all yours, but . . ." he began, and could not finish.

La Mendosa picked up a vase and flung it at the closest glazed window. The room filled with the sound of tinkling glass falling onto the cobbles below.

So the windows in the downstairs hall had fallen victim to a temper tantrum, it would seem. But what, exactly, had caused the actress's wrath on that occasion? I sensed that Miss Mendosa's display of jealousy was a performance, based not on true affection for Mr. Brownly, but on a whim to frighten, to amuse, to keep at bay any sense of reality. Katya Mendosa's entire life was a play filled with lies.

But smashing windows was too much. Let her play-act all she wanted; I did not think it suitable to endanger horses below in the street. I would end this latest temper tantrum.

"I saw your old friend a few days ago," I said quietly, steadily staring her down. "Mr. Wortham. He sends his regards."

Katya Mendosa turned red and then white. Her nostrils flared. She looked covertly at Edgar Brownly, who was still on his hands and knees fetching pieces of lunch from under the furniture. He had not heard my comment.

"It is time for you to leave," she whispered. Her manner became almost polite.

So Edgar Brownly did not know his mistress was acquainted—very well acquainted—with his brother-in-law, Preston Wortham.

That knowledge might prove useful. But it seemed wise to end the interview at that point, so I rose.

"I'm sorry your lunch was spoiled," I said, and for

one of the few times in my life I was completely insincere. "There is still marzipan, of course," I said, pointing to the tin.

"I hate marzipan." Edgar Brownly pouted. "That was a gift from Wortham. He must have assumed I would enjoy it because my sister enjoyed marzipan. He's a stupid fellow."

My heart raced. The marzipan had been brought from France by Preston Wortham? Digby must have confused the presents and thought Dorothy had brought a box of bonbons for me. Relief flooded through me. Of course Dorothy would never wish to harm me.

The relief was short-lived.

Who had Mr. Wortham intended to be the recipient of that box of marzipan now down at the police office, waiting for the chemist's test? Or perhaps my imagination was racing, and there was no connection at all between the marzipan and Mr. Mapp's death?

"I would not eat the candy," I told Edgar and Katya. "I think it has gone off. In fact, you should discard it."

"Take it!" Katya shrieked, flinging the box at me.

Back in the dark stairwell, with the door slammed resoundingly upon my departure, I remembered I had not left the invitation I had come to deliver. Well, I would not go back in there just then, for with my ear to the door (yes, dear reader, I admit it: I eavesdropped) I could hear Edgar and Katya quarreling viciously. The voices rose and fell and Katya repeated over and over, "You do not love me! You never send me love letters, never!" and Edgar protesting, with some indifference, it is true, that she was the light of his life.

I wondered if Edgar would have the sense never to put his declarations in writing for her. Such a woman would not be above using them when he grew tired of her, and a lawsuit could well follow, publicity of the worst sort.

Written declarations.

Why had I not thought of it sooner?

Chapter Sixteen

Danger in the Fog

As fate would have it, one Mrs. Giles Milton was passing by the door of Edgar Brownly's studio just as I was leaving. I could tell it was Mrs. Milton by the extravagant number of daughters in her carriage—eight, at last count—and by the booming voice with which the older woman greeted me. Mrs. Milton was a woman who never spoke softly but always yelled, since she herself was hard of hearing and refused, out of vanity, to use an ear trumpet.

"Louisa! Is that Miss Alcott!" Mrs. Milton roared.

"Oh, Mama, it is!" roared back her daughters. "And isn't that where Mr. Brownly keeps his studio?"

There I stood, unchaperoned, blushing, and carrying a box of sweets that, at that moment, could have been confused as a gift from a gentleman.

I wished for a miracle: that the fog would suddenly grow so dense that I would disappear in it, that there would be an earthquake to swallow me or that Mrs. Milton's horses would take fright and bolt . . . without harming any of the children, of course. After a few minutes in company with Katya Mendosa, I was weary of hysterical women who insisted on misreading situations.

"Why, Louisa, my dear, I didn't know you were on intimate terms with dear Mr. Brownly," Mrs. Milton gushed so loudly that the other passersby turned and stared.

The fog did not grow denser. The earth did not tremble. The horses did not bolt. Mrs. Milton, the worst gossip in Boston, would have to be faced. Hastily I donned my hat, which I had removed despite the rules of calling attire for the afternoon. I put my shoulders back, thrust my hands deep into my pockets, and strode over to the carriage.

"Why, Mrs. Milton, what a surprise," I said, which was the only greeting I could think of that would not be an out-and-out lie. Certainly it was not at all nice to see her. "Whatever brings you to the wharves?" I asked, hoping to distract her from asking the same question of myself.

"Mr. Milton is suffering the gout today and we were expecting a shipment, so I drove down," the woman gushed. "Oh, how hard I am worked! How hard! Girls, do stop giggling. . . ." Mr. Milton owned a dry-goods shop that carried items from England, and so he spent some time at the harbor, checking on stocks in his warehouse.

"Indeed, you are hardworking," I agreed. "Well, I must be on my way. Good day, Mrs. Milton." And I turned away, moving with such alacrity that I estimated the fog would render me invisible in half a minute or so.

"Louisa! Miss Alcott! You have not said . . ." Mrs. Milton called after me. "You are here alone, unchaperoned?"

Alone. Quite. Looking, well, you know how women look when . . . I knew Mrs. Milton would say such things about me all that day and the next. For Mrs. Milton was a woman of considerable energy, and even her many children did not quite expend her resources. What strength was left she devoted to gossip.

I walked on without responding. It was none of Mrs. Milton's business what my visit to the Brownly heir had been about. But I knew it would be all over Boston by the next morning that I had been walking—and visiting—alone, and that simply was not done. I frowned and whistled as I walked, feeling even more rebellious because of those stupid rules that so stringently dictated what young women could and could not do with their free time.

And because I was in a bad temper, and because harm had already been done, I decided, *In for a dime, in for a dollar*. I would visit, unchaperoned, the Wortham mansion on Commonwealth Avenue as well. Digby, as a rather powerful member of the servant class, since gentlemen's gentlemen ranked in the top of the downstairs hierarchy, might have some leads on positions for Queenie. And he might have some answers about Preston Wortham as well, if I could pry them out of him.

By this time there was no choice about taking a public coach, since the city horses had been stabled for the rest of the day; otherwise the coaches would be knocking into each other and pedestrians, the fog had grown so thick. Only an extremely stout hater of exercise such as Mrs. Milton would risk a horse and carriage in such a pea souper.

So I walked north through the drizzle, pondering what could drive a person to murder another human being, much less a sweet and loyal human such as Dorothy. I had come to the realization that the guilty party must be either Mr. Wortham or Mr. Brownly, and that money had to be the catalyst for the crime. Yet both men were well housed, well clothed, and well fed. What need had they of more money? It was true what Father often said, that the wealthy never had enough.

I had begun to suspect, though, the true reason why Preston Wortham was already out of funds, and I would now confront Digby with my suspicions.

Half an hour later I rang the bell at the Wortham mansion.

When Digby came to answer my ring at the door, he was less obnoxious than upon my first visit immediately following the murder. He was, in fact, deferential and even solicitous.

"Miss Alcott! Out in such weather! Will you come in?"

"Thank you, Digby, I will," I answered, stepping over the threshold. The house seemed eerily still, as if it were waiting for something. Gone was that atmosphere of days past, of illicit gaiety upstairs, the creaking floorboards and hushed whispers of a waiting unseen companion.

"However, Mr. Wortham is not at home," Digby stated gravely when I took off my sodden coat, indicating I would stay at least a few minutes.

"I know, Digby. He has been incarcerated. Let us go into the parlor, shall we? I wish to speak with you."

Digby started to say something, then closed his mouth, thinking better of it. Somewhat meekly, he followed me into the parlor, the place of my last visit, the place of Dorothy's tea parties.

All had been set in order in that room. No more shawls and assorted women's garments draped themselves over the parlor sofa. No scent of cheap perfume hung in the air.

In fact, the room was almost empty. The settee, table, and several chairs were gone, and all of the paintings, fairly good Turner imitations of seascapes, had been taken down from the wall, exposing darker squares of red flocked wallpaper where the sunlight had been blocked.

"Is Mr. Wortham relocating?" I asked.

"I couldn't say, miss," the servant answered. "His banker was by yesterday, and ordered the removal of the missing items."

"Well. I'm sure you are busy," I began, sitting in

one of two remaining upholstered chairs, "but there are some questions about Mr. Wortham I would like to ask."

"It is not my place, miss," Digby answered with another grave little bow.

"Please. Just for a moment." I balanced the box of marzipan on my lap. I had considered tossing it onto a rubbish heap outside, but reconsidered, since street children and beggars rummaged through such heaps. I would have to carry it home to dispose of it.

"As you wish. For a moment." He stood in front of a window, on the far side of the room. The street gas lamps had been lighted, and the flickering yellow radiance cast harsh shadows into the room. The curtains, too, had been removed.

"I have heard distressing things about your employer," I began.

"You must not believe everything you hear." Digby stood stiffly, his white-gloved hands tense at his sides.

"Of course not," I gently agreed. "You knew him perhaps better than the rest of us. Except for Mrs. Wortham, of course."

"Of course."

"I have heard that he went to visit his mistress, Katya Mendosa, as soon as he returned from his honeymoon. That must have been very distressing for Mrs. Wortham."

Digby stood even straighter. "A patent falsehood, miss. He did no such thing."

"Not even once?"

"Not even once."

Digby, as good manservant, would lie about that, of course, I thought. I would try a different tactic.

"I'm so relieved to hear that," I said. "Of course, in Europe he stayed devotedly by his wife's side. Is that how you would describe Mr. Wortham's nature? Devoted and loyal?"

"His nature?" Digby considered. "Of course."

"So you did travel in Europe with them."

"He required my services, yes, miss."

"How cold it is today," I said, rubbing my hands together to warm them.

"Exceedingly, Miss Alcott," he agreed.

"And very wet." I stared about at the flocked walls as if distracted. "When did Preston Wortham first employ you, Digby?"

"Upon his engagement to Mrs. Wortham. I am skillful at setting up domestic arrangements, and as a new husband he would need to make . . . certain changes . . . in his living arrangements once he brought his new wife home."

"You would not be willing to supply more details about those certain changes?"

"No, miss."

"No matter." My imagination could very effectively supply the domestic differences that would perforce be needed in Wortham's living arrangements once he made the transformation from bachelor to husband.

"You have been helpful, Digby. You might be interested to know that I had employment inquiries from a gentleman who expressed particular interest in you. Unfortunately, he has died rather unexpectedly."

"Ah. That would be Mr. Henry Mapp. I read his obituary. He asked particularly for me?"

"He did. He was most impressed with you."

Digby frowned. "I am flattered, of course. But the position would not have suited me."

"You refer to the inquiry of five years past." Mr. Henry Mapp had been called before a court to answer charges of embezzling funds from a club for which he had been secretary. "He was cleared of all wrongdoing in that matter," I said.

"Yes. But the mud clings, miss. Once something like that is made public . . ."

"His peers have largely forgotten, since he was innocent of wrongdoing," I said somewhat hotly. But it would not serve my purpose to lose my temper, so I softened my voice and began again. "I know of a young woman seeking employment, Digby. Could you help?"

"Is she of impeccable character, miss?"

I sighed. It was useless. By Digby's standards, Queenie could hardly be described as a woman of character. It wouldn't matter that Brownly had drugged and raped her.

"If not . . ." he began, but the air in the room grew charged and the servant did not finish his sentence. He was staring somewhere beyond me, over my shoulder.

I was certain I would be dismissed any moment. I could no longer hesitate.

"Perhaps, Digby, you can tell me who has been blackmailing your employer," I said.

"I don't quite understand, miss," Digby blustered.

"Of course you do. All the signs point in that direction. A young man of poor reputation and estranged from both his family and his family's wealth, a known seducer, marries a wealthy young society girl. It's a perfect setup for blackmail. I already know that Mr. Wortham was . . . busy . . . for several summers in Newport, and I'm sure most of Boston, high and low, knows it, too. Certainly the papers have not hesitated to print all the old gossip. If he was not being black-mailed, why, then, was he always out of funds, even after marrying a rich wife?"

The silence that followed was longer than it should have been. I looked up from my teacup and saw Digby frowning at something behind me.

"Don't badger my servant, Miss Alcott," a man's voice growled.

I turned, and saw Preston Wortham standing behind me, glaring.

He wore his stylish brown velvet Roman coat and

black top hat and carried a walking cane, as if he had been out for a walk and just returned. Which, indeed, was the case, as I was startled to discover.

"There was no evidence. I was released yesterday," he said, answering my unspoken questions.

Preston Wortham looked murderous at that moment. His wet hair clung to his face in dripping tendrils, his face was flushed, and his eyes glittered with mad impulse. Incarceration, even for a brief time, seemed not to have rehabilitated Preston Wortham but set him more deeply in his rogue ways.

"You are returned, sir. Well, well. May I take your coat?" Digby took Preston's hat and cane as well, and with a gentle hand at the elbow, led his employer to the remaining comfortable armchair, then placed a footstool for his feet.

"Why are you badgering my servant?" Wortham repeated angrily from the depths of the chair. "What is this nonsense about blackmail?" If he felt any gratitude for my kindness to him at a time when everyone else had abandoned him, he did not show it at that moment.

I studied him closely. He resolutely avoided my gaze and stared at the ceiling.

"It isn't nonsense," I said softly. "It is the truth. Who is blackmailing you, Mr. Wortham?"

He ignored my question and, instead of looking at me, studiously wiped the damp from his face. He moved his feet closer to the grate and leaned heavily into the chair with the possessive gesture of a man who had been temporarily deprived of his own hearth. "Surprised to see me at home, Miss Alcott? Perhaps you were the one who accused me in the first place, in that anonymous letter," he said finally.

"You don't believe that. I have been your friend throughout this ordeal, and I will continue to be your friend as long as you will let me, for not even the worst of us deserves to be denied the grace of friendship."

His eyes, dark, opaque, glittering, met mine briefly, and then resumed their study of the ceiling.

"There is no evidence against me," he said. "The writer of the anonymous letter has written a second one, saying the first was a prank with no truth to it. It was received yesterday, and I was released yesterday. Ask Constable Cobban. He received the letter and showed it to me. Moreover, my tailor has come forward and explained that I spent most of that afternoon with him. I was nowhere near the waterfront when Dorothy . . ."

Suddenly he seemed exhausted. His shoulders slumped and his chin fell forward onto his chest, as if even the effort to sit upright required more strength than he possessed.

"Died. Dorothy is dead," I whispered. "She was murdered. Isn't it time for the truth, Mr. Wortham?"

"Forgive me, sir. It now seems the right thing to do." Digby stepped forward, still holding Preston's cane and sodden coat and hat. "Mr. Wortham was being blackmailed." He addressed himself to me. "He was, for a time, in great danger himself. That is now in the past."

Wortham looked up at Digby with an expression of great relief.

"Well. It is out." Wortham sighed.

"Who is the blackmailer?" I asked.

"It is over. What does it matter?"

"Mr. Wortham, have you ceased to believe in justice?" I asked. I noted, for the first time, that a brown leather valise, puffed and heavy-looking with contents, had been placed behind the drawing room door. Was Mr. Wortham planning a voyage? "I notice this room has been relieved of much of its appointments. It must be painful to sell off such beautiful possessions," I said.

"My beautiful possessions—I use the term 'my' loosely—have been returned to the leasing company,"

Wortham said. "You spy my valise, there in the corner. I will leave this world, or Boston, depending on how the wind blows. This is no home to me."

"Then perhaps a crime has been committed against you, as well as Dorothy," I said.

"Miss Alcott, thank you for your kindness. For speaking to me, and visiting me, at a time when all others had abandoned me. But I now wish only to put this behind me. Good day, Miss Alcott." Wortham's voice was firm.

When I stood, he noticed the box of marzipans, now tucked under my arm.

"A gift?" he asked, and his grin was like his old one, boyish.

He truly seemed to have never seen it before. Perhaps he had simply forgotten it. Or perhaps he was even more skilled at the thespian arts than his friend Katya Mendosa.

Digby stepped forward. "I will see you to the door." He gave a solicitous glance over his shoulder at his exhausted employer and politely showed me out.

And so once again the ornate, heavy door of 10 Commonwealth Avenue was hastily shut, and I was left perplexed.

It was, by then, very late afternoon, and the streets were very dark, almost black, in those sections that did not contain gaslights. A bad time of day to be walking alone. It would be a long and wet walk home.

I trudged through the cold twilight, lost in thought. I had much to reflect on. And between memories of Dorothy rose up the small but nagging irritation that I would have to purchase a new umbrella, for a sudden stray wind turned mine inside out as soon as I left Wortham's front step, and it was useless now except as a walking cane. Well, events would prove it not entirely useless. But at that moment the thought of the expense of a new one saddened me, for it came just at a time when I had given up all unessential expenses and begun a penny bank for Queenie. I could not put aside much money for the girl, but every nickel, I knew, would help keep her a moment longer from complete destitution and disgrace, once her time at the home had elapsed and she was required to leave.

It was not of Queenie I thought, however, during that sodden walk. Much as I had dreaded to think that Dorothy might have been murdered by her own husband, I now realized that if Wortham were not tried for the murder, nobody would be. There were no other suspects other than the victim's own brother, and the justice system would never accuse the Brownly heir, with or without direct evidence. Dorothy's murderer might go free.

I was not particularly pleased to see Mr. Wortham released from jail, as much as I had argued against the circumstantial letter that incriminated him and that, indeed, turned out to have been some sort of deadly practical joke. Who had sent that letter? And why had the sender changed his mind and sent a second, rescinding the first?

Now the police had no suspects.

And that did not sit right with me. I had been brought up to respect justice even more than the laws, for the two so often are unrelated, and I wanted justice for Dorothy, which meant I would ask, and think, and consider, till Dorothy's murderer was brought to justice—if it took the rest of my life, which, at that moment, seemed a likelihood.

Even more worrisome was the problem, as unresolved now as on the first day of my investigation, of why Dorothy had been murdered. Too many motives were as bad as too few. And there were far too many. Greedy husbands, money-driven sibling rivalries, jealous mistresses . . . hadn't Dorothy a single friend or protector who wished her well?

I was her friend. She counted on me. I had let her

down once, that first day when I did not stay and insist she talk to me about her problems then and there. But I would not fail her a second time.

I had already walked as far as the Common, and was only another half mile or so from my own home, when I grew aware of footsteps behind me in the thick drizzling twilight, keeping time with my own. I slowed my pace. The footsteps slowed.

And when I turned to look, no one was there.

I walked on, a little more quickly, but not much. I was not given to panic. I listened, picking out the noise that was not part of the rain and the distant booming of the foghorn. A man's steps, heavier than a woman's, the heel of the boot making a thud that echoed slightly. Another sound. Wood knocking against brick and cobble. An umbrella or a walking cane.

He wanted to be unseen, but not unheard. He wanted me to know he was there. He wanted to frighten me.

I sensed his desperation, his anger, now directed at me. If only I could see his face! I was convinced I would see the face of Dorothy's murderer. I turned quickly, just in time to see the tall, dark shape of a man in a black hat and black greatcoat sidestep into a doorway. But when I turned to walk on, the footsteps behind me resumed.

I began to walk faster then, eager to reach the busier streets at the bottom of Beacon Hill, for this part of Boston was isolated and empty, with huge trees looming overhead making the twilight even darker. The fog grew thicker with each step, closing me in, decreasing the distance between myself and him, and my heart began to beat faster. I had driven the beast from his cave. What did he intend to do? A pulse sounded in my ears like a drumbeat . . . and all the while, a different part of my now-frightened consciousness was thinking, *I must remember this sensation and write it down as soon as I am home.*

The bells of a coach sounded, a horse's rhythmic steps, its snorts and breath close by. A carriage! The presence of others—reassured me. I was not alone with a murderer. However, the fog was so thick that the coach might be only a couple of yards away, and I still couldn't see its shape in the gray, wet, moving dusk.

Running footsteps, coming closer. No longer in time with my own. He had made a decision.

Raising the broken umbrella as a defense (a ploy even I laughed at later when telling the story), I spun around in the mist to face him. I struck out with the rattling umbrella, its cloth folds black as bat wings in the twilight, and felt a momentary satisfaction as the tip of the umbrella prodded something soft, flesh perhaps. But the prod was inadequate. I felt a push. I was in the road, stumbling, falling to my knees, the umbrella clattering some feet away, and now I saw the coach almost upon me, the startled horses snapping their heads up, their hooves flashing white. They passed within inches of where I fell, the carriage wheels kicking up stones.

"Damnation!" the driver yelled, pulling on the reins with all his might. The hooves came down inches away from me. The horses skittered sideways, their eyes huge and white with panic.

I instinctively put up my arms up to shield my face, and then began flailing, for another hand pulled at me, lifting me to my feet, and I wondered if he now meant to throw me completely under those frightened horses.

"Miss Alcott! Are you all right? Come out of the road," a familiar voice said. It was Constable Cobban. Even the fog and twilight could not dim the bright red of his hair, the pinkly freckled complexion, and I remembered thinking, at that moment, that a man with Constable Cobban's particular coloring could never attempt secret acts in the dusk, that noon would be as suitable as midnight for him. That aspect of Dorothy's murder had confounded me; she had been struck down in broad daylight.

"Damn foolish thing, walking in the road," the driver of the coach shouted down.

"I wasn't walking in the road. I was pushed." My voice shook a little, which embarrassed me, for Cobban was looking at me strangely.

"Probably a pickpocket," Cobban said. "You shouldn't be out walking alone. Come, I will see you home." He picked up my umbrella and the candy box.

"How do you happen to be here?" I asked. He took my arm, for I was visibly shaken.

"You are trembling. Here, lean on me, Miss Alcott. I was out for a walk. What are you doing out in this weather?"

"I have been to the Wortham home." I did not correct his impression that a common pickpocket had bullied me. However, the fear I felt at the incident and the force of my intuition convinced me the attack was more serious and sinister.

"Ah."

"Yes. Ah. Mr. Wortham came in while I was there."

We walked on together, the coachman having resumed his errand. I noted that the footsteps that had followed me were now gone. Instead, Constable Cobban's gait thudded along with my own lighter steps.

"You have not been following me, have you, Constable?"

He blushed, turning a shade of scarlet visible even in fog. "Of course not," he grumbled.

"Well. Your coincidental arrival is interesting." He did not reply. I tried a different tactic. "I understand that Mr. Wortham's tailor is supplying an alibi?" I pressed.

"An alibi? Miss Alcott, you have been reading the popular press. He is. I suspect that for a fiver, he would say anything."

The popular press. I couldn't hold back a smile, reflecting on what Constable Cobban would think of my blood-and-thunder stories, should he ever read one.

We continued our walk in silence for some moments, the fog creating an eerie sense of isolation about us. My knee was beginning to ache and I suspected it might be cut, but I walked staunchly on without complaint. Abba would see to it once I was home.

"It is a strange world, is it not, Miss Alcott?" Cobban said when we had rounded the corner and begun to climb Beacon Hill. His voice was weary. He might almost have been talking to himself. "My father grew up in County Cork. His father worked a farm there. And one day the landlord came and beat my grandfather so badly he never walked straight again. And there was no one to stop him, for my father and his brothers were just little ones and my grandmother was only a weak woman, and the hired man had run away. So the landlord beat him and beat him and my father could only stand and watch. He tells me that story every week, on Sunday night. So that I'll never forget about the weak ones of the world, who need strong ones to protect them, and the poor who have to be protected from the rich . . ." He pronounced the word *rich* with heavy bitterness. "It comes down to simplicities."

"It seems to me that true justice is anything but simple," I said.

I winced at each step and thought of many things to say but decided against voicing any of them.

"We have no evidence against Mr. Wortham," Cobban concluded when we were almost at my house. His hand at my elbow grew less gentle. "You're partly responsible for that, Miss Alcott. I checked your crab-cake seller. She insists there was no quarreling lady and gentleman that day at the wharf. The information in the anonymous letter was false. And then the writer sent a second letter, admitting he had invented it."

There was anger, frustration, accusation in his voice.

"Would you hang an innocent man?" I protested.

"Are you so certain Preston Wortham is innocent?"

"No. *Innocent* is a word few of us genuinely deserve." Mr. Wortham was a seducer, probably a blackmail victim, but never an innocent. Greedy, yes. But was his greed great enough to resort to murder? "There is much at stake here," I said. "We must be certain, and build a case upon evidence that assists justice rather than tricks it."

"Perhaps you are getting close to that evidence of which you speak. Perhaps, Miss Alcott, you should leave this alone now. It may be dangerous. Your friendship with the Worthams leads you into peril."

"You include Mrs. Wortham, Dorothy, as a danger? Why?" I asked. There had been a note of disgust in his voice.

"It is dangerous," Constable Cobban repeated.

"I dropped a box of bonbons at your office earlier today and asked that it be tested. Did you get that request? How soon will the chemist examine the marzipan?"

"He has submitted a chit for materials for his laboratory, and the testing chemicals must be purchased. It takes time, Miss Alcott. We are a new organization."

"You may give him that box, as well," I said. "The first box was from Mr. Henry Mapp's house. This is from Edgar Brownly's studio. I fear both may contain substances other than those promised by the manufacturer."

Cobban carried the second box of candy a little more gingerly.

"Time," I said, "is something we seem to be running out of."

Several hours after sunset I limped into my home, leaning heavily against my escort, the very pale Constable Cobban.

Abba's eyes opened wide, but she did not scream or swoon, as other mothers might. Instead she helped me into the parlor, where, ashen-faced, I lay down on the sofa.

"Will you have a seat, Mr. Cobban?" Even in a crisis she was polite.

"He must be on his way," I dismissed rather hurriedly. "Thank you, sir, for your assistance." I met his cool gaze.

"Well," he said, clearing his throat. "You are safe now. I'll be on my way."

Chapter Seventeen

Interlude

"It is dangerous," Abba said, wrapping gauze around my skinned and already swollen knee. "Louy, you must stop. Let others resolve this."

"Abba," I responded sadly, "when has danger ever prevented an Alcott from doing his or her duty to the truth?"

Abba, of course, could not respond to that, since her own husband was, almost at that very moment, endangering himself by aiding the fugitive slave Anthony Burns, who had been captured and taken to the courthouse and was probably sitting in the very room that Preston Wortham had recently vacated.

"Then promise you will be more careful, and not take so much on yourself, or at least to have someone with you when you go on these strange errands," Abba pleaded.

"I promise," I agreed. I also promised to spend the next day in bed, for a fierce head and chest cold was already beginning to set in, and what with the newly acquired limp and nascent sniffles and sneezes—moreover, a large purple bruise was taking shape across my forehead—I looked miserable indeed.

Rather than one, I spent several days in bed, fever-

ish and low in spirits. Notes were sent 'round saying
that I was ill and the children should not come for
lessons for the rest of the week. The curtains were
drawn in my bedroom to shut out the gloom, and my
little writing desk in the attic grew dusty from disuse.

It seemed to me that the world and its evil had
bested me. I could not help Queenie, nor could I discover the content of Dorothy's last unspoken message
to me. I had asked every question I could think of,
and I had arrived at a brick wall. There seemed to be
other questions needed to get at an answer, but I did
not know what they were, despite all my pondering.

Even Abba's advice that to discover the nature of
the person was to discover the truth of any situation
seemed to be failing me. What if their nature were
undiscoverable or unformed? Surely there must be
some other way to acquire information about crimes,
other than witnesses, who were unreliable or down-
right liars; other than motives, which could be hidden
or confusing; other than human nature itself, which
was often unpredictable. Pondering was often the only
way to solve crimes, and I speculated about a time
when other means might be at the disposal of the
investigator, perhaps even a trace of identification a
criminal might leave behind at the scene of the crime.

I suspected that someone who wanted more money
had murdered Dorothy, and not someone who merely
wished to buy a loaf to feed a hungry family. A poor
person would have stolen her expensive gold coat and
card case and sold them, but Dorothy had been murdered, not robbed. So, this had been a crime of greed,
not of true need. Nor had she been murdered by a
lunatic; her murderer had been cunning and secretive,
not raving. Moreover, he moved in the upper classes,
not the taverns and brothels of the typical criminal
class. Someone of the lower criminal classes would
never have had the brazen courage to murder her in

broad daylight for fear that his (or her) face would already be known to the constabulary.

How to find such a person, who had acquired a perfect camouflage, who moved through my world and Dorothy's world as confidently and lethally as a lion moved through the plains of the African Serengeti? Who might, in fact, be a friend, or at least an old acquaintance?

Certainly the study of phrenology offered no assistance, for according to that dubious science all people of criminal mentality were low of brow, large of nose, and coarse of complexion. Neither Edgar Brownly nor Preston Wortham possessed the protruding ears and massive jaws, the stooped posture and slouching gait said to mark the true criminal.

Nor were the theories of the alienists particulary useful, for they claimed that crime was a product of a diseased mind, and that the diseased mind was easily discovered by the ravings and bizarre behavior of the lunatic. Mr. Brownly and Wortham were queer, indeed, and certainly of a low moral fiber. But they neither ranted nor raved.

Guilt or innocence was as difficult to establish in 1854 as it was in 1554, when women accused of witchcraft were thrown into ponds to see if they would float or not. Wiser in method, to me at least, was the ancient Chinese practice of putting rice in the accused's mouth; if he spat it forth moist he was innocent, but if it was dry he was guilty, the theory being that fear stops the flow of saliva. But I could not very well parade around Beacon Hill asking the Brownlys, Preston, and everyone else to spit out rice for me.

I realized that most crime began in the mind and stayed its own secret, as unique as each person capable of wanting more than they had, or lusting after a neighbor's wife, or simply enjoying acts of violence against another. Crime, I reflected, was an abnormality of the soul, not the face, or even the social manner and behavior. And to find the criminal I must find the steps, the landmarks that led back to the soul.

For at this time, as I tossed feverishly in bed, drifting in and out of bad dreams, I considered that an added complication had crept into this affair: Constable Cobban.

The Boston Watch and Police was not yet a year old, and there were many in Boston who complained that the tax money spent on it would be thrown away for nothing, that the city should have retained its older, less expensive system of guards and night watchmen, most of whom had been volunteers.

If the new police force could not even solve a domestic murder with plenty of suspects from which to choose, how would they earn their salary? Cobban, I sensed, was determined to find a suspect to try and hang. And if I did not point him in the direction of the truly guilty person, an innocent one might die in his place. There would be two murders, not one.

But I had asked every question that seemed pertinent, and the truth had not revealed itself.

What more was there to ask? What final question would present an answer, a truth?

While I feverishly tossed and fretted at home, Mrs. Milton lost no time spreading word that the Alcott girl had taken to visiting men alone at the docks. It was not long before Abba heard the story making its rounds through Boston, and even I myself soon afterward heard the story from Sylvia.

The one unfortunate consequence, for me, of what my father termed "the unseemly, irrelevant gossip of idle minds" was that Abba insisted I attend the ball announced in Sylvia's honor. I had hoped my illness would excuse me from mundane social tasks, but a combined effort by my parents, and my weakened physical state, forced me to realize I would simply have to make an appearance. Even I grudgingly understood that an entrance at one of the finest balls of the season, in one of the oldest homes of Boston, would help mend the serious rent in my reputation caused by that visit to Edgar Brownly. And even an authoress must give some credence to the importance of reputation.

But while, after the week of my illness, life had returned to normal, I had not. My original sadness over Dorothy's death had given way to a desperate urge to find her killer, and Abba knew I must uncover the answer soon, or it would be lost forever and I would never know, and never fully recover from this particular grief.

"But what question is left?" I asked Sylvia whenever we spoke of Dorothy.

"Other than who did it?" my friend asked, uncomprehending.

"No, Sylvia. The question that will provide the answer to that question. The one I haven't thought to ask, the key."

On the day of the ball, I arrived early, as promised, and a little out of sorts. Sweet, shy Lizzie hadn't wanted to attend the ball. "Poor Louy," she had said in sympathy.

But "Lucky Louy!" May had exclaimed. "I am invited?" May, our butterfly, loved nothing better than dancing and dressing up, but she was too young for a real ball, and Abba had asked her to stay at home that night. Mother and Father were expecting a family of "travelers," and we knew what that meant. The Alcotts were to contribute blankets, a change of clothes, and a food basket, and Abba needed help.

How it rankled with me to have to be away that evening!

Sylvia didn't seem in much better spirits. I could tell

from her expression that she and her mother had fought bitterly over some insignificant detail of the evening. I've noticed that such events, intended to be amusing, perhaps even relaxing, often have the opposite effect.

I took one of the lounge chairs in Sylvia's sunroom and tipped my face up to the uncurtained window with eyes closed. Two weeks had passed since my visit to Edgar Brownly and Wortham, since the "accident" in the street.

"No polkas for me, I'm afraid," I said to Sylvia.

The bruise over my right eye from my misadventure had almost faded, but I still moved with a hint of stiffness in my right knee.

"We will have the band play all waltzes," Sylvia said, sitting next to me. "That won't bother your knee as much."

"I was thinking again of Dorothy," I said. "Not dancing."

"Poor Dorothy." Sylvia leaned back in the chaise and put her arm through mine. "I think for me the truth is just becoming evident. I'll never see her again. That is what death means, isn't it? I mean, unless you are a Spiritist and expect Dorothy to come at night because we are sitting in a circle and holding hands. No, Dorothy would never participate in anything that dubious. I will never see her again."

"And I will never know what happened."

"Surely at some point, Louisa . . ."

"No. Constable Cobban has talked to everyone in the family at least twice, and has come to an impasse in his investigation. The afternoon that Dorothy was murdered, Mr. Wortham was with his tailor until he returned home, and Digby says he did not leave the house again. Edith and Sarah were shopping together until they went to the Wortham home for tea. Miss Alfreda was tending to her sister, Mrs. Brownly."

"Edgar Brownly?"

"He confessed to Constable Cobban that he was with Katya Mendosa. Wisely, I might add. The truth is always better than a lie. Moreover, Miss Mendosa will have less incentive to attempt future blackmail with him, since the affair is already confessed."

"Would she, do you think?"

"That is how such affairs usually end, I believe."

"The family are all accounted for, then," Sylvia sighed. "As well as Katya, who was with Edgar."

"Yes. All accounted for. Though, of course, one or two of them are lying. And we shall never know which." I opened my eyes again and stared unhappily into the muddy landscape outside. The gardener went by just then with an armload of gray pussywillow branches arranged in a pretty blue-and-white vase. There had been a miracle during my two weeks at home recovering from injuries and the Slough of Despond. Spring, finally, had triumphed, the snow and frost had been abolished, and things were growing again. Dorothy had loved pussywillow.

"A tramp has been arrested," I told Sylvia, who did not read the daily papers. "He was sleeping homeless by one of the piers, and the day before Dorothy's murder he had been inebriated and made a commotion of some sort. So now the Boston police have arrested him and charged him with murder."

"Hanging seems an unfair punishment for being homeless and prone to tipple," Sylvia agreed.

"It grows worse. Constable Cobban is beginning an investigation into a new case," I said, rising from my chaise longue. "A prostitute who was murdered on Wharf Street."

"Isn't that near Edgar Brownly's studio?"

"It is. But don't get your hopes up." I smiled ruefully; strange concept to have one's hopes rise at the thought that an acquaintance is a murderer. "There are many artists' studios in that area, many brothels

and taverns, and from what the constable has gathered
so far, the poor girl was not particular in her choice
of clients. Mr. Brownly, if he knew the girl, would
have been one of dozens, I understand."

I sighed again and jammed my hands into my pockets. "No. What this means is not more intelligence
about Dorothy's death, but simply that Constable
Cobban has given up and begun a new investigation,
and a person innocent of the crime of murder may be
hanged. I have this feeling, Sylvia, that he is withhold-
ing something from me, something important. Whenever Dottie's name is mentioned, his eyes get very
hard. And I don't know why." We both stared, perplexed, out the window for a long while. The gardener
passed by again, his arms empty this time. Where had
the pussywillows gone? Perhaps into his own wife's
sitting room. I hoped so. Sylvia's mother could afford
a roomful of orchids; the gardener's wife should at
least enjoy pussywillows.

"Shall we choose our dresses now?" Sylvia asked,
trying to distract me. "Wear the pink dress," she said,
leading me upstairs to her rooms. We were of the
same size, and when necessary I, who could not afford
fancy outfits, borrowed frocks.

"The green, if you don't mind," I answered thoughtfully. "Pink seems a bit lighthearted for me today."

Sylvia rummaged through the piles of lace and silk
laid out on her bed, searching for the green satin. "Do
you think Preston might come, Louisa? He did come
to your house for supper so soon after Dorothy's
death. Mother is so fearful that he might attend, after
all, and ruin her evening."

"Forgive me if this sounds a criticism, but you know
your mother tends to flights of fancy. He is not particularly sensitive, but I don't think Mr. Wortham would
appear at an event where he is blatantly unwanted. I
suspect he wishes a little privacy at the moment, for

despite his many faults he does seem to have had some affection for Dorothy. Are you wearing that? Oh, how lovely, Sylvia."

She held up a white dress embroidered with yellow roses. "Yes, I'm wearing this. And I shall powder. What a scandal there would be if we both went downstairs with powder on our faces!"

"Poor Dorothy would be shocked, too. She had that perfect peaches-and-cream complexion. . . ."

"And that lovely, full figure," Sylvia added. "She never had to sew flounces inside her dresses to fill them out, the way I did. Poor Dottie . . ."

That was, I recalled later, the very last time we put a *poor* before Dorothy's name. After that evening I would be free to remember Dorothy as sweet, as shy, as gentle and loyal; as all the good things she was before she had been made into a victim. My one final question and the all important answer would occur to me in the middle of a fandango.

Chapter Eighteen

Revelation at the Ball

The guests began arriving at five, as was the custom. We would dance for a couple hours, have a buffet supper at seven, and then dance more until ten, or until the last guest disappeared, which was often much later if the champagne and fruit punch were particularly good. Parties required stamina in those days.

Even I admitted to stirrings of enthusiasm as the girls in their glittering party frocks and dancing shoes, and the young man in their evening suits of black jackets with tails to their knees and jaunty bows at the throat, arrived. There was something quite pleasant about seeing girls dressed in their prettiest gowns, with their swansdown boas draped over bare shoulders, or in the case of poor Jennie O'Connel, a thin scarf of possum, and their satin skirts hitched up to show red petticoats. The young men, awed and often bamboozled by such blatant displays of feminine charms, put into practice their oft-rehearsed best manners, some of which even verged on gallantry. When young Robert Baldwin, only a very distant cousin of the piano family, arrived, he left his top hat on a moment too long, and, blushing red with embarrassment, he actually went back out and rang a second time at the bell to repeal that faux pas.

But despite the gaiety of the scene, I could not give myself over to joy.

I stood solemnly in the reception line, a pale, grave young woman in a borrowed green frock, plainly preoccupied with decidely unmerry thoughts. I had dreamed of Dorothy again the night before, of Dorothy in her blue-and-white-striped sport dress and carrying her tennis racket. "You have looked, but you have not seen. See me!" my friend had pleaded. "Louisa, look and see me!"

What was it Dorothy wanted me to see?

"Perhaps," Sylvia suggested, "it was just a dream with no significance."

"Perhaps." I sighed without conviction. "But I have overlooked something. I know I have. There is a strange atmosphere to this evening, Sylvie. I feel it in my bones. Something will happen."

"No more carriages trying to trample us," Sylvia said hopefully. "No more suspicious French bonbons, though Mother suspects all things French."

I had a dance card tied around my wrist with a pink ribbon, as did all the unwed women, but it did not interest me. I did not carefully hold my hand and wrist in midair so as not to crush the card, as did the others, and when a young man asked to put his name down for a waltz I had already lost my little silver pencil.

But when the rooms grew crowded and warm and soft with candlelight, when the band began with a lively rendition of "Buffalo Girls," some of the preoccupation began to lift from my brow. My spirits lifted. My foot tapped and I could not stop it.

By six all the guests had arrived and been greeted, and Sylvia and I were free to dance. There had been some tense moments during those greetings, especially when Mrs. Milton and her daughter arrived and pointedly refused to acknowledge me, for by that time gossip had me running half-clad in the street, chasing

Edgar Brownly, who refused to embrace me, rather than merely leaving his studio with my hat off.

Sylvia smoothed over that awkward moment by announcing, in confidential tones yet loudly enough to be heard, that I was wearing that lovely garnet brooch that Margaret Fuller's family had given me. And since Margaret Fuller upon her death had been a countess, and since Mrs. Milton was a name-dropper of the worst kind, that reminder of my proximity to nobility ended the problem and the gossip.

Robbie Baldwin asked for the waltz—Annie Potter glared in fury—and I was whirled away. Sylvia did not see me much for the rest of the evening, not until suppertime, when we shared a bench as we ate shrimp and oysters and cucumber salad. The window had been opened slightly and I thoughtfully nibbled shrimp as I watched the first spring moths singe their wings in the candle flames. One fell onto my slipper and I bent forward to pick it up, but the insect was dead.

I was breathless, for I had danced often, despite my injured knee.

"The evening is a success," I pronounced without enthusiasm. "Your mother will be so pleased. Have you danced, Sylvia?"

"I have. My toes will testify to that, since I danced with a young man by the name of Christopher Holt, from New York City, who has not yet learned left from right. What he lacks in skill he makes up for in enthusiasm. In fact, if a boy with black hair and black eyes and a jacket too short in the sleeves approaches, you are not, under any circumstance, to relinquish your place on this bench next to me. Promise."

"Dorothy would have enjoyed this so much. Will none of my dearest friends be lucky in love?" I whispered wistfully. The band had been ordered to play calmer tunes during supper for the sake of everyone's digestion, and the sad strains of "I Dream of Jeannie with the Light Brown Hair" now floated through the air. "Perhaps Dorothy was too loyal."

"Have you tried the strawberries, Louy? Do take a plate. But why do you say Dorothy was extreme in her loyalty?" Sylvia said.

"I'm not hungry anymore. Not even for strawberries, though I can't imagine how your mother obtained them, and in such quantity. Money is an amazing thing, Sylvia, in its limitless ability to obtain anything from strawberries to husbands. I speak of Dorothy's loyalty to Mr. Wortham, of course. Despite everything, she seems to have stayed by him. I want so much to ask her why, but I must figure it out for myself."

The black-eyed boy who had outgrown his evening jacket had spied us and was approaching. Quickly we fled back into the candlelit ballroom.

At ten o'clock, after the supper table had been laid waste and the musicians were replaying the tunes of the first hour, just as the first matrons were preparing to leave, we realized the unknown event that we had awaited was upon us.

Constable Cobban was announced by a very startled doorman.

Cobban, blushing and looking extraordinarily uncomfortable, was in the same plaid suit in which he seemed to make all of his appearances. It was a handsome enough suit for ready-made, but Sylvia sighed when she saw him, and I knew what she was thinking: No woman could ever really love a man who had but one suit to his name. He stood in the doorway, lit from behind like garden statuary at twilight, twisting his hat about in his hands and looking furtive.

"Who is that extraordinary young man?" Sylvia's mother asked. The band was playing a lively cotillion and only the hardiest dancers remained on the ballroom floor. Sylvia had finally asked her mother, as courtesy required, to sit with us and have a cup of punch. "Did you invite him, dear?"

"No, Mother."

"Oh, perhaps it is Preston Wortham's driver! Is he here? Is that terrible man here?" She fanned herself so vigorously that the feathers of her boa stirred like palm fronds in a storm.

"I don't see him, Mother. Stay calm." Sylvia gave me a sidelong glance. "I will discover this visitor's purpose and then ask him to leave."

She did no such thing. She gave his coat to a servant and brought him a glass of champagne, which he refused.

"I'm not here for pleasure," he said, and then blushed. "Not that I don't take pleasure in your acquaintance . . . I mean . . ."

With the constable's entrance, the atmosphere of the evening changed. Whereas before it had felt slow, like swimming underwater, now it sped up and felt out of control, like a horse that will not be reined in. I felt the change and looked up to see Constable Cobban's eyes staring directly into my own.

I felt the faintest thrill of fear. The time had come; I felt it in my bones. The final revelation would be made, and I would know Dorothy's story, as surely as if I had told it myself. Somehow this young man had become twisted in the coils of this tragedy, and it was only through him that the truth would be revealed. But I was no longer certain I should know. This inability to let go of the errors of the past could destroy, I thought.

But in that fatal moment, when Constable Cobban and I gazed at each other, truth seemed the only possible good. The cotillion was followed by a slower two-step, and Cobban shyly approached me. I left my little group and gave him my hand so that he could lead me onto the dance floor. The card dangling from the ribbons on my wrist tangled in his fingers; when he did grasp my hand it was with too strong a grip. I cleared my throat, and he relaxed his hold somewhat.

"We meet again," was all he could think of to say. He nervously tried to pat his ginger curls flatter. They sprang back up, forming a kind of halo around his head, a most bizarre effect for a young man hardly worthy of canonization.

"As you seem to have planned, Constable Cobban," I answered with a gentle smile, "since you have not mentioned any urgent business. You have come for the dancing?"

"No. Yes. I mean . . ."

"Let us be friends, shall we?" And I meant just that, though he would not realize it till later.

"I would like that," he said.

As Mr. Cobban was of the school of dancing theory that counts aloud to the music, conversation was somewhat limited. I decided we should sit out the rest of the dance at a table in the card room. The entire party would soon be gossiping about me, since I was walking hand in hand with a young man in a checkered suit, so we might as well sit in the very eye of the storm. Mrs. Milton, fortunately, had already left by that time.

"That evening, two weeks ago . . . when I saw you, and you had fallen into the road . . ."

"I was pushed," I corrected softly. "Evil is omnipresent, Mr. Cobban. You may temporarily lock part of it behind bars, but another part will always walk freely among us. And perhaps the worst part is the unseen, the unknown."

"You always rise to his defense. One would think—"

I interrupted him. "I never defend crime, not even when it is sanctioned by our own government, Mr.

Cobban. If I argue that evil may not stop at Mr. Wortham's front door, I am simply stating a truth as I reason it."

My admonishment made him blush, for he was not fool enough to overlook another fact. "Well," he admitted. "I have been thinking about that evening, that if you didn't trip into the road then you were pushed, and that maybe it wasn't a simple pickpocket who pushed you."

"That idea had also occurred to me."

"And I think you have been useful in this case, and I don't wish you to think me ungrateful, but it is time for you to leave well enough alone," he finished in a rush. "If anything should happen to you, Miss Alcott . . ."

"You have tested the marzipan," I guessed. "Did the chemist's supplies arrive?"

"No. They weren't needed, after all." He stopped and again tried to flatten his copper curls. "His dog found the opened box and ate the last piece, and the powdered sugar as well. The dog is dead, Miss Alcott. There are two murders, Miss Dorothy's and Mr. Mapp's. You must leave this to me. You see, I think there is a fondness between us. . . . I certainly feel fondness, that is, although you have strange friends and I should expect you to see less of them, if you see them at all, after—"

"Mr. Wortham is not so very strange," I said, discreetly leading Mr. Cobban away from the conclusion of his speech, which seemed to intimate that he might wish to take me walking on Sunday morning and perhaps even speak to my father. "He is, as are many criminals, more pitiable than strange, being a person whose ambition exceeds his moral intelligence."

"I was not speaking of Mr. Wortham, for his nature is not at all strange but simply criminal," Constable Cobban said. "I was speaking of his wife, of Mrs. Wor-

tham. I wouldn't have believed you to be friends with
a woman like that, and I hope there are no more like
her in your set."

My heart skipped a beat. With every instinct, I knew
the key was now to be presented. And he did not even
seem to be aware of the significance of this moment.

"What do you mean?" I asked, forcing my voice to
remain calm.

"I mean the baby that was born to her before her
marriage."

"The baby." I repeated the words slowly, as if they
were foreign. And then they took on meaning.

"You did not stay to the end of the autopsy," Cobban said.

"No, I did not stay. I thought Sylvia was going to
faint, so we left. What did I not see, Mr. Cobban?"

"It is common, during a postmortem on a female, to
examine the, uh, the womb." He blushed, but continued.
"Mrs. Wortham had given birth some years before.
Years before she was married. I thought you knew, but
I see now you did not, and I have been clumsy." He
shook his head with disapproval. "The things women
hide from each other. And their families. I'm assuming,
of course, that Mr. Wortham did not know of the child."

"No," I said. "I don't believe he knew." I formed
the words slowly and carefully, tasting their bitterness,
the surprise in them that should not have been a surprise. We had been friends. And I hadn't known. I
hadn't seen. *See me,* Dorothy had said in my dream.

"That is why your friendship with Mrs. Wortham
surprises me. She was a woman of dubious character,"
Cobban said.

I have a temper. I have never lied about this, and
a lifetime of trying to tame it has not been successful.
"Dubious?" I said. "Because she gave birth? You are
a cruel judge, Constable," I said, and my voice was
not sweet. "Do you judge her partner as harshly, or
is the guilt all the woman's?"

He blushed and stammered. "Of course, she was a child herself. She was badly used. . . ."

"Yet you call her 'that woman' and judge her."

We grew awkward with each other. Neither of us knew the way out of this terrible moment. Cobban decided to try a different topic of conversation.

"Too bad for that alibi of Wortham's," he said almost cheerfully. "It seems we have another motive on his part. Wouldn't you say? Money isn't the only motive, Miss Alcott. There is honor and pride and jealousy to consider, and it seems his wife tested him sorely on those points."

"Yes. It would be provoking to learn that Dorothy had had a child earlier and not told him."

"I suppose I could bring him in for more questioning. And check on that tailor of his perhaps. He will admit to the lie."

"Yes. Perhaps. A child . . ." I repeated, still stunned and feeling, in that very moment when society would have me hate and disdain my old friend's very name, more love than I had ever before felt for the gentle, sad Dorothy. Dorothy, with the great sadness, the maternal nature, the full, womanly figure. Oh, what a weight of secrecy had pressed on those tender shoulders!

"Then, too, it's not looking so good for Edgar Brownly," Cobban mused. "His sister had begun her family, it seems, though she kept quiet about it. Even an illegitimate child may be given some legal and familial rights, so there would be more competition for the family fortune."

"The family fortune? Or what remains of it. They are looking distinctly down-at-the-heels to me," I said.

"Perhaps, then, you will relinquish your relations with that entire family," Cobban said. "I would rather you acquired different friends."

I rose from my seat and stepped away.

"Mr. Cobban, it is time for you to leave. Not even

my father dictates my friendships. You overstep. Good night."

Again, the blush and stammer. Then he too rose, turned on his heel, and stalked out.

The rest of the evening seemed a blur. I danced. I attempted small talk and pretended to be interested in the latest styles from Paris. Minutes passed. Hours passed. At midnight, almost at the same time as the stroke of the clock in the hall, I had it figured out, and wondered that I hadn't seen it sooner.

I stood up so quickly my chair fell backward. The lingering whist players in the room where I had sought some calm and quiet looked up, shocked.

Sylvia, who had just arrived with a glass of champagne for me, looked wide-eyed and alert, despite the late hour.

"Sylvia, may I use your mother's coach?"

"I'll have to find Jenkins and have him bring it from the stables. Jenkins is not known for his agility and quickness of pace."

"Then I will run instead," I said.

Chapter Nineteen

The Nursery

I hitched my gown to my knees and charged into the night, forgetful that I had promised Abba to attempt no more errands alone in the dark and trying vainly to ignore the throbbing in my knee. Why had I danced so much? Now I could barely walk, and I was in such a hurry.

In addition to limping, I was completely out of breath from the effort of half running while costumed in a heavy gown, wooden hoop, and thin velvet slippers. But there was an errand that required my immediate attention. The puzzle pieces had been jostling against each other, ready finally to fit into place. Dorothy was going to tell Mr. Wortham about the child. Surely that was what she meant that day when she said, "I must tell him I am in terror. . . ." There was a phrase I remembered from a letter she had sent me from Rome. *God designates one true husband for each woman, and I have been united with mine.* That part of the letter had been splotchy, as if she had been crying. Could there have been a re in front of *united*?

Four blocks from Sylvia's house, a phaeton with two swift horses caught up with me. I cringed, remembering the carriage that had tried to run me down in the fog, but Sylvia waved from the coach and ordered the driver to stop for me.

"I thought your mother's carriage was in the stable?" I asked breathlessly.

"It is. This is Mr. Baldwin's. We have borrowed it. Right, Jenkins?"

The driver grinned and tipped his hat.

"Always at the service of a damsel in distress," he said, revealing that he, too, was a fan of the popular press.

"Then to Mrs. Brownly's house," I said, taking Sylvia's hand and ascending the carriage steps.

Stars shone overhead. The night smelled of spring. But I, deep in thought, was oblivious to everything but the jolting of the carriage and my own thoughts. I took some moments to explain to Sylvia about the baby, Dorothy's child, and then braced myself as we bounced over the cobbles.

The Brownlys' downstairs maid was not pleased to open the door to us at midnight. She stood in the doorway, her hair tucked under an old-fashioned mob, a candle in hand, glaring like a guardian dragon.

"Everyone is in bed. Come back in the morning," she said as she rubbed sleep from her eyes. "Even Master Edgar," she added, inadvertently making it clear that Master Edgar was not accustomed to keeping early or regular hours.

"Tomorrow morning may be too late. I must see Mrs. Brownly now," I insisted. "It is urgent." It must indeed have appeared urgent. I stood there, hatless, my wind-tousled hair and bedraggled silk flowers plastered against my face, my—Sylvia's—green dress dark with dew and stained at the hem from trailing through the puddles that always gathered at the bottom of Beacon Hill even in fine in weather.

"Oh, all right, then." Grudgingly the dragon-maid opened the door wider and led us into the dark front parlor. "Wait here."

The house was in complete darkness, and she lit only a single lamp in the room. We sat closely together within that cold circle of light, not speaking. Sylvia was filled with questions but knew she must wait a bit longer for the answers, for I had such a look of studious concentration on my face she dared not interrupt my thoughts.

As we waited, I observed the condition of that parlor and saw in the light of the solitary lamp that the curtains were mothy, the carpet stained. There, against the window overlooking the garden, was the blue-and-white sofa, the one that Mrs. Brownly could not recover in yellow paisley because of the expense. I saw the brighter patches of wallpaper where pictures had been removed.

The furnishings were long past the point of replacement, and not even the argument that goods were not as well made as they were fifty years before could justify the negligence of this room and its appointments. The Brownly fortune was being spent elsewhere. Following my eyes, watching the speculation flicker in her subtle changes of expression, Sylvia opened her mouth, unable to postpone the questions. I held a finger before my lips, indicating she was not to speak.

A quarter of an hour later Mrs. Brownly came down in her nightclothes, looking stern and forbidding despite the frilled white lace cap and voluminous chenille robe. She gave Sylvia a chilly greeting, but when she saw me sitting there, her expression changed. The formidable Brownly matriarch suddenly looked like a tired old woman.

"You have a reputation for perspicacity." She sighed. "I knew you would be back, Miss Alcott. Return to bed, Mary," she said to the maid who stood behind her. "I will handle this." With a parting angry glance, the maid turned and disappeared into the dark hall.

"May I see Agnes?" I asked gently after a few minutes, when the sound of the maid slapping upstairs to the attic in her slippers died away. "I won't wake her," I promised. "I merely wish to see her."

Sylvia looked questioningly at me, but knew that to interrupt my train of thought at that moment would be useless. Biding her time with increasing impatience, still Sylvia kept quiet.

Mrs. Brownly, however, did not share her confusion. She nodded and sighed once again. There was weary resignation in her eyes, but a note of relief in the sigh.

"What a burden such a secret must be," I whispered.

"We shall go upstairs then, and you may see my burden," Mrs. Brownly said.

She carried the lamp. We followed, making slow progress through the dark halls and up several flights of stairs. It was an eerie journey through a house and a family history we had thought we had known and now realized we had not.

At the top floor, night-lights burned in several niches, and I remembered sharing a bed with Anna, telling secrets in the darkness, knowing Mother was just steps away. This child had no such comfort.

"Here," Mrs. Brownly said, opening a door.

The nursery still smelled of cough syrup and menthol steam, although it was weeks now since Agnes had fallen into the water down by the docks.

"She has weak lungs," Mrs. Brownly whispered, leaning over and gently pulling a cradled cloth doll from the sleeping girl's face. We stood in a circle around Agnes's little bed, and looked down.

"Just as Dorothy had as a child. Poor thing," Mrs. Brownly added.

And there she was, with her little button nose, white-blond hair, pale face. Sylvia finally saw what I had already known we would see . . . that startling resemblance to Dorothy, a resemblance we had been willing to accept as a sisterly one, when all along it had been a child looking like her mother. Dorothy's daughter. *See me,* Dorothy had said in the dream.

"So like Dorothy," I whispered, and with the lightest of touches stroked the child's blond curls.

"Yes. Very like Dorothy. No sign of the father, whoever he might be. Dorothy never said," Mrs. Brownly added, and her voice was bitter.

"Else the father would have known about the child," I whispered. "He did not know."

I leaned closer to the sleeping child, holding my breath so that she would not be disturbed. Agnes seemed to be dreaming. A sweet smiled played across her pale mouth. Dorothy's child. My heart swelled with love. While children could be tedious in the classroom, I have always loved them, and my bond with Dorothy's child was instant and lifelong.

Leaning closer, delighting in the warmth of the child's even breath on my face, I saw the locket around Agnes's neck. It was a tawdry souvenir piece, ten-karat gold already wearing thin, with a picture of the Pantheon engraved on it.

"Dorothy brought it back from Rome for her. Agnes will not take it off. She lost it one day and was inconsolable till it was found again . . . well, we'd better continue this downstairs."

Mrs. Brownly made the tea herself, rather than wake the maid. It was a conversation she wished no one to overhear. The entire house and the city around it slumbered, finally, and we had the eerie night sensation of being the only alert people in a world of sleepers. We sat in the kitchen, close to the stove, where stoked embers gave some warmth against the night.

"I will do that," I protested when I saw the stately Mrs. Brownly stoop to put a scoop of coal into the stove.

"My dear," the older woman said, "you can't imagine how I have longed to do that for the past three decades. I grew up on a farm, you know. One of ten. My favorite chore was loading the stoves . . . oh, the noise the coal makes as it slides down the scoop and lands in the embers, and just for a second the room lights up like midsummer evening with its fireflies. But once Mr. Brownly made his fortune . . . well, those chores were beneath me, he said. We had maids to do everything. And most of them couldn't do their chores half as well as I." She smiled. Then she remembered where she was, and why I was there, and her face grew stern once again.

"You will have questions," she said, carefully putting a chipped Limoges teapot on the table. And then, "That color suits you, Louisa. I approve. Did the dance go well? I know how desperately Sylvia's mother wishes her to wed." She gave my friend a pitying look. "I myself have forgotten, if I ever knew, why it is we mothers are so eager to marry off daughters." She sighed and stirred sugar into her tea, but did not lift the cup to drink. Instead she folded her thin, arthritic hands on the table in a posture close to prayer.

"The dance was charming," I began softly. "But Constable Cobban dropped by to say hello. It was he who told me Dorothy had given birth some years earlier."

"Ah. The young man with that terrible red hair. Information discovered at the postmortem, I suppose. I begged them to leave poor Dorothy alone."

"Yes."

"And you understand why I wished it to be kept secret."

"Yes. But keeping that secret must have been devastating for Dorothy."

"Yes. No." Mrs. Brownly sipped her tea and

thought for a moment. "The true devastation began when Dorothy was fifteen, and seduced in Newport. You remember that summer, Louisa. You, too, Sylvia. The three of you went boating together in the afternoons."

"I remember," I answered, and I thought of Dorothy, her pale hair loose on her shoulders, laughing and trailing her hands in the water and then falling silent and dreamy-eyed in the middle of her sentences.

"She loved him, the foolish child, and she never named him. There she was, beginning to swell up, and she would not even tell us his name. She said he had not truly loved her, so she would not force him to marry her." Mrs. Brownly sighed again. "Love. You young people think too much of love. But how brave Dorothy was. She never wept, you know. Not then." A smile of pride played across the mother's tired face.

"So you took her to Rome," I said. "To have her baby in secret."

I heard a clock ticking in the hall. Time passing. Life and death, second by second. So many secrets in this house.

"Yes. And when the baby was born in Rome, Dorothy . . . Well, the birth affected her greatly. Motherhood often does. She threatened to throw herself in the Tiber if I did not bring the child back with us, so she could be raised in Boston, where she might be close to her. I had planned to leave her with a Roman family. A noble family, though much reduced in circumstances. They would have raised Agnes well. But Dorothy insisted. Oh, how she clung to that baby when we tried to part them. Clung and wept and shouted. She gave me no choice. I had never known her capable of such passion."

Mrs. Brownly sighed and chewed on a nail, and for a brief moment I saw that farm girl from long ago. Then she remembered herself and folded her hands

in her lap. "Edgar saw at once, of course, when we
brought the child back. He was older, knew more of
the world. He saw immediately that Agnes was Dorothy's child, not mine, as we claimed."

"But you decided to raise the child as your own
rather than send her to another family. Dorothy must
have been grateful."

Mrs. Brownly smiled, perhaps remembering how
her granddaughter had burrowed into her daughter's
chest, perhaps remembering her own passion for her
children. "I had grown fond of her, too, you see.
Edgar was displeased, of course. But then, he couldn't
very well give orders to his own mother. He tries.
Oh, how he tries. But I made the decision and that
was that."

So many things were now comprehensible: Dorothy's sudden departure for the continent, her personality change when she came back, the way she had of
seeming preoccupied, older than the other girls of her
set. To be a mother at sixteen, to have to deny the
child, all to suit the harsh and arbitrary norms of society. And that terrible animosity between sister and
brother.

"How sad," I whispered.

"Yes. How very sad," Mrs. Brownly agreed. "And
now Dorothy is dead and I wonder sometimes how
the world grew so cruel. It didn't used to be. I almost
lost Agnes, you know."

"When Agnes fell into the water at the docks, it
was Dorothy who rescued her, wasn't it? That's why,
when she came home that afternoon before the tea
party, she was wearing a new set of clothes, to replace
the ruined ones."

"Yes." Mrs. Brownly nodded. "That's how it happened. When she returned home from the tour of Europe she came here almost every day to see Agnes.
She had missed her so. She told Wortham she was
going shopping, or visiting. When she came that day

and learned that that foolish nurse had taken the child out, she was terrified. She had discovered, you see, that the nurse had a male friend who was a ship's factor, and the woman liked to spent time at the harbor, though I had forbidden it. She didn't watch the child closely."

"Was that the day Agnes lost her locket, Mrs. Brownly?" I asked, cupping my hands around the hot cup of tea. The embers in the stove were dying down, and the kitchen was growing cold.

Mrs. Brownly looked at me with dawning admiration. "How quickly you see things as they are. Yes. The child was brought back here, soaked to the skin and already feverish. I told the nurse not to bring her to the docks. . . ." Mrs. Brownly was beginning to repeat herself, and growing increasingly distraught.

"The nurse was let go." I remembered my earlier visit to this house, the complaints of the maid that the nurse was to leave, and so there would be more work for everyone else.

"Yes." Mrs. Brownly nodded. "I had been displeased with her even before I discovered she was spending her afternoons at the dock. She spent her weekly evening off at the theater, though I had forbidden that as well. I don't like members of my household to waste their time and money in such places. Not at all. Was Agnes sleeping soundly, Louisa? I don't remember. Perhaps I should go back upstairs."

"She was sound asleep, Mrs. Brownly," Sylvia said gently. "Drink your tea. It will warm you."

"After Agnes was carried home," Mrs. Brownly continued, "we gave the child a hot bath and doused her with syrup, and then Dorothy saw the locket was gone."

"And that's why Dorothy went back to the docks the next day. To see if she could find the locket. She discovered it. . . ." I finished.

"She found it, and sent it back with her maid. I

never saw her again. That was the day my poor girl was murdered."

Mrs. Brownly closed her eyes with grief, but did not allow herself to cry.

I reached over and touched her hands. We sat in silence for a long while. But it was not yet over. There was more to be said, more to be brought into the light.

"You and Dorothy were being blackmailed," I said gently but firmly.

Mrs. Brownly withdrew her hands from the table, where I had put mine over them for comfort. She tried to pick up her teacup, but her hands trembled so severely she had to place it back in its saucer.

"Your mother always boasted you were clever. Yes. It began just after we returned from Rome. A letter, a plain envelope, no return address, no name. Only instructions. He said he had proof, eyewitnesses who had seen Dorothy in Rome. She went out very little, but I could not very well lock her in her room. The doctor there said she must have mild exercise or else."

Mrs. Brownly did not need to finish. I already knew firsthand what a delivery could be like for a girl who was not in excellent health at the beginning of labor.

"Dorothy would go out walking at twilight, in the Trastevere, where the other Americans did not go. Still, she was seen by someone, some American who knew who she was, and not even the largest cloak can hide that condition in its last months."

"May I ask how much money he required of you?"

"Fifty dollars every month."

Fifty dollars. What many workers earned in a year. And they had been paying it since Dorothy returned from Rome years before. No wonder the draperies were moth-eaten.

"A fortune," Mrs. Brownly said. "But there were Sarah and Edith to consider, as well as Dorothy. Their reputations were also at stake. You know how society can be, Louisa. The sins of one sister would ruin all three. And perhaps Edgar as well, though I wonder if there is much of his reputation left to save."

"And where was the blackmail money paid?" I asked.

"I was to go to Trinity Church on the first Wednesday of the month at eight o'clock and sit in the fourth pew of the left side, and leave it there. I left it without ever looking behind me, though I imagined sometimes I saw a man in a greatcoat, a tall man, occupy that pew as soon as I left."

I began to pace, hands behind my back, chin leading forward, deep in thought, fitting all the pieces together.

"I believe Dorothy was going to openly claim Agnes as her own, Mrs. Brownly. Dorothy had decided to let it all come into the open, so that she might have her daughter with her. But if she did, the blackmailer would lose his hold over her . . . and over you. That's why she was murdered."

"That was what I feared," Mrs. Brownly said. She looked up and what had a moment before been a glance of distracted age and sad motherhood was now a look of such hatred that Sylvia and I flinched before it.

"Or perhaps the blackmailer had found a new and easier way to claim the entire inheritance. Perhaps he married Dorothy. And then murdered her," Mrs. Brownly said, and her voice trembled with rage. "But we caught him in his own trap. Not a penny."

"You think Preston Wortham was the man blackmailing you?" I asked.

"He had such an evil reputation, and he showed strange interest in Dorothy. And one day, when I visited them, there was mail to be posted in the hall. I . . . looked. An envelope addressed to . . . to Edgar. I knew the handwriting, for I had received a similar envelope. From the blackmailer. He has been black-mailing Edgar as well, hasn't he, Louisa? Oh, I know Edgar thinks he has secrets from me. About the studio. About the women who come and go. Of course. Do you think Mrs. Milton could resist repeating such gossip, even to his own mother? And his own brother-in-law is now blackmailing him."

"I admit Mr. Wortham's reputation is bad. But is it possible that he might have truly loved Dorothy? And having loved Dorothy, wished no ill for her family?" I asked.

"Love. That word again."

I took a deep breath. "Mrs. Brownly, I believe Preston Wortham is the father of Agnes. That was why Dorothy insisted on marrying him once he finally returned her affection and proposed. She had been in love with him for years, since that summer in Newport. I don't think she ever loved anyone else. It was her nature to be faithful."

Mrs. Brownly and Sylvia stared at me in amazement. "Preston? Agnes's father?" they said simultaneously.

"Wortham is the father?" Mrs. Brownly repeated. "Then he killed his wife, the mother of his child. Oh, the devil." She slumped forward in her chair, collapsing.

"Mrs. Brownly, let me ring for your maid. I don't want to leave you alone, but I have another task to see to. And I need Sylvia. Your family is still not out of danger."

I pulled the bell cord and waited for Mary to come back down, to sit with her mistress, and the wait seemed an eternity, for I sensed, with an infallible instinct, that the continued danger to the family I had spoken of was real and imminent.

Jenkins was enjoying himself that night, for his second set of instructions was to rush at top speed, even if he risked loosening a wheel.

"Where to, misses?" he asked.

"I will go to Preston Wortham's house on Commonwealth Avenue. And then you and Miss Sylvia have a different errand. You must find Constable Cobban and bring him to me at Wortham's. As quickly as possible," I said.

"Giddap, Bessie," Jenkins shouted gleefully to the horse, cracking the whip over the animal's head. Her ears twitched with irritation, but she once again paced herself for a trot and we jolted through the night over the rain-slick cobbles.

Chapter Twenty

A Culprit by Any Other Name

Wortham's Commonwealth Avenue mansion was completely dark when I arrived. I hesitated before the heavy front door. Instinct told me to wait for Cobban, but sense told me there was no time to be lost. There had been that packed, half-hidden valise, the emptying of the house of most of its rented furnishings. I raised my hand and lifted the brass ram's-head knocker, bringing it down heavily against the door.

No one answered. I stepped back into the street and looked up. Yes, there was a light coming from a second-floor window.

My sense of urgency grew even stronger. I took the door handle in my hand and tried it. It was unbolted.

I opened the door and peered into the long, dark hall. Drizzle and fog swirled into the entrance, making the unlit interior even darker. I waited a moment for my eyes to adjust, and when they did the first object I recognized was the luminous fur collar of Preston Wortham's Roman coat hanging on the coatrack. His gleaming beaver hat rested on the table.

So the escape had not yet been effected; surely he would not leave that coat and hat behind. But why did Wortham or Digby not attend to the unbolted door? Perhaps because he knew I had discovered his secret. Perhaps he was waiting for me, as he had waited for Dorothy, at the docks.

My heart was pounding so loudly I rocked slightly with the force of it as I stood absolutely still in that hallway, almost in the very place where Dorothy had stood that day she had come home, that day he had lied and said she had gone out to replace her lost Paris chapeau.

He had known that Dorothy had gone to visit her daughter, that she was getting braver and weary of living the lies, and soon would claim the child as her own. He had stood there, in that parlor off to the side, and thought, I will kill her. I shivered.

I waited a minute longer, hoping to hear the clatter of Jenkins's carriage out front in the deserted street, and Cobban coming up the front steps. Through the still-opened door came the sound of a dog barking at some other night disturbance, the fog making it sound hollow and very faraway. There was no sound of carriage wheels coming over the cobbles. No other noise disturbed the night. I was alone with whatever evil cowered in this dark house.

"Mr. Wortham?" I called, gently at first and then louder. "Mr. Wortham?" No answer. Digby did not respond to my call, either. I shifted my weight and a board creaked underfoot.

Perhaps he had fled after all, leaving that fine coat behind.

Pressing through the darkness, my hands before me like a sleepwalker, I moved deeper into the hall, near the twin arched doorways, one of which led into the dining room, the other into the front parlor. The room was cold and silent as a tomb; not even embers glowed in the fireplace. Beside a pile of torn newspapers on the mantel I found a candle and matchbox. I won-

dered what it would be like to tear paper into kin-
dling strips and see a front-page box of yourself with
the announcement *Murderer!* under it. The scratch
of the match striking the sandpaper on the side of
the tin box was startlingly loud, since all else was
so quiet.

By candlelight I saw that the room was almost emptied, the few remaining pieces of furniture draped with
cloths. But the packed valise was still there. He hadn't
left yet.

The emptiness had a strange feel to it.

And I knew then, with all of my senses alert and
in alarm, that he was watching me, waiting. I realized now how vulnerable I was, standing in the surrounding darkness, made visible with that candle in
my hand.

Quickly I blew out the candle and moved closer to
the wall, sheltering at least my back from the attack
I knew was to come. For underneath those perfect
manners, that suave calmness, was the nature of a
murderer, and I had come to accuse him, to stop him
from leaving before justice could be done. And he
would try to stop me.

Where were Cobban and Sylvia? Why didn't they
hurry?

My silk skirt rustled in a sudden draft and I pressed
closer to the wall. A door had been closed somewhere.
I peered into the darkness, and as I shifted my weight
a board creaked underfoot, the same board that had
creaked under my foot in the hallway. He had closed
the front door, locking me in.

I stood statue-still again, waiting. Another board
creaked, closer.

"I know you're here." I spoke into the darkness,
forcing my voice to be steady. "Let us talk and make
an end of this. It is over. You can do no more harm
to that family. You must leave them in peace now."

"It is indeed over," a man's voice whispered in the darkness. "I don't hope you expect gratitude from me, Miss Alcott."

"Redemption is yet possible. Evil can be turned away," I whispered, for I knew he was very close, and coming closer. Yet another board creaked and I heard the stiff leather crackle of his polished shoes, smelled the rich fragrance of imported French cologne.

"Redemption!" He stepped in front of me, looming, a figure darker than the darkness of night because of his black suit, and I realized too late that the wall that had protected my back now entrapped me. I was too far from the front door; I would never reach it in time.

I raised my hand and the candlestick it held, attempting a defense.

Effortlessly, as though I were no more than a child playing with forbidden toys, he forced the candlestick from my grasp. I felt his fingers, gloved, powerful, strong enough to circle my throat, to strangle Dorothy's throat, the windpipe broken . . . that hand closed over my own, taking me prisoner.

"Redemption," he repeated, stepping close enough now that even in the darkness I could see his face.

He raised the candlestick.

"No," I said. He still held the candlestick in midair, poised to strike me down, and I knew a blow of that heavy silver against my head could be lethal. How to stop him? Not physically. *No, think*, I instructed myself. *His nature. What is his nature? Vanity. He is vain and proud.*

"You were so clever," I said quietly. "You had so many people fooled and terrified for so long. You had such power over them."

The hand holding the candlestick lowered an inch. "It could have gone on longer," he said after a moment. "Why did you interfere? I warned you."

"Why Dorothy?" I asked.

"She was an opportunity. A good businessman never misses an opportunity." The candlestick came within inches of my head, but crashed into the wood paneling behind my right ear. I felt the cold breeze of it, heard the wood splinter, but knew he hadn't missed. He hadn't meant to hit me. He wanted to strike me down, but was unable, for the moment, at least. Why? Because for the first time he could talk freely? Perhaps I was simply not a good business opportunity. Perhaps his nature, for all his crime, was not yet thoroughly calcified, and murder came harder to him than he expected.

I sensed an opportunity for life, for escape. Talk. Words.

"You followed me . . . that night in the street . . ." I said, keeping my voice as calm as possible, trying to draw him out.

"I apologize for the push. Very bad manners, I know. But necessary. You ask so many questions, Miss Alcott." He wrenched the candlestick out of the wood paneling and raised it once again. His black-clothed arm was silhouetted in the darkness, his mourning coat darker than the night itself. And the very hand that had killed Dorothy was now raised against me. The silver candlestick gleamed.

"Tell me about Dorothy, about Mrs. Wortham," I said. "Tell me how you knew."

"I suspect you already know all there is to know about Mrs. Wortham, and what happened that day," he said. The candlestick was still raised, ready to strike.

"Tell me anyway," I said. "I'm sure there are things I have overlooked."

"You think me a fool," he sneered. "You and your kind have looked down your noses at me for far too long. But I have a long journey ahead of me, so I must excuse myself, Miss Alcott."

His nature—vain, but also with a strong sense of practicality. The night was disappearing, and the day must find him elsewhere.

The candlestick finished the arc of its swing and I saw that this time it would not land in the wood paneling. My vision filled with exploding red, and then black. My last thought was that he would get away. We hadn't been in time.

Ten minutes later, Sylvia, Cobban, and Jenkins found me crumpled on the parlor floor of the empty Wortham mansion. Fog-thinned moonlight glistened on a trickle of red running down my forehead and over my left cheek. My hands were ice-cold, but something was tickling my nose.

"She's breathing," Cobban said, taking away the feather with which he had ascertained that fact. In the confusion of throbbing but renewed consciousness I wondered if he always carried a feather in his pocket for just such a reason, and how strange the life of a constable must be.

Cobban, aided by Jenkins, carried me to the cloth-draped couch and chafed my wrists while Sylvia fetched a vial of salts from her reticule and held it under my nose. I sneezed fiercely and flailed at the air.

"No, no," Cobban said gently, holding my wrists to restrain me, "you are safe, Miss Alcott; you are with friends."

"Have you got him?" I asked, staring about wild-eyed. "Is he here?"

"Don't move so quickly," Constable Cobban said. "Lie back down, Miss Alcott, or you'll faint."

"I don't faint," I protested. "Not unless someone thwacks me on the head. Have you stopped him?"

Jenkins cleared his throat. "If you mean the gent that rushed down the street past us and almost knocked me over, why then no, we don't have him, miss."

"We didn't think to grab him. We were just thinking of you," Sylvia said somewhat apologetically.

I sighed heavily and lay back down, rubbing my forehead. "Gone," I said. "Why didn't you go after him?"

"Don't worry," Cobban said. "He won't get far. We'll send telegrams to all the stations and ports with his description, and Wortham will be in custody by tomorrow evening."

"Wortham?" I sat up again.

At that very moment we heard a groaning rise from somewhere deep in the back rooms of the house.

Cobban cocked his head to one side, listening.

"Isn't it Preston whom we must pursue?" Sylvia asked, thoroughly confused.

"That is Wortham you hear now," I said with weary patience. "It is Digby who has made good his escape."

"Digby?" said Cobban, Jenkins, and Sylvia in unison.

I held my head and rubbed at the lump on my forehead. "Of course. Jenkins, you must report this immediately to the night watch, and give the officers a description of Wortham's manservant, Digby. Tall, black-haired, dark-eyed. He will, again, be wearing Wortham's own hat and coat. He has a penchant for borrowing his employer's items of clothing. He may be traveling with a female companion."

And so Jenkins went off again into the night to make a report, as a confused Sylvia and Constable Cobban helped me search the mansion.

We found Wortham locked in the back pantry. He was bound and gagged and was more in need of smelling salts than I, for even after he was released from his ropes his teeth chattered with fear.

"Oh, Mr. Wortham." I sighed, stroking back the hair from his forehead. He, like I, had a bleeding gash on the side of his head and a black eye as well, and bruises about the mouth.

Preston grinned ruefully, relief lightening the pain of his injuries. "You don't know the worst of it. He was going to murder me; I have no doubt of it. But then he heard a noise—you, Miss Alcott—so he left me for the moment. You saved my life."

"Digby," Cobban said, still piecing it together. "Of course. He would have murdered you, I have no doubt, had not Miss Alcott arrived and provided a distraction. Though I do wish you had waited for me," Cobban said, frowning.

"I couldn't. I knew he was about to fly and there was no time to lose."

"Digby?" Sylvia repeated.

"Yes," I said. "All the signs were there; it just took me time to see them. Who else is better situated to blackmail someone than a trusted employee?"

"I need not ask what he was blackmailing you about, considering your reputation." Cobban looked harshly at Wortham.

"No. You need not ask. Especially not in front of ladies. But to murder Dorothy just to further terrorize me . . . Wasn't it enough that he forced me to take him into service, into my very household, where he went through my income with an ease even I could not manage? But why murder Dorothy?"

"You really do not know," I said, shaking my head.

"No. But something in your voice tells me I will need the swooning couch in a moment." Wortham's battered face grew yet more somber.

"Be brave, Mr. Wortham," I said. "You suspected it yourself. There was another person in Dorothy's life, and Digby was blackmailing her."

Wortham grew so pale the blood on his forehead seemed black against the whiteness of his skin. He drew his lips into a tight, furious line and was unable to speak. He was the very image of that dreadful dime-novel terror, the jealous husband who discovers his wife has loved another. For a moment he looked truly capable of murder.

I pressed forward, eager now to say all that needed to be said, all that had been kept in darkness, all that had harmed this family so terribly.

"That other person was a child, Mr. Wortham. Dorothy had a child. Digby had been blackmailing her as well, and her mother, Mrs. Brownly. He murdered Dorothy because she was going to tell the father about her past and bring the child into her home. The blackmail would end."

"A child?" he said.

"Mr. Wortham, the child was your own. Agnes." There. I had said aloud what had been kept hidden for six years. A deep sense of relief washed over me. I sensed that Dorothy would have been pleased.

"Mine?" he asked, stunned.

"Yours. From that summer in Newport. Did you really think that, once in love, Dorothy would ever be disloyal, or forget that love? There was no other man coming between you, only a little girl whose mother had been forbidden to acknowledge her."

Wortham looked faint . . . as would any man who learned he has a six-year-old daughter, not a six-year-old sister-in-law.

"My child," he repeated in a kind of stupor.

We left Wortham in his emptied mansion. The news of his child had overpowered his physical pains and agitation. "A child," he kept repeating to himself, running his fingers through his hair.

With Jenkins off to file a report, Sylvia and I had no choice but to walk home, despite our exhaustion and my bloody gash. Cobban offered to escort us, and since it was late and I was dizzy, I accepted his offer.

"That makes it a different matter altogether," he admitted with an apologetic smile as we closed the door behind us and went again into the night. "Wortham was the father and she married him."

But I remembered what he had said earlier that evening, that cutting comment about "a woman like that."

"Indeed," I said somewhat coolly. "Does Dorothy meet your standards now, Constable?"

He blushed fiery red and mumbled that perhaps he was harsh in his statements about young Mrs. Wortham's character, but I was still concerned with a more immediate matter.

"Do you think Jenkins has arrived at the station yet?" I asked, sorry now that I had not gone along with him and unwilling to admit that my head injury was causing me some distress. I could walk only with assistance.

"Most likely. As soon as you are safely home, I'll go to the station and file my own report. We'll find Digby. Don't worry," Cobban said.

Abba was a light sleeper, well used to late-night knocks on the door. She sighed and shook her head under its crooked, old-fashioned lace nightcap and went to fetch a bundle of gauze for my wounds. On the hall table was the basket of food and clothing prepared for the "travelers" and I hoped Cobban would not remark upon them. He did not, or at least pretended not to see them.

"Is it over yet, Louisa?" Abba asked. "You can't take much more, I fear."

"It is almost over. Now we can only wait and see if Digby is caught."

"Thank God," she said. And then, "Digby? I would never have thought."

"Good night, Constable," I said, holding my hand out to him. "Thank you for your help. Now file your report and make sure Jenkins is safe."

"Good night, Miss Alcott. Louisa . . ."

Abba gave him a sharp glance for that intimate use of my given name. He backed out the door and disappeared into the night.

Chapter Twenty-one

The Business Concludes

"Sylvia, what do you think of our Dorothy now?" It was a week later, and Abba had finally allowed me to resume my much-missed walks. The sun was shining, and spring seemed truly, finally, on its way. We were back at the Smokers' Circle and I was discreetly studying the men and the gray clouds of smoke they blew.

"That she was braver than I ever suspected. What she went through . . ."

"Yes. And for love of Wortham."

"The world is a strange place, isn't it, Louisa?"

"It is. Strange, and too often unjust. Sometimes, though, there is justice, Sylvia. Divine justice." For Digby had not been captured, yet he had been stopped. In his hurried flight he had pressed a hired cab to an unsafe speed, and had been overturned on the road leading south, to New York. He probably had planned to board a ship there under an assumed name and make his escape back to Europe, where he had first noticed the young American heiress, Dorothy Brownly, unwed at that time and plainly pregnant.

Digby's body had been crushed in the accident. His traveling valise had been filled with gold and silver

coins, Brownly and Wortham wealth both, mixed together. His traveling companion, Katya Mendosa, was
only sightly injured. I had visited her in the hospital
the day she received the good news that the family
was not going to press charges against her.

" 'Ardly out of charity," she had snipped, her Latin
accent completely gone and the Irish brogue thick as
soup. "They just don't want it in the papers."

Her child was with her that day, a pretty little girl
with Wortham's dark eyes and long limbs. She had
the brown complexion of a child raised in the country,
probably in a humble foster home. I was happy to see
mother and child reunited, even if some of the money
that enabled the reunion was ill-gotten.

"I have to admit that in this case, as in many, divine
justice is better than the man-made variety," Sylvia
said. "Think of what the trial would be like, when all
those secrets would come to light, all those old wounds
would be reopened."

Mrs. Brownly certainly seemed relieved that the
matter was concluded without a trial.

"She is still protecting Dorothy's reputation," I said.
"For Agnes's sake, if not her own. Justice is not always about punishment, but about ending a reign of
terror," I mused that day. "If only we could convince
the plantation owners of that."

We had just visited Agnes earlier that morning and
played a rousing game of blindman's buff with her,
for her congestion was finally passing and she was in
good health again. With the blindfold over her eyes,
twirling about, hands before her, she had reminded us
so much of Dorothy as a child that we had both shed
a tear. But they had been happy tears, for it seemed
we had not completely lost our friend.

"I should have seen it sooner," I said, walking with
my hands clasped behind my back. I had brushed my
hair lower than usual over my forehead to hide the

plaster over the blue-and-red gash left by the candle-stick, and I had spent an amusing hour with my schoolchildren, making up stories about how I had acquired that injury.

I sniffed contentedly at the spring air. "All the signs were there years ago. Dorothy's personality change, her sudden maturity and preoccupation, even the way her figure changed. Motherhood was the only explanation. And I completely overlooked it."

"What mystifies me is how Preston could have over-looked it," Sylvia said. "I suppose that as the very self-involved person he is, all those signs you noticed he would not have noticed simply because he did not wish to. He visited me this morning, you know. He is leaving Boston. Can't say that I blame him. He has not exactly been warmly welcomed in society. Going west, I believe, upon the advice of Horace Greeley."

Preston Wortham had made the front lines of the morning edition one last time, the day before, as his innocence in the murder of his wife had been declared.

"Is Mr. Wortham taking Agnes with him?" I asked, thinking then of the child I had come to know and love, and of Sylvia's cousin, who had broken off all his social connections except those of immediate family.

"No. He has agreed to leave her with Mrs. Brownly for the time being. She requested that, and he readily agreed. Fatherhood will not suit him, especially with-out Dorothy to prop him up."

"Someday Agnes will have to know," I said. "She needs to know what a wonderful person her mother was, how brave."

"Yes. But I need to know, Louy. How did you de-cide upon Digby as the blackmailer and murderer?"

I smiled. "Little things at first. His shoes were much too expensive for a valet's. That was the first aspect of Digby that made me consider. Vanity in not uncom-mon in gentlemen's gentlemen, but to have the financial resources to act on that vanity . . . that is rare. And he had a strange effect on Wortham, and Miss Alfreda seemed absolutely afraid of him. I suspect she somehow had discovered his identity and he had been blackmailing her as well."

"Miss Alfreda?" Sylvia asked, more than a little surprised. "Whatever for?"

"Sylvia, she has not always been old. I suspect as a young woman she had her share of indiscretions and incautious moments . . . perhaps even more than her share, since she seems to read only romances. She has lived, and not always wisely, I'm sure, and she does have that penchant for pocketing expensive little items when she thinks no one is looking. The day I went to Wortham's house to fetch his wardrobe items, she was just leaving, remember. Perhaps she had gone to plead with Digby to relinquish his hold over her, to give up whatever old letters or personal history he used for blackmail."

Sylvia fell silent. She seemed perplexed by the notion of Alfreda Thorney as young and passionate. I continued.

"And then the Worthams and the Brownlys seemed, for all their wealth, to be having difficulty with their finances," I continued. "That sofa that Mrs. Brownly could not re-cover, the moth holes in her curtains . . ."

"And Dorothy and Preston quarreled over money that day of the tea party. He criticized her for hat shopping or some such thing."

"Yes. When she came in wearing a different costume, and was confused that we were there. I suspect Digby had purposely told her the wrong date and time for the tea party, to make the lady of the house look unstable. That was also the day that Agnes fell into the water and Dorothy rescued her so, of course, the clothes she had left the house in would have been sodden, unwearable. She had changed into an older costume stored at her mother's house. And that was why Dot smelled of cherry cough syrup that day and why there was no money in her purse; she hired a carriage to take Agnes home and stopped at a pharmacy on the way.

"Agnes's accident terrified her," I continued. "It made up her mind that she was going to tell Mr. Wortham about the child, his child, that she would end Digby's reign of terror. Dorothy was going to defy her family and convention. She had had enough of deceit. Digby had sensed the change in her, and followed her the next day."

"But didn't he realize that with Dorothy dead his secret income source would come to an end?"

"No. He could still blackmail Mrs. Brownly, who would not want Boston to know of Dorothy's illegitimate child. He could still blackmail—and threaten— Preston Wortham."

"For his many sins?"

"For murder. Digby purposely wore Mr. Wortham's coat the day of the murder, in case he was seen. I strongly suspect it was Digby who sent the anonymous letter accusing Wortham, and then the second one, exonerating him. It was his way of saying, 'I have complete power over you.' "

"He was a villain, a true villain," Sylvia said in awe. "You have taken notes, haven't you, Louisa?"

"Evil is misused genius," I answered. "Digby was fond of reading the society pages, it seemed. That was how he found employment with Mr. Wortham: when the engagement was announced. He had already been blackmailing Dorothy and Mrs. Brownly for years. Achieving a position in Wortham's household completed his web of control. If only that intelligence had been put to good use!"

"I'm still not quite certain how you know it was he," Sylvia said, twirling a curl that had escaped her bonnet. "Surely shoes are not enough to incriminate."

"It was that chance remark that Mr. Mapp made.

Poor Mr. Mapp. He told us he had seen Digby in Rome the year that Dorothy was there with her mother. Remember?"

"Now I do. Though I didn't remark it at the time. I must pay closer attention to your conversations in the future, Louisa. And speaking of poor Mr. Mapp, I may assume that the poisoned bonbons were a gift from Digby, not Preston or Dorothy?" Sylvia said. "He suspected that you suspected, or were getting close. But if he was also a skilled poisoner, why did he murder Dorothy in such violent manner? Why not a quiet case of undetected poisoning?"

"I have thought of it," I said, no longer smiling, no longer feeling contented. The world held such a burden of evil made manifest in different personalities, different natures. "Digby couldn't be certain that only Dorothy would eat the sweets. Perhaps Preston would, as well. And then his blackmail income from that source would have ended. He was diabolical. It didn't matter to him that my family might have shared the tin of marzipan, and died. It is quite difficult to think about, that part. I endangered Abba and Father and my sisters."

My beloved family in danger! It didn't bear thinking about. May, of course, had been thrilled by this proximity to danger, when I had revealed all of these events to my other family members. Lizzie shook her head, disbelieving. Father lectured me soundly, and then congratulated me on my successful application of reason to a series of mysterious events. Abba hugged me, and gave me a basket of stockings to mend.

"And what of Katya Mendosa, Louy? How did you connect her with Digby?"

"Her fragrance, attar of roses, which I smelled in Wortham's parlor the day after Preston had been incarcerated, the day there was a woman upstairs and Digby seemed so distracted. Her shawl, too, the same shawl in the parlor and in her dressing room. Sylvia, have you yet figured out her true name?"

"True name?"

"Sylvia, you must stop repeating. Katya was Marie Brennen. Yes, the maid whom Wortham seduced and got dismissed. She'd had a child and he had sent her money all these years, but apparently that wasn't enough to appease Marie Brennen. She was the one who pointed out Wortham's engagement when it appeared in the papers. She pointed out the blackmail opportunity to Digby, for who better than Marie Brennen knew all the trouble that Wortham had caused that summer in Newport?"

"Marie Brennen? How did Preston not know? He seduced the same woman twice?"

"I suspect the second time she seduced him, as part of the blackmail scheme. Woman change considerably in six years, Sylvia. Look at the difference six years made in Dorothy. Miss Brennen colored her hair, adopted a false Latin accent, grew taller and heavier. She grew from a girl to a woman, and Preston did not recognize her. Remember, too, if we can believe him, that after that summer in Newport, after his engagement, he spent only one evening with Marie, who was by then known as Katya."

"Well," Sylvia said, thinking and trying to digest all this. "I am glad, then, that she was able to fetch her child back home to her. It would seem that Miss Brennen has had her revenge."

"It would seem," I agreed, not completely saddened.

We walked in silence for some time, admiring the new tips of pale green growth on the oak trees, the noisily honking geese overhead, the sheer exuberance of the season. Dorothy had loved the spring. Someday we would tell Agnes how one spring day in Concord her mother had stripped off shoes and stockings to wade in a little stream, how she had climbed a tree in her best dress and torn it . . . how lovely she had been at fifteen, when she had first fallen in love. . . . There would be so much to tell little Agnes.

"As poor and unhappy as Queenie is, at least she has been able to keep her child," Sylvia mused.

"It is a compensation for all her suffering," I agreed.

"What will happen to Queenie, do you think?"

I stopped in my tracks, and I'm sure Sylvia saw the hint of mischief in my smile. "Haven't I told you?" I said, knowing full well I hadn't. "Edgar has agreed to endow Queenie with enough money to leave Boston and set up a boardinghouse in San Francisco."

Sylvia pondered this for a long moment, attempting to borrow some of my own methods of logic. "He is not generous by nature," Sylvia decided. "Therefore, someone else helped him come to this decision."

"Perhaps." I began to whistle, a habit Abba had never been able to break me of.

"Ah," Sylvia guessed. "You have reached an agreement with him. He will pay; you will not tell his mother."

"We had a discussion; that is all. If he made incorrect assumptions, I did not see it as my duty to enlighten him. He will be furious, eventually, when he learns his mother already knows about his studio, his art, his models. He will be furious to learn that he suspected me of a blackmail I could not commit." My pleasure in the fine spring day returned. "But he does not know yet. *'Honi soit qui mal y pense.'* Shame on him who thinks evil."

"So both Preston and Queenie are going west," Sylvia said as we completed our circuit of the Smokers' Circle.

The Commons was crowded with beribboned, ringleted children and nurses running after them, watching over them. Robins sang in the tree branches, and ducklings paraded after their proud duck mothers. My lethargy of late winter had lifted, and I filled page after page with blood and thunder during my late-evening and early-morning writing hours.

"Perhaps Preston and Queenie will take the same train," I said. "If so, wouldn't you love to hear that conversation? Oh, if only I could be there to take notes . . ."

"Speaking of strange couples, young Constable Cobban has been honored with a dinner and a pay raise for his investigation," Sylvia said. "He sent me flowers. Did he send you flowers as well, Louy?"

"He did. I gave them to the Home." I hadn't forgotten his harsh early judgment of Dorothy. We never really made up that quarrel, for he was stubborn and would never, ever admit he had been completely wrong in his character assessment of Mrs. Wortham. Sweet Dorothy. Laid to rest.

Never had the opera house been so full as now, gallery after gallery filled, and still the crowd poured in, for the fame of the lovely singer had flown far and wide, and hundreds gathered there to wonder and admire.

The purple curtains were open in the box of Beatrice, but the painter Claude stood with folded arms in the shadow of the gallery opposite, and watched with a strange interest. . . .

"And so does Beatrice get her revenge on the faithless Claude?" Sylvia asked. We were in my attic workroom once again, discussing the story I had begun weeks before but put aside when a friend was murdered.

"She does," I said, putting down my pen. "A somewhat cruel revenge. A blood-and-thunder revenge.

Claude will repent and spend his life regretting the wrong he did her. This story is for Dorothy."

"It is finished?"

"Quite. See?"

I handed her the manuscript. An envelope mixed in with the pages fell to the floor and I hastily picked it up and tucked it safely into my pocket. It was a letter from the editor of the *Saturday Evening Gazette*. My story would be published in an autumn issue.

For an excerpt from the next
Louisa May Alcott mystery,
please read on. . . .

Dunreath Place
Roxbury, Massachusetts
March 1887

Gentle Readers,

It was the summer of 1855 when I first began to associate potato cellars with corpses. Dear. That does sound strange, doesn't it? Especially coming from the famous Miss Louisa May Alcott. But in 1855 I was still the unknown Louy Alcott and I was badly in need of wholesome air, sunshine, and serene days, having spent the previous Boston winter investigating the murder of my close friend, Dorothy Brownly, and being almost run over by carriages and threatened at knife point by a blackmailing valet.

I was twenty-two years old and that sad and dangerous winter had awakened in me pleasant childhood memories of Concord, of racing through meadows, climbing trees and spending entire days out of doors, reading and daydreaming—activities impossible to fulfill in the narrow lanes and busy streets of Boston. Moreover, I wished for more time and energy to write. I had sold a couple of "blood-and-thunder" romance stories under a pen name, and a collection of children's fables, but I had a nagging sense of non-arrival, of not yet writing what was most important for me to write, what only Louisa Alcott could write.

There was a name, Josephine, and an image of a tomboyish young woman surrounded by a loving, but difficult family, but I had no more than that. Little Women was still quite a way from its conception.

I remembered that restless time again today, when Sylvie visited. She has grown plump with the years and looking at her now, with her cane and her several chins and her strict schedule of naps, it is amusing to remember her as she was decades ago, lithe and eager for adventure, my companion in danger.

Perhaps her perceptions of me are similar. I am no longer the unknown, struggling authoress in her chilly and dark attic. I took a bit "the grand dame," I fear, though my cuffs are still ink-stained.

Sylvia arrived with a package that had been waiting for me downstairs on the hall table.

"It's from London, Louy," Sylvia gasped, breathing somewhat heavily from her climb up the stairs. She sat opposite me and leaned forward with such eagerness I thought she might open it herself. The brown package almost disappeared into the folds of her bright green plaid dress. Sylvia has buried two husbands, but refuses to wear black.

"London! Yes, I know the handwriting," I said, taking the package. "It is from Fanny Kemble. Dear Fanny. There is a letter, and another voume of her memoirs."

Fanny Kemble, if you are of that group that does not recall names easily, was, in her day, the finest Shakespearian actress on both sides of the Atlantic. She was one of the few of her profession who could play both wicked Lady MacBeth and girlish Juliet with wondrous credibility. To see Fanny onstage, wringing her hands and sobbing "Out, damned spot! Out, I say. Yet who would have thought the old man to have had so much blood in him?" why, that was to know great acting. Especially when she gave us a private enactment of that scene, in Walpole, where there was indeed a great deal of blood in the cellar.

She was a great friend of the family and one of the joys of my girlhood was to see pretty Fanny standing behind Father, hands on hips or pointing at invisible causes and perfectly mimicking his expressions and mouth movements as he earnestly expounded on his principles.

"Fanny visited you in Walpole, didn't she?" asked Sylvia. "I think I remember her there, in that summer of '55. This morning I have been thinking of Walpole, and potatoes."

I patted Sylvia's hand with great affection. Only a friend so old, so true, could say "I have been thinking of potatoes" and feel confident I would understand exactly what she meant.

"Yes," I said, reaching for the scissors in my sewing basket. "When we had our little theater." I cut the string and the brown paper fell away. On top of the volume (so new I could smell that wonderful fragrance of printer's ink!) was a likeness of Fanny. She looked much the same except that like Sylvia, her chins had multiplied and her black hair looked unnaturally so. She must have had it dyed. I passed the photograph to Sylvia and a moment later the maid arrived with a tea tray "Four lumps, right?" I asked Sylvia, picking up the sugar tongs.

"One. I'm trying to slim," she said. "But you are too thin, Louisa," she said sternly. "You must eat more." She stirred her tea and eyed the little cakes that sat beside the white teapot. They had been frosted with pink icing, which I found very disagreeable but Sylvia obviously found tempting.

"I need little," I protested, "and eat as appetite demands."

"Not like the old days," said Sylvia. "Remember those breakfasts you put away in Walpole? Bacon and ham and porridge and toast. Then eggs. You ate like a field hand and stayed slender."

"Perhaps because I had to eat quickly before Father returned from his morning ramble and found me in the kitchen gorging on forbidden meats."

We laughed, thinking of Father's stern vegetarianism and the ruses the rest of the family had used to avoid that strict regimen. Sylvia eyed the pink cakes again and looked so wretched that I put one on a plate and handed it to her.

"If you absolutely insist, Louy," she said, eagerly attacking it with a fork.

Outside the window, past the shoulder frills of Sylvia's plaid frock, I watched the gardener clear away a thick mass of last year's leaves from the lavender beds in preparation for spring, and it reminded me of the lavender bed beside the kitchen door in Walpole, New Hampshire, and just steps away from that country garden, the ravine where I ran each morning.

I was revisiting in my memory those granite cliffs, the clear blue sky with hawks circling overhead, when I heard Sylvia sigh and was brought back to the parlor, to the red plush chairs and carved table and striped wallpaper.

"I can't quite remember, Louisa. That summer, did you perform your comic scene before or after the body was found in the potato cellar? What a strange place to find a body! I still feel faint which I think of it."

"It did put us off potatoes for quite awhile, as I recall. Another cake?"

"I couldn't. Well, maybe a small one. Perhaps you

should write about that summer in Walpole," she suggested. "Do you still have your journal from that time?"

I did, but even without my diaries I remembered clearly what I had written about that summer. It was a sketchy entry, which meant of course there was much I did not say. "Pleasant journey and a kind welcome. Plays, picnics, and good neighbors."

Good neighbors indeed. Except for the occasional murderer.

In June of that year I had received a letter from an uncle who owned a farm in Walpole, New Hampshire, inviting me to come spend time with him. Yes, he was the unfortunate owner of the already mentioned potato cellar, but I must not rush the story. Pacing is important.

I received a letter. An invitation, handed to me by Abba, my mother, who had been concerned for me, since in the weeks before I had endured far too many hours exploring the darker and often dangerous side of family life when large fortunes are at stake.

"It is from Uncle Benjamin," I said, hanging my damp cloak on a hook and sniffing the pot of soup simmering on our old black stove. We still, at that time, lived in the little, somewhat rundown house on Pinckney Street of Boston's Beacon Hill, though even the rent for that modest residence was becoming difficult to meet. It had been a winter of hard work and vegetable broths.

That day Abba was cooking potato soup, I'm afraid to say, though I did not yet know the association I would soon make with that vegetable. "I haven't had a letter from him for years. What can this be about?" I sat on a stool near the warm stove to dry off my skirts and tore open the envelope.

"I have no idea," said Abba, stirring the pot and looking, to use a phrase, like the cat that has swallowed the canary.

The letter was on old shipping letterhead, for Uncle Benjamin had done well in that industry before settling in Walpole with his books and various hobbies. It was also brief. "Come visit, my dear," he had scrawled. "I could use some companionship. Fine weather up north, though I understand it's sodden in Boston. I've a litter of kittens for you to play with."

"Does Uncle Benjamin know my age, Abba?" I asked, looking up.

"He can be forgetful," she admitted. "Widower's get that way." Uncle Benjamin had been married to Abba's sister, who had died a few years before. "But there's more, Louy. He wrote on the back side, as well."

I turned the paper over. "There's a theater here as well," the old-fashioned spidery writing with the arabesque capitals continued. "The Walpole Amateur Dramatic Company, a flock of young people who would look kindly upon your joining them."

Abba was humming as she stirred and looked up at the cracked, flaking ceiling.

"You've arranged this," I said, giving her a quick hug.

"You need time away." Abba, with her free left hand, sketched a circle in the air that encompassed my household duties, the little school I ran to earn a little money, my baskets of take-in sewing with which I earned a little more money. Father was a philosopher and while they make for very interesting conversation, philosophers do not provide much of a secure living for their offspring.

"I will go, then," I said. And in my mind, I was already thinking of the plays I would write and help produce with the Walpole Amateur Dramatic Company. They would all be comedies. I'd had enough of tragedy, and death.

It would seem, though, that they hadn't had quite enough of me.

About the Author

Anna Maclean is the pseudonym of Jeanne Mackin, a professor of writing at Goddard College, award-winning journalist, and author of several historical novels. She has traveled extensively throughout the world and lives in upstate New York with her husband and two cats.